The Morning Fox

Stories of Love, Loss, and Hope

John P. Weiss

Dedicated to the memory of Stephen D. Walpole, and the hospice professionals who bring dignity and comfort to those hovering between this world and the next.

Blurb

"There's a meditative, artful quality to John P. Weiss' writing—whether the subject is personal or philosophical, his words always feel valuable."—Charles Schifano, Desk Notes

Contents

Introduction

I write short stories about love, loss, hope, redemption, and more. When the stories succeed, readers share what I felt. The following stories are favorites, curated from my books and website journal. Some of the stories are previously unpublished. Fiction often captures the truth of life, illustrating our shared hopes, dreams, and humanity. May the following stories warm your heart and speak to your soul.

John P. Weiss
Henderson, Nevada
September 2024

Chapter One

We Love the Things We Love for What They Are

The lip of the steel beam glistened in the moonlight, and her toes barely gained purchase.

She breathed heavily, glancing at the empty abyss below and then back to the approaching headlights. The fog made everything slippery. Her aching right arm bent around the bridge railing.

Her left arm held the crying baby.

Beyond the diffused glow of the headlights, she discerned the outline of the vehicle as it slowly came to rest. Squinting, she saw the emergency light bar and spotlight, which suddenly activated, blinding her.

She looked away and cursed.

Tonight was a private thing, her final, defiant act. To show everyone she rejected life.

And now some cop was going to mess it all up.

***

Sergeant Timothy Swanson was a bear of a man, and his colleagues nicknamed him "Big Tim." But beneath his stout frame beat a tender, gentle heart.

He lost his dear wife, Ann, four years ago.

The drunk driver who slammed into Ann's car was uninjured in the crash. It often went that way, Tim thought. Drunks walk away unscathed, leaving carnage, destruction, and stolen dreams.

Ann was his high school sweetheart, and they married young, despite family members telling them to wait. "Wait for what?" Tim used to say. The lines of a Robert Frost poem he memorized in high school English class always buoyed him:

"We love the things we love for what they are."

And Tim knew to the core of his being that Ann was the love of his life.

They were married for 25 happy years until a drunk, angry young man ignored the bartender's offer to call a cab. Witnesses said the Dodge truck ran a red light, and the violent collision turned Ann's little Mazda into a contorted heap of smoking wreckage.

Even now, less than a year from retirement, Tim felt that familiar ache in the pit of his stomach. Losing a loved one is hard, but losing the love of your life in a violent accident is nearly unbearable.

At least the work kept him occupied.

Especially nightshifts when the bars emptied and drunks drove home. Tim became an expert at spotting irregular driving. He was the king of DUI arrests in his police department. Everyone knew where his motivation came from.

But on this night shift, in the chill and fog, the dispatcher's call was not a drunk driver but a suicidal woman on a bridge.

And the incident would forever change his life.

***

Tim grabbed his MagLite, radioed dispatch that he arrived on scene, and slowly approached the edge of the bridge.

He noticed an old compact car, with its front and rear doors left open, parked just before the bridge. At the entrance to the bridge, he saw a pair of shoes and an overturned purse lying on the ground, its contents scattered about.

High above, in the misting fog, bridge lights cast a diffused luminescence. It was just enough light to make out a figure clinging to the outside railing.

And that's when he heard the cries of the baby.

He could see the woman now, barefoot, clinging to the outside rail, her other arm clutching a frayed, bundled-up blanket. The blanket held little movements and the cries of a baby.

"Stay away from me!" the distraught woman yelled.

"No problem. Is it okay if I stand here, just to talk?" Tim said.

"It isn't supposed to happen this way. You're ruining everything! Nothing ever goes right. I can't even get this right!" The woman's eyes were fierce, her voice sharp, and her movements jerky and trembling.

It scared Tim.

The thin metal edge she was standing on, and the cold railing she clung to, were both slippery with moisture. Tim radioed for a cover unit and ambulance, advising that they stage thirty feet from his location. He didn't want to startle the woman.

"May I ask what your name is?" Tim said.

"No, you may not! This isn't your business. Why are you even here?" The woman was staring at Tim now.

"Someone called. I think they heard you scream," Tim said.

The woman cursed several times. Her left foot slipped, and she leaned into the rail to steady herself.

"I don't want you here. I want to get this right. I don't want to mess this up. For once in my life!" Her voice trailed off.

"My name's Tim. I don't want to upset you. I just want to help, if I can."

"It's too late for that, Tim. When Joey was beating me up, where were you? When my baby girl was in foster care, where were you? Hey, maybe you were the pig that locked me up over my addiction. Was that you, Tim?" Her voice was sarcastic. Angry. Desperate.

Tim tried to remember his professional training. The things he learned in hostage negotiation school. What did the instructor say? Oh yeah, ventilation. Keep them ventilating. It was a fancy term for talking.

"Sounds like you've been through a lot. How old is your baby girl?"

"She's one. And you know what, Tim? She and I don't need your help. Because you don't know the first thing about hardship."

"Well, I don't know about your hardships, you're right. But I lost my wife four years ago. Car accident. So I know hardship. I know loss. It's terrible."

The woman stared at Tim. Her demeanor changed slightly. She looked down, and then back at Tim.

"Okay, then you know how pointless it all is. I tried, I really tried. But everyone is gone now. My parents, even my little brother. There's nothing left, and I don't want my baby girl to face this crappy world."

"Yeah, it does feel pointless sometimes. I hear you," Tim said, as he felt his phone buzz in his shirt pocket. He slipped it out and glanced. It was a text from his Lieutenant, stating, "I just arrived on scene, about forty feet back by the trees. Good job, keep her talking."

"Oh, I'm sorry, Tim, am I boring you? Gotta check your Instagram?" The woman's voice was biting and sarcastic.

"I'm sorry, it was my boss. He's not far away, and he said he's here to help, too, if he can."

"Well, tell him to go home. I'm sure your boss doesn't have any redeeming qualities. I haven't met any cops who do."

"Well, I like to think I have a few," Tim said.

The woman switched position, transitioning the baby to her other arm and turning to face Tim.

"Oh yeah, just what redeeming quality do you have, Tim?"

"My bald spot," Tim said.

She didn't expect to hear this, but Tim blurted it out. It was the first thing that came to mind, and it surprised him, too. He wasn't sure, but he thought he saw a brief smirk on the woman's face.

"What do you mean, your bald spot? Are you kidding me?"

"Well," Tim said, "my bald spot keeps me humble. I'm a CrossFit addict. I work out regularly. I also like English literature. The guys at work say I'm Mr. Perfect, but I know I'm not. And my bald spot keeps my ego in check."

The woman stared at Tim for a long time.

Then she looked down at the dark void below, and back at Tim.

"Just my luck. I'm trying to wrap things up, and along comes Mr. Nice Cop with a bald spot. See what I mean? The world is just a big load of random crap."

"Well, we might live in a broken world, but there are still good people in it. Hidden behind all the pain and suffering, we still have some beauty, laughter, and hope," Tim said.

"You really believe that?"

"Yes, I do. But it took a while to feel that way again after I lost my wife."

"What was her name?" the woman asked.

"Ann. Her name was Ann."

And suddenly the woman began crying.

***

The fog was getting thicker and the temperature was dropping.

The woman continued sobbing, then looked at her baby and said, "Did you hear that sweetheart, his wife's name was Ann."

Tim felt his phone buzz again, and he risked looking down. "Keep her talking. Try to get her to give us the baby," the text message from his Lieutenant said.

"There's a poem I memorized in high school by Robert Frost, called Hyla Brook," Tim said, to keep the woman talking.

She wiped her runny nose and red eyes, then looked quizzically back at Tim.

"What?" she said.

"It's a poem about a brook near the poet's farm. Some frogs bred there. The brook came and went with the seasons. Anyway, what the poem is really about is that everything should be loved for what it is, rather than what it ought to be," Tim said.

The woman looked at her baby, and then back at Tim. She was listening, which was a good sign.

"Limitations are part of everything, and that shouldn't stop us from loving to the fullest. Like I loved my Ann and you love your baby girl. And love should be unconditional. We have to accept the strengths and weaknesses in everything. The good and the bad." Tim let his words hang in the air.

"Well, my life has been more about bad than good," the woman said.

"And I'm sorry for that. But look who you're holding. She's the good part. She's everything, isn't she?" Tim said.

"But the bad ruins what good there is," she said.

"It may feel that way, but I'm not so sure. In the Robert Frost poem, he talks about this beautiful brook, but then a drought comes along, and it's all dried up. It's not very beautiful anymore. Despite the present condition of the brook, Frost declares his unconditional love for the brook. He remembers when the brook was beautiful, and that's enough." Tim stopped and tried to read the woman's expression.

"We love the things we love for what they are," Tim said, adding, "That's the last line of the poem. Things don't have to be perfect to love them. Life doesn't have to be perfect, to love it."

The woman smiled at Tim.

"I think you're a good man, Tim. Maybe you can teach my baby girl to love the best of who I was, and to love the world like that poet loved the brook."

She kissed her baby's forehead, adjusted the blanket, and then carefully raised the baby over the rail, setting her gently on the safe side.

And then the woman stepped off the bridge, into the dark, empty expanse below.

You can't save everyone, and their last moments haunt even the most stoic police officers.

Tim participated the following week in the team debrief and mandatory counseling sessions. His Lieutenant and others called him a hero.

"But she jumped. I lost her," Tim told them.

"No, Tim," his Lieutenant said. "You saved her baby. She already made up her mind. Don't you see? She was going to take the baby with her. And you prevented that. You and your poetry, no less!"

In one of Tim's mandatory counseling sessions, he told the therapist, "It's weird, before the incident, I always felt this empty, sad, stillness inside me. A sort of dull, persistent ache."

"The loss of your wife, Ann?" the therapist asked.

"Yes. But the moment I picked up that baby girl on the bridge, and her tiny hands latched onto my uniform, the stillness and the ache inside me vanished. I mean, instantly. What is that? What does that mean?"

The therapist handed Tim a tissue to wipe his eyes.

"Maybe it's hope, Tim? Maybe it's acceptance of your loss? I'm not sure, but time will hopefully tell," the therapist said.

Tim dreamt of Ann that night as she smiled and said, "It's okay, darling. You know what you have to do. Do it for both of us."

***

Tim awoke the following morning like a man on a mission.

The adoption process took time, but it was less complicated than he imagined. The woman on the bridge had no next of kin, and the father of the little girl died of an overdose the year before.

"We love the things we love for what they are," Tim kept telling himself throughout the process, knowing his late wife would be proud of him. He knew from the moment that baby girl latched onto him he would love her and give her the life her mother wanted. Tim was at the station visiting his Lieutenant one day when the phone call came, notifying him that he could officially take home the baby girl.

"I'm nervous," Tim told his Lieutenant.

"Don't be, Tim," the Lieutenant said. "You're going to be an amazing father. Come on, I'll take you to the Division of Child and Family Services."

When they arrived at the County Building, a few patrol officers were already there, waiting for Tim and his Lieutenant. They held little pink balloons that said, "It's a girl."

"Cute," Tim said.

Tim was greeted inside by two of the Family Service employees. One was holding the baby girl, who looked like a little angel to Tim.

"Would you like to hold your daughter?" the employee asked.

"Yes, I would, very much," Tim said.

"Be gentle now, big guy. Try not to break her," Tim's Lieutenant joked.

When Tim held her in his arms, the baby latched onto his shirt and started cooing contentedly.

"By the way," the adoption employee said, "We finally confirmed all her records. It took awhile because her mother moved around a bit."

"Do we know what her name is?" Tim asked as he smiled at the baby.

"Ann," the adoption employee said. "Her first name is Ann."

Chapter Two

The Old Jesuit

O nce again, the dream awakened him.

He was covered in sweat, his heart racing. He sat up, reached for the plastic water bottle beside his bed, and gulped its contents. He wiped his brow and waited for his heart and breathing to slow.

The past was still chasing him, tormenting him.

It seemed a small thing, just a moment of impatience so long ago. But something in the child's eyes haunted him, even after all these years.

He grabbed his rosary and with each bead recited the prayers. Then he closed his eyes, asking God for guidance.

The room was stale, so he slipped out of bed and wrenched open the window. Cool morning air rushed in. Across the street, in a tree, a lone mourning dove cooed softly.

The old Jesuit stared at the bird and listened to her gentle sounds. Then he closed his eyes, and whispered, "Thank you, Lord."

He knew what he had to do.

***

Lucy was the front office manager for Our Lady of Fatima. In her sixties and widowed, she was a reliable and trustworthy Catholic whose devotion to the church was above reproach.

Lucy always arrived early in the front office, where she turned on the heat and made coffee. She knew the old Jesuit, Father Michael O'Flanagan, would soon join her. She admired him, not just because he was a disciplined old Jesuit with an impressive, academic mind.

She admired him for his goodness.

Father Michael lumbered into the office. He was a bear of a man, standing 6' 3" and weighing nearly 250 pounds. Yet he was the most gentle of men, known to cradle lost kittens and tenderly hold babies.

Lucy handed Father Michael a mug of black coffee, which he took but placed on the desk. He seemed distracted.

"Good morning, my dear Lucy. Might you be willing to dig up an old file for me?"

"Of course, Father. Did you say an 'old' file?"

"Yes, I think the boy's last name was Fitzgerald. The Fitzgerald family were parishioners here in the late 1970s. We should have the boy's confirmation records. What I'm after is a current address."

"May I ask what this is about?" Lucy said.

"It's about atonement," Father Michael said.

And then he began rifling through a file drawer in the corner of the office.

"Oh no, those are tax records. Let me get my keys and I'll check the files in the tombs," Lucy said.

"The tombs?" Father Michael asked.

"Yes, you remember. The little office in the cellar. We moved all the old records down there last year to make more space in the main office."

"Oh yes, that's right," he said.

Lucy found her keys, went downstairs, and began digging through files. Twenty minutes later she found the Fitzgerald family file, and the confirmation records for their son, Matthew. Victorious, she climbed up the stairs to the main office. She opened the door, holding the file above her head, stating, "Here you go, Father."

But Father Michael was gone, and he hadn't touched his coffee.

***

In the Catholic tradition, Holy Communion includes the priest placing the Sacred Host (Eucharistic bread wafer) on a communicant's tongue.

Many past church leaders believed that only the priest's hands should touch the Sacred Host, to ensure it wasn't dropped or desecrated in any way. But modernity invites change, and some churches allowed receiving the Sacred Host in the hand. The Holy See (Pope) granted dispensation to American churches on June 17, 1977, allowing priests to administer Communion to the hand. Communicants could still opt to receive the Host on their tongue, but many switched to their open palm.

During young Matthew Fitzgerald's Catholic Confirmation training, he had received the Sacred Host on his tongue. So this new option, to receive the offering in his hand, was unusual and unfamiliar.

Matthew noticed how many in the church had chosen to receive Holy Communion in their hands, so he decided he would too.

What Matthew didn't know was that upon receiving Holy

Communion in the hand, after saying Amen, one must continue to face the altar while placing the Host in one's mouth. On that fateful day, Matthew said Amen, but then turned from the altar as he put the Host in his mouth.

And that's when he felt the firm grip of Father Michael's beefy hand on his right arm, jerking him around toward the altar.

"Respect for the Lord!" Father Michael hissed sharply, adding, "Face the altar when you receive Holy Communion. Respect for the Lord!"

With this, tears began to well in Matthew's eyes, and by the time he returned to the pew where his family was seated, he tried to muffle his cries. Matthew's mother asked him what was wrong, but all Matthew could do was cry. She took his hand and led him out of the church.

Back then, Father Michael was an idealistic, young Jesuit.

He was deeply faithful and conservative in interpreting religious doctrine. He read and agreed with the *Memoriale Domini*, which directed priests to place the consecrated bread on the tongue of communicants. And he agreed with his hero, St. Thomas Aquinas, who wrote in his Summa Theologiae:

"...out of reverence towards this Sacrament, nothing touches it, but what is consecrated; hence the corporal and the chalice are consecrated, and likewise the priest's hands, for touching this Sacrament. Hence, it is not lawful for anyone else to touch it except from necessity, for instance, if it were to fall upon the ground, or else in some other case of urgency."

As a Jesuit, Father Michael had taken perpetual vows of poverty, chastity, and obedience. So he accepted the Pope's dispensation allowing the Host to be placed in the communicant's hands, but he did so begrudgingly.

Father Michael believed in tradition, and he felt like the old ways were being eroded. And that day, when the boy turned away from the altar and popped the Host in his mouth like candy, Father Michael did something the kind man rarely did.

He lost his patience.

And though he didn't know it at the time, he did more than lose his patience. He lost a young parishioner, who tearfully told his mother later in the parking lot that he never wanted to come to church again.

***

Lucy entered the main church and found Father Michael sitting in a pew, on his knees in prayer.

He heard her approaching, made the sign of the cross, and then sat back in the pew.

"Father Michael, is everything alright?" she said.

"Oh Lucy, I'm sorry. I don't mean to alarm you. This old Jesuit needs to try and fix the mistake I made when I was young and impetuous."

"I don't doubt you were young, and you're still young at heart. But...impetuous? I don't see that in you, Father," Lucy said.

"Oh, I had my moments. I guess time, maturity, and God's grace softened the rough edges of my character." He spied the folder under Lucy's arm.

"Is that the file?" he said.

"Yes, and the boy's name is Matthew. There's an address listed, but I don't know if the family still lives there."

"Thank you, Lucy, what would I do without you?"

"Do you want me to reheat your coffee?" she said.

"What coffee?"

"The coffee I handed you in the office that you didn't touch."

"Oh dear, I must have forgotten. Yes, I'd love some coffee," he said.

And that's when Lucy first began worrying about Father Michael's memory.

***

The bread was burning again, and Karen Fitzgerald clicked off the oven and threw her baking gloves in the sink.

Her mother was gifted in the kitchen, always able to transform the simplest ingredients into delicious meals and baked goods. But not Karen. Somehow any semblance of culinary talent eluded her, despite her best efforts.

"So much for the bread," she said to herself. "Maybe I'll order Chinese tonight."

The doorbell rang.

Karen slipped off her apron and made her way to the front door. Beyond the frosted glass slats of the door, she saw the outline of a large person, dressed in dark clothing and wearing a fedora.

"Yes?" she said without opening the door.

"Oh, hello, yes, I'm here to speak with Mrs. Fitzgerald. My name is Father Michael O'Flanagan."

Karen opened the door but kept the security chain attached.

"I'm sorry to bother you, and I'm happy to come back if this is not a good time," Father Michael said.

"May I ask what this is regarding?" Karen asked.

"It has to do with your son, Matthew, Mrs. Fitzgerald. He was a parishioner in our church, Our Lady of Fatima, many years ago."

"We were all parishioners back then," Karen said.

"Forgive me for asking, but is that freshly baked bread I smell?"

"Yes, Father. Well, it was. I burned it. Again."

"My mother used to say the trick to baking bread is to keep your yeast, salt, and sugar separate when adding to your mixing bowl. The sugar and salt can kill the yeast which will reduce the effectiveness of the yeast if they come into contact at the early stages of bread baking," Father Michael said.

Karen blinked.

"Father, you said you had some information about my son Matthew?"

"Not so much information but a desire to apologize for a misunderstanding. No, that's not right. I want to apologize to Michael for frightening him when he was a little boy. He was receiving Holy Communion and I admonished him for improperly stepping away from the altar. It might sound odd after all these years, but I never forgot it. I must have scared away your entire family because I never saw you in church again."

Karen unlatched the chain and invited Father Michael in. She led him into the living room to sit down. She sat across from him.

"Father, I'm not sure how to tell you this."

"Oh, I'm accustomed to hearing just about anything," Father Michael said.

"Well, you see, Matthew passed away three years ago," Karen said.

***

The words stunned Father Michael, and he felt like a man suddenly lost at sea.

Mrs. Fitzgerald kept talking. Something about a late-night

party. A drunk driver. Paramedics and police officers. The doctors said his injuries were too great.

But mostly Father Michael was swimming in a fog.

How can he apologize?

How can he find atonement if the only person who can grant it has left this earth? For a moment, Father Michael felt shivers of despair. But then, fragmented lines from Hemingway's "The Old Man and the Sea," came to mind: "But man is not made for defeat," and, "A man can be destroyed but not defeated."

"A man can be destroyed but not defeated," Father Michael whispered.

"Excuse me, Father? What did you say?"

"Oh, I'm sorry Mrs. Fitzgerald. I'm sorry for your loss. Oh dear. The last thing I want to do is bring you and your family more pain. Just know that all these years, I have prayed for forgiveness. I have prayed that one day Matthew would forgive me for scaring him away so long ago."

"Oh Father, I'm sure Matthew forgot all about it. I don't remember the incident at all. I know our daughter Melissa fell under the spell of one of her high school teachers, an agnostic scientist, and I think Melissa was the reason we stopped coming. We got tired of arguing about it. I don't remember, it was years ago," Karen said.

"Thank you for taking the time to visit with me, and may God bless you, your family, and Matthew's soul."

"Thank you, Father," Karen said, adding, "Can I walk you out?"

At the front door, Father Michael thanked Karen again, shook her hand, and left. Outside, the wind had picked up. The air chilled, and Father Michael strolled over to a park bench.

"Dear Lord," he said to himself, "Please send me a bit of your grace. A bit of hope. Please forgive me and tell Matthew how sorry I am."

He stood up, settled his dark fedora on his head, and returned to his car. His afternoon was free, and he wasn't sure what to do. He recalled seeing a pub a few blocks away and decided a pint of ale might steady him and soften the sadness in his heart.

***

Late that afternoon, Lucy began to worry about Father Michael.

It wasn't like him to be gone this long, and she was about to call Philip, a long-serving Deacon in the church. Just as she picked up the phone, someone knocked on the front office door.

Lucy opened the door, and her heart sank.

Two young police officers, a man and a woman, stood outside. Their faces were serious.

"Hello, I'm Officer Fuentes and this is Officer Webster. We're looking for a woman who works here named 'Lucy.'"

"Yes, that would be me. Is this about Father Michael, I'm terribly worried about him," Lucy said.

"Yes, ma'am. Father Michael has been taken to County General Hospital. He was at a local pub and folks there said he collapsed."

"Oh dear," Lucy said. "Father Michael isn't one to get inebriated."

"No, ma'am. He wasn't drunk. It seems to be some kind of medical issue. When the paramedics were loading him into their rig, all he said was, 'Tell Lucy, at the Church.'"

"Thank you, Officers. I'll lock up, get my bag, and go see him immediately."

***

When Father Michael opened his eyes, he was in bed in a hospital room.

Across from him was an elderly woman with white hair and kind eyes. She smiled at Father Michael and said, "Ah, the good priest is awake."

"I don't feel like a good priest," Father Michael said.

"Yes, I know. You still feel bad about Matthew and your impatient behavior as a young priest," she said, adding, "I wouldn't worry about that, there's always more to the story."

"How do you know about Matthew?"

"Oh Father, you do chatter a bit when you're asleep," she said with a soft laugh. "By the way, my name is Catherine."

"Michael. Father Michael O'Flanagan," he said.

"Pleased to meet you," she said.

"You know, I had an Aunt Catherine. My Dad's sister. But I never met her. She lived out of state and died before my father.

"Tell me about your father," Catherine said.

Father Michael still felt dizzy but found it relaxing to converse, and Catherine had a gentle, kind disposition.

"My father and I didn't get along. He was a university professor and disapproved of my decision to enter the priesthood. He was a staunch atheist and said I was a fool, believing in all that fairy tale nonsense."

"Fairy tale nonsense. Yes, it's easy to dismiss mystery and the unknown. I've met many people who never opened their hearts and minds to the numinous. To the breadcrumbs of divinity that can be found around us, if only we'd slow down and be open to their presence," Catherine said.

"Well put," Father Michael said. "Dad and I never did see eye to eye. I loved him, and I tried to tell him as much, but then he was diagnosed with cancer and slipped away in 1985."

"Oh, don't you worry about your father. He loved you, and was proud of who you became."

"And how do you know that?" Father Michael asked.

"Divine intuition," Catherine said, adding, "And what about this business with the boy? What was his name again?" Catherine asked.

"Matthew. Matthew Fitzgerald. When he was little, I scared him away from the church. It was foolish of me. I chastised him for improperly receiving Holy Communion. I've wanted to apologize to him all these years, but I learned today that he was killed a few years ago in a drunk driving accident."

"And here we are. They said you fainted in a pub," Catherine said.

"Well, it wasn't from the ale. I'd just had a few sips when a fog descended over me. And the next thing I knew, two paramedics were stuffing me into an ambulance. But it doesn't matter. I feel like something's wrong with me. I'm forgetting things. And now that I know Matthew is gone, I feel defeated. I've been to confession. Fellow priests have absolved me, but I can't seem to forgive myself. And so my road ahead feels dark." With that, Father Michael closed his moist eyes.

"Do you remember Peter Pan, Father? What you need is some good 'ol pixie dust," Catherine said.

"Pixie dust?" Father Michael said.

"Yes, indeed. There's a line in Peter Pan: 'All the world is made of faith, and trust, and pixie dust.' Your being a priest and all, I think you can appreciate that line."

"Funny you should mention Peter Pan," Father Michael said. "When my Aunt died they sent us some of her things. She had no other family. And one of the things she owned was an old copy of Peter Pan."

"Good taste," Catherine said.

"I think my aunt and I shared a sensitivity for things unseen."

"I would agree with that," Catherine said.

There was a knock at the door. It creaked open, and a young woman peeked inside the room.

"Excuse me, but I'm looking for Father Michael O'Flanagan. I was told this is his room." The woman was elegantly dressed, with long dark hair, slender features, and intelligent eyes.

"I'm Father Michael. What can I do for you?"

"I was hoping to steal a minute of your time. I heard you came to visit today, about Matthew." The young woman walked into the room and pulled a chair up next to Father Michael's bed.

"How do you know Matthew?" Father Michael asked.

"He was my brother."

***

Melissa Fitzgerald crossed her legs, opened her handbag, and slipped a photo from her wallet.

"Here's a photograph of Matthew. It was taken a few months before his death." She handed the photo to Father Michael.

"He's a handsome young man. A jovial face. I barely remember his features, from when he was a boy. What I remember most were intelligent, penetrating eyes," Father Michael said.

"Are you sure, Father?" Melissa said.

"What do you mean?"

"Well, are you sure it's his eyes you remember?" she said.

"I remember grabbing his arm. I remember jerking him around. Those intelligent, intense eyes, with a bit of confusion and fear," Father Michael said.

"Oh Father, those eyes didn't belong to Matthew. He had sweet eyes, full of life and playful passion. Those eyes that you remember were not his."

"Not his?" Father Michael said.

"No, they were mine."

***

So much of life unfolds around us, and we often fail to make sense of the interconnections and deeper meanings.

For the next hour, Melissa filled in the gaps of memory that had confused Father Michael. It was she, not Matthew, that he had chastised that day in church. And how after that fateful day, she never wanted to go to church again. How she rebelled against religion and celebrated her biology teachers and anyone who rejected the notion of God in favor of science and secularism.

"Oh my dear, I'm so sorry. Won't you please forgive me? I was a young priest back then, too wrapped up in the rules and traditions of the Church to understand my deeper role," Father Michael said, reaching out to hold Melissa's hand.

"Your deeper role?" Melissa said.

"Yes. My job was to help you see and know God. To open your heart to that whisper in your soul, that transcends science and secularism. My job was to protect your soul, not drive it away. And I can see, even now, something in your eyes. I don't know what. Pain. Loss. Uncertainty."

"It's probably the pain of my divorce. He was cheating on me, but that's another story, Father," Melissa said.

They were still holding hands.

"My dear, please allow me to apologize. I've prayed for forgiveness. I never meant to hurt you. Somehow I confused you with your brother. I want you to know that I became a priest to help people. To help them to know God. To know that their lives have meaning. And that God loves them with all His heart."

"Oh Father Michael, I forgive you. You were always kind to me and my family. It was just that one day, at Holy Communion, that you frightened me. But really, I was already on a rebellious path back then. In some ways, what happened became an excuse for me to rebel even more."

Father Michael exhaled and leaned back against his pillow.

Forgiveness is a gift we give others, but also ourselves. And when Melissa saw the relief and peace that seemed to wash over Father Michael, she felt a kind of serenity wash over her as well.

And then she giggled out loud, surprising herself.

"Careful," Father Michael said, "You don't want to wake up my roommate, Catherine."

"Catherine?" Melissa said. "Who's that?"

"Well, she's in the bed next to me. She's been chatting with me about Peter Pan," Father Michael said, as he started to sit up a little and look over to his left.

But there was only an empty bed across from them.

***

Lucy arrived at the hospital and sat down with Father Michael's doctors. She was on the list as family, even though she was not a blood relation. Deacon Philip was on the list as well.

"I'm afraid Father Michael is very ill," the doctor said. "He has a form of dementia caused by plaque on the brain. And he also has a neurological disorder that we're still investigating. We think he had a transient ischemic attack back in the pub. We'll need to do more tests."

"Poor Father Michael," Lucy said. "He's been so forgetful lately, I was worried about him. Now it all makes sense."

After the meeting with the doctors, Lucy phoned Deacon Philip and told him everything.

"Oh Lord," Philip said. "Okay, I'll call the Bishop. Poor Father Michael."

When Lucy went to Father Michael's room, Melissa greeted her.

"Oh, hello, I'm Father Michael's church secretary," Lucy said.

"Hello. I'm Melissa Fitzgerald."

"Melissa is my guardian angel," Father Michael said. "And she's forgiven me for being a young fool so long ago. Come sit down, Lucy, and we'll explain everything."

Lucy sat down, and through tears and laughter, Father Michael and Melissa explained all that happened so long ago. And then Deacon Philip showed up and joined them. And they talked more, and for the first time in many years, Father Michael felt a deep sense of release.

Because forgiveness is a powerful thing.

It can free the soul.

***

One week later, Father Michael's condition deteriorated.

A doctor sat down next to the old Jesuit and tried to explain the neurological disorder and complex medical issues afflicting Father Michael. The doctor was young, and he was nervous. How do you tell an old priest that he's dying?

"Doc, it's okay," Father Michael said. "One of the blessings of being a man of God is that death doesn't hold sway over me like it does others. And anyway, I've already glimpsed a few miracles."

"Miracles?" the doctor said.

"Yes. My Aunt Catherine visited me the other day. We talked

about Peter Pan and pixie dust."

"Pixie dust?" the doctor said, writing a few notes about adjusting medications.

"Yep, pixie dust. That magic elixir that transcends this world and the next. I breathed a bit of pixie dust, Doc. And I forgave my father. And Miss Melissa forgave me. And I said a prayer for young Matthew's soul. And I've realized that being a priest was my calling. Old J. M. Barrie got it right when he wrote 'It is not in doing what you like, but in liking what you do that is the secret of happiness.' And I've liked being a priest. So I guess what I'm saying, my dear doctor, is that I'm finally at peace."

The doctor sat back in his chair and closed his notebook.

"I envy you, Father. It can be hard in life to truly find peace. I know I'm still searching."

"All you have to do is keep an open mind. Be open to a little pixie dust," Father Michael said.

"Yes, a little pixie dust. I'll do that, Father," the doctor said.

In the following weeks, there were many visitors to the old Jesuit.

Longtime parishioners. Old priests from back in Father Michael's seminary days. Lucy and Deacon Philip. Mrs. Fitzgerald and Melissa also came to visit.

Mrs. Fitzgerald brought a freshly baked loaf of bread. "You were right, Father," Mrs. Fitzgerald said. "I kept the yeast, sugar, and salt separate."

During his final afternoon, Father Michael heard Catherine's voice in the bed next to him. "Oh Michael, my dear boy, there's so much you won't believe. So much pixie dust, you will feel like such joy and peace are more than one soul can take."

"Thank you, Catherine. Thank you for being here with me. Stay with me," Father Michael said.

The last thing Father Michael remembered hearing was the

hospital chaplain praying beside him. "May Holy Mary, the angels, and all the saints come to meet you as you go forth from this life."

And outside his hospital bedroom window, as the last rays of sunlight disappeared over the horizon, a gentle mourning dove sat on the ledge, cooing softly. Lovingly.

Calling the old Jesuit home.

Chapter Three

The Daffodil Painting

The old gentleman knew that more years were chasing him than remained. His beloved Cynthia had passed away last December. It was awful.

He awoke that chilly winter morning and found her in his art studio, on the floor. A teacup shattered beside her frail body. And in her left hand, his recent painting of daffodils.

It comforted him immensely. That in her final moments, she had picked up his little flower painting. Cynthia loved the garden and especially daffodils.

"They don't ask anything of nobody. You just put them in the ground. In decent soil. Then let them do their thing." He could still hear her lyrical voice saying that.

"I love their brilliant yellow. They look like a cup and saucer. So up-lifting. So full of promise and renewal, don't you think?" He smiled at the memory of that. "Yes, Cynthia, I do think you're right," he said to himself. "It's why I painted the daffodils for you."

The inevitable transition
Later that spring, he heard the familiar sound of his son's truck

pull into the driveway.

"Hey, Dad, sorry I didn't call. Thought I'd check in on you." The old gentleman let his son in the front door.

"Where's Pamela and the kids?" he asked.

"Oh, they're at the shopping mall. Pamela said something about a new Coach purse." But the old gentleman knew it was a lie. Benevolent, but a lie nonetheless. In reality, his son had come for "the talk."

"It's just that with Mom gone now, there's no one to look after you, Dad. And besides, you've seen those apartments at Oak Street Villa. There's enough room for you to set up your art studio. It's a nice retirement community."

His son meant well. But he wasn't old enough to understand the long shadow of grief that accompanies the loss of a spouse. Or the pain of facing the inevitable transition. Leaving the home you spent a lifetime in, only to descend into a community of the irrelevant and forgotten.

"Come on, Dad, it's not like that. You'll have company. You won't have to cook. You'll be closer to me, Pamela, and the kids."

And so, with that, he looked at his son. "Okay, I guess it's time. Time for Croak Street Villa."

His son frowned. "No Dad, Oak Street Villa, not Croak Street Villa. That's not even funny."

Memories are roses in our winter

The move went as well as expected. Going through Cynthia's old clothing and things was hard. But he was settled into the new apartment now, and his son was right. There was sufficient room for his art studio.

Still, he missed Cynthia terribly. At night, she'd come to him in his dreams. They were young again and laughing. He mused about his artistic ambitions. She'd emerge, smiling, from the daffodils in her garden.

But then he'd awake, to the solitude.

At least he still had his art.

The staff at Oak Street Villa were kind enough and arranged for several of his pieces to be hung around the facility. Maria, one of the nurses, asked him about Cynthia, and how he dealt with her loss.

"I don't think I have dealt with it," he told her. "I just go to bed at night, hoping. Hoping that she'll come visit me."

And then he said this:

"Memories are roses in our winter. I read that in a George Will column once. Never forgot it. Because it's true. In the autumn of our lives, well, we still have our memories."

Maria's eyes welled with tears when she heard that.

Who will be my Mendelssohn?

The old gentleman often joined the others in the dining hall. He was known around the place, due to his artwork. One old chap, a retired history professor, had taken to calling him "Monet."

"Hey, Monet, I saw that new garden painting you did in the front lobby. Beautiful piece," said the professor.

"Well, my wife kept a beautiful garden. It reminds me of her." It was all the old gentleman could think to say.

The professor suggested he paint more pieces for the many halls and lobbies at Oak Street Villa.

"What's the point," the old man said. "No one is interested in an old man's flower paintings. People today like that modern stuff."

With that, the professor became quite serious, and said, "Johann Sebastian Bach's music wasn't broadly appreciated until after his death, 80 years later. When another composer, Mendelssohn, played it all over Germany. Same with Thoreau.

His Walden Pond wasn't embraced by the public until after his death. So, you just keep painting. You never know when or how your art will impact others."

The old gentleman smiled and said, "Well, I don't know who my Mendelssohn will be."

The healing power of art

A few years crept by and the old gentleman did his best to paint, but arthritis and cataracts were his enemies now. His son and family would visit, but something inside of himself said it was time.

He dreamed that final night of a daffodil garden, and in the distance, he saw her. Cynthia was sitting on a bench, smiling and waving. Beckoning.

In the weeks after his death, his son and family cleared out the apartment and said their goodbyes to the staff. It was poignant for everyone.

A month later, another family arrived with their elderly mother. She had lost her husband and was terribly afraid of change.

She felt so very alone in this new place. The kind nurse, Maria, told her that a wonderful artist used to live in her apartment. But the old woman was still afraid.

"Tell me your story," Maria asked. "What did you used to do?" And the old woman said, "I raised my children while Carl, my husband, worked at the bank. Oh, and I gardened. Tulips, roses. And especially daffodils."

The second night in her new apartment, the old woman sipped some tea and continued unpacking. At one point she sat down and wept.

Change was hard. But then she clicked the light on in her closet, and noticed an object on the top shelf. Using a stool she reached up and slid out a small painting. She took it down into the light.

Gazing at it, she began to feel a sense of peace wash over her. "It's so beautiful," she thought to herself. "This must be a sign. Maybe I'll be okay, after all."

The next day she visited the front desk and asked if there was a frame shop in town.

"Why do you ask?" said the girl at the desk.

"Because I have the most lovely daffodil painting, and I want everyone to see how splendid it is."

Chapter Four

A Perfect Graveyard of Buried Hopes

Whenever he visited Annie, he always smuggled in a flask of whisky.

Her mind may have been deep in the woods, wandering down deer trails of old memories and dreams, but her taste for whisky remained faithful. Sometimes, it even summoned glimmers of lucidity, and the old Annie would emerge from the depths of dementia and gift him moments of clarity.

They'd sit on the bench down by the lake, on the grounds of the care center, with a blanket over her legs to stave off the autumn chill. He'd look over his shoulder, to make sure the nurses and cameras were a sufficient distance away. And then he'd slip the flask out of his pocket.

"Here you go, Annie, my love," he'd say with a wink.

And somehow just the sight of the flask awakened dormant synapses in her brain. She'd smile widely.

"Ah, bless you, Walter. Nectar of the Gods," Annie would say with a grin.

Of course, his name was Peter, not Walter. Walter was her long-deceased brother. But at this stage in the game, any conversation was welcome.

His wife may have succumbed early in life to the curse of Alzheimer's, but at least he could still talk with her. For a little longer, anyway. Her body held other maladies, and the doctors felt that time was growing thin.

She sipped the whisky a bit, until a warm radiance washed over her. It made him happy to see her ensconced in the glow of whisky. She seemed to relax and settle into herself.

Sometimes, she even laughed.

It took him back to their youth when they visited the movies on Friday nights and tossed popcorn at their friends in the seats below. Annie would giggle until laughter erupted out of her. Peter missed those moments of joy and frivolity.

He missed everything about their life together before her illness stole their happiness and future.

And so he visited every other day, to see her and pray for moments when Annie's mind surfaced from the depths of confusion and fog. Moments when, however fleeting, he felt pieces of their old life.

"Oh, Annie. You take care of yourself. I'll see you in a few days," he'd say.

***

The work helped.

Peter volunteered at the local tutoring club. They didn't have much money to pay tutors, so he waived the meager salary. He leveraged his experience as a retired literature professor to help students make sense of writers like Melville, Hemingway, and Dostoevsky.

Peter knew Annie would have approved. Before her illness, she was an elementary school teacher. Peter and Annie both had a soft spot for kids.

In the evenings, the house was quiet and lonely. So Peter would walk down to Flannigan's, the local Irish pub. It was always festive with music and the staff all knew him.

What they didn't know was that Peter was gravely ill.

***

"Evening, Peter. The usual?" Eddie Flannigan said as he held a glass below the Guinness tap.

"Absolutely, Eddie. I wish to find sympathy and feeling," Peter said as he slid into a booth near the bar.

"Sympathy and feeling?" Eddie said.

"Oh, Eddie. If you paid more attention in school instead of chasing the lasses, you'd remember my literary friend Fyodor's observation: 'And the more I drink the more I feel it. That's why I drink too. I try to find sympathy and feeling in drink...I drink so that I may suffer twice as much!'"

"And what do you have to suffer for, Peter? What I'd give to be retired like you and free to do as I please." Eddie walked around the bar and handed Peter his pint.

"I'd happily go back to work and abandon all this idleness if Annie were well and home again," Peter said.

Eddie slid into the booth. "I'm sorry, Peter. We'd all sacrifice what we could if it would restore Annie. How's she doing?"

"She's existing, Eddie. I slip her flasks. Sometimes she laughs. But her mind is adrift. Each day she floats further away."

"I'll keep praying for her, Peter."

Eddie was a kind man. The son of Thomas Flannigan, who originally owned and operated the pub before heart disease ended his life at age 62. And so Eddie took over the place.

"Now leave me be, Eddie," Peter said as he sipped his Guinness. "You've got customers, and I've got my thoughts to reflect on."

Eddie smiled and returned to the bar.

Peter reached inside the small book bag he carried, and slipped out a well-worn copy of Saul Bellow's "Dangling Man." He flipped the pages, re-reading underlined passages and his marginalia notes.

Peter thought of his recent cancer diagnosis. The oncologist, Dr. Sullivan, was optimistic. She had a treatment plan. Without it, he would surely die. With it, the cancer could be arrested. Perhaps even permanently.

But he told her no.

No to the treatment. No to more time. No to more empty days without Annie and their old life. He knew Annie's time was short, and perhaps the best thing now was to bow out. To drift away together.

"Well, aren't you the sad old man, huddled with your beer and books."

Peter looked up to see Father Ryan slip into the booth. The priest looked over at Eddie, held up his finger, and Eddie nodded.

"I see you're lingering over Saul Bellow," Father Ryan said. "I don't know what you see in him. Joseph, the dangling man, is discursive. Too closed in on himself. What was the line? Ah, yes: 'Some men seem to know exactly where their opportunities lie; they break prisons and cross whole Siberias to pursue them. One room holds me.'"

"I can relate to Joseph. I'm dangling like him, sometimes,"

Peter said.

"You remind me of Anne Shirley," Father Ryan said.

"Anne Shirley?" Peter looked confused. "Is she one of your parishioners?"

"Don't tell me the great literary professor hasn't read L. M. Montgomery's Anne of Green Gables? Marilla Cuthbert and her brother tried to adopt a boy to help on the farm, but there was a mixup with the orphanage and they got a little girl named Anne Shirley instead. And one day Anne says to Marilla, 'My life is a perfect graveyard of buried hopes.'"

"Please tell me you're building up to something profound," Peter said as he took another sip of his beer.

"Well, you remind me of Anne Shirley. In the story, she goes on to explain that she read that line about buried hopes in a book, and she repeats it often to comfort herself whenever life disappoints her."

"It doesn't sound comforting," Peter said.

"Exactly. You see, some people think there's romance in dreams forsaken in the name of sacrifice. Playing the 'what might have been' game sometimes blinds us to what is. Ever since Annie's illness, you seem to view your life as over, Peter. A graveyard of buried hopes. I'm worried that you can't see the future, and your part in it." Father Ryan looked up as Eddie walked over and handed him his beer.

"Peter, you seem a bit withdrawn," Father Ryan continued. "Not yourself. I'm so sorry about Annie, and God bless you for all your visits. But what about you? Are you doing okay?"

What Father Ryan left out was that he knew Peter had cancer. It's a small town, and when oncology doctors confess frustration over a patient refusing treatment, a good priest has to explore options and solutions.

"I'm fine. I just wish God spared Annie," Peter said.

"So do I, Peter. But then, we see so little here. In all of space and time, perhaps we'll never understand God's designs. The connections, reasons, and consequences of things." Father Ryan sipped his beer, letting his words linger.

"You'll forgive me if I hold a less charitable outlook about God's plans," Peter said.

"I understand, Peter." Father Ryan knew that hardship and loss sometimes turn people away from God and faith. And that some folks hold no religious beliefs. All he could do was try. "By the way, I have a favor to ask, Peter. You're probably the only one who can help."

"What's that, Father?" Peter said with a wary eye.

"We have a youngster from Sacred Heart orphanage who was recently adopted by the Sweeney family. You might recall Mary Sweeney was never able to have children, so they adopted."

"And?" Peter asked.

"And the child they adopted is 14 years old and underperforming in school. Struggling with English and writing. I know you volunteer at the tutoring center. Would you be willing to meet with the kid?"

"What's the kid's name?" Peter asked.

"Stacey. Great kid, but a bit remote and hard to figure out," Father Ryan said. "If you'd be willing to work with Stacey, it might get your mind off your troubles. Maybe you'll find some breadcrumbs."

"Breadcrumbs?" Peter asked.

"Yeah, breadcrumbs. Those unexpected, little signs that tell you all is not lost. That life has meaning, hope, and God's grace."

"Well, I don't know."

"Please, Peter. We need your help. Let's give this kid a chance." Father Ryan finished the last of his pint. He was a hard man to say no to. Peter remembered how often Father Ryan visited during the early days of Annie's illness.

Peter gazed down at his Dangling Man book, a sort of philo-sophical diary novel. A story about a man, Joseph, caught be-tween civilian life and induction into military service. Caught between two worlds, free for the first time, facing a year of idleness. He is a dangling man. But then freedom, when not properly used, can sometimes become a hangman's noose. Per-haps, Peter thought, he is caught between two worlds. The past and the future. Dangling. Just like Joseph.

"Okay, fine. Send the kid to the tutoring center after school on Monday," Peter said.

"Bless you, Peter. Bless you," Father Ryan said.

***

"What in the devil is she doing?" Peter asked himself.

There was a woman across the street, in a parking lot, walking one way and another, her hands swinging back and forth as if she were shooing away imaginary ghosts.

It was Monday afternoon, and Peter was en route to the tutoring center for his first session with Stacey. But curiosity got the best of him. He crossed the street to get a better look.

And then he saw.

There were several quail chicks, scampering this way and that, unable to hop over the short brick wall separating them from their squawking parents. The woman was desperately trying to help.

"Can I give you a hand?" Peter asked, adding, "There's an opening near the end of the wall. If we work from both sides, we can direct them through."

"Oh, that would be lovely," the woman said. And in no time,

they ushered the little birds through the gap, where they reunited with their parents.

"Hey, aren't you Peter Burke?" the woman asked.

"Yes, I am."

"Your wife, Ann Burke, was my school teacher. She inspired me to chase my dream of veterinary school. And now I'm a veterinarian. How is she?"

"I'm afraid she has Alzheimer's disease and is in poor health."

"Oh, I'm so sorry. My grandfather had that. But you know, there were days when he remembered us. Little moments of grace. Well, thank you. And please know how special your wife is." The woman readjusted her purse, waved goodbye, and strolled off.

"Breadcrumbs," Peter thought, remembering Father Ryan's comment in the pub.

Peter double-timed his steps, not wanting to be late at the tutoring center. A few more blocks, and despite being out of breath, Peter swung open the door. He walked into the front lobby, where Claire, the receptionist, looked up and said, "Oh, Peter, there's a young student named Stacey waiting for you in room two."

"Thank you, my dear," Peter said.

He strolled down the hall, readjusted his book bag, and opened the door to room two. Inside, sitting quietly at the study desk, was Stacey. Peter took a moment to study his student. Short brown hair, dark eyeliner and lipstick, and a black tattered T-shirt with an image of Edgar Allen Poe on it. Also, a small lip ring pierced the upper corner of Stacey's mouth.

Peter didn't know if Stacey was a boy or a girl, but he didn't care. Much of society is awash in gender debates, but Peter learned long ago that such matters could easily be resolved with the Golden Rule. Treat others as you'd like to be treated. With basic dignity and respect.

"So, you're a Poe fan?" Peter said.

"Of course. Romanticism and the macabre fascinate me," Stacey replied.

With that, Peter knew instantly that this child possessed an advanced intellect. And most likely psychological wounds. To dress so differently, to unapologetically proclaim one's individuality in a sea of conformity is to mock derision. Sometimes people with wounds do that. Because in a way it strengthens them. It shows others that they can't be hurt anymore.

"My name is Peter. And I believe you're Stacey?" Peter said.

"That's me," Stacey said.

"Okay. Tell me about school. I hear you're struggling with English, yet you seem to be a reader?" Peter said.

"It's the teacher. She doesn't like the way I look."

"Then maybe we should start there. I'd love for you to write a short essay discussing your style, what it means to you, and why we should never judge a book by its cover."

"That might get me in trouble with the teacher," Stacey said.

"No, it won't. I know the teacher and the principal. As long as you're considerate in your essay, you'll be fine."

"Well alright then," Stacey said with a grin.

***

Peter and Stacey worked together for a few months.

Stacey proved to be exceptionally well-read. Because books were an escape from the orphanage. The library was a portal to other worlds, and Stacey found wisdom and solace in literary travel and exploration.

Together they worked on the roadblocks preventing Stacey

from success in the classroom. Peter even visited the teacher and explained Stacey's background and how impressed Peter was with Stacey's intellectual and literary knowledge. The teacher begrudgingly admitted that she hadn't given Stacey a fair shake, wrongly assuming that Stacey was "one of those sulking, anti-authority types."

"Well, sometimes those sulking, anti-authority types are the ones we need to be the most charitable with. Because you never know, they might surprise you," Peter told the teacher.

Before long, Stacey reported that things improved in the classroom, and she was at the top of her class.

The entire experience surprised Peter. It renewed him. His outlook was changing. Perhaps old Father Ryan was wiser than he realized.

Then Peter got a phone call.

***

"Peter, it's Dr. Keegan. I'm afraid I have some bad news."

It was the phone call Peter dreaded. The phone call he knew would come someday.

Annie's funeral was a modest affair. A few family relatives showed up, as well as Eddie Flannigan, and the blokes from the pub. Even the veterinarian, whose name he forgot, showed up. And Father Ryan officiated.

Most pleasantly, Stacey attended the service.

"Hi, Peter. I'm so sorry," Stacey said. "I don't know what to say. People at school tell me your wife was amazing. She encouraged students to embrace learning."

"Yes, she was passionate about helping students fall in love with learning," Peter said.

"Then I'll bet she would have appreciated Edgar Allen Poe's poetry. He once wrote 'Ah, not in knowledge is happiness, but in the acquisition of knowledge!'" Stacey smiled at Peter, and he could do nothing other than embrace Stacey in a bear hug.

"Thank you, Stacey. Thank you. You're a special person," Peter said.

***

Our lives can be a mystery.

We think the trajectory is set, but then adversity strikes. Annie's death devastated Peter, and it would have been easy to let nature take its course with his declining health.

But sometimes there are breadcrumbs.

Little, inexplicable events that make you wonder if maybe, just maybe, something grand and beyond your understanding is at work. Something that challenges all your assumptions, conclusions, and plans.

The other day Peter was walking to the tutoring center when he heard a rustling sound. He looked over at the bushes and there they were. The quail family. The parents were leading their brood, minus a few who likely succumbed to predators.

"Well look at that," Peter said to himself. "I guess the veterinarian and I did our good deed. You're all a fine-looking family today."

That evening, Peter checked his message machine before heading to the pub. Folks teased him about his antiquated message machine, but it had been a gift years ago from Annie, and he couldn't part with it.

There was only one message. It was from Dr. Sullivan, the oncologist.

"Hello Peter, it's Dr. Sullivan. I haven't heard back from you and I'd really like you to reconsider treatment. I think we can prevail. Please call me."

Peter put on his coat and headed down to Flannigan's pub. The usual gang was there.

Father Ryan was in a cheerful mood. "Our Sunday collection was especially generous this weekend," he said. "Let me buy you a round, Peter."

They slid into a booth and sipped their Guinness pints.

"I got a phone message from Dr. Sullivan," Peter said.

"And?" Father Ryan said.

"I'm going to call her back tomorrow and begin treatment. I think Annie would have wanted that. Not to mention Stacey. And an annoying priest I know. Maybe even the quail family."

"The quail family?" Father Ryan asked.

"Yes, the quail family. You'll have to ask the local vet. She'll explain. They're breadcrumbs, Father. Breadcrumbs of grace."

And the two of them sipped their beer, knowing that some hopes are never buried. Some dreams live on, evolve, and become something else.

But they're still beautiful.

Chapter Five

The Prisoner

Sometimes dreams don't come true. The best of plans unravel and life takes you on an unwanted detour.

For Benjamin Foster, that detour led straight to the Barstow County Correctional Center. As most prisoners know, "correctional center" is just a softer word for "prison."

Benjamin used to be a good kid. He played little league and was a decent student. He loved computers and drawing and dreamed of becoming a video game designer.

But things changed. His Dad ran off with his secretary. After his parents divorced, Benjamin lived with his mother. Dad infrequently visited and Mom had to work more to make ends meet.

Idle hands are the devil's workshop

Benjamin used to walk home after school and usually had the house to himself. He'd try to get his homework done but often was distracted by television and doodling.

Then one day after school he ran into Sid, a fellow high school student who lived in the neighborhood. Soon the two were inseparable. It wasn't long before Sid introduced Benjamin to alcohol and marijuana.

Benjamin's grades began to slip and arguments ensued with

his mother. She lacked the support needed to raise Benjamin.

Marijuana and alcohol led to mushrooms, LSD, rave parties, and then methamphetamine. Benjamin's life quickly unraveled.

They say idle hands are the devil's workshop. If that's true, then methamphetamine is the fuel that powers the devil's workshop. Benjamin's addiction to meth led to shoplifting, burglary, and crime.

Benjamin's mother was exhausted and defeated. Her son had been in and out of Juvenile Hall and even participated in a substance abuse program. But it was all to no avail.

In his early twenties, Benjamin worked part-time at a car wash. The perfect place to deal drugs. Until he got ripped off by some dangerous clients and owed money to his suppliers.

The bank robbery was supposed to be the answer to Benjamin's predicament. How could he know two off-duty cops would be in the bank that day?

The court process played out and Benjamin's public defender did what she could. In his favor, Benjamin hadn't used a gun (only pretended to have one) and didn't hurt anyone.

Benjamin's mother cried at sentencing and when he was escorted out of the courtroom in chains. He was sent to Barstow County Correctional Center. He was no longer Benjamin Foster.

He was Inmate 27409.

Meeting Rembrandt

Prison frightened Benjamin. Everywhere there were hardened men with tattoos, built-up bodies, and hidden alliances.

The prison noise was relentless. Alarms, slamming doors, arguments, buzzers, screams, and yelling. It was a concrete hell.

Navigating this new world required effort, luck, observation, bartering, and time. Unfortunately, his four-year sentence provided plenty of time.

Benjamin sought jobs that helped him avoid trouble and pass the time. His favorite job was working in the prison library.

Years later, he would reflect that the job in the library probably saved his life. Because that's where he met "Rembrandt."

Benjamin's first encounter with Rembrandt was near the rear of the prison library. It was there that Benjamin found a seventy-two-year-old inmate, seated at a desk with several art books opened around him. Also on the desk was a sketchbook filled with amazing pencil drawings.

Benjamin conversed with the old man and learned that everyone called him "Rembrandt."

"It's funny because I don't even paint," Rembrandt told Benjamin. "The prison budget cut back on paints, so all I've got are sketchbooks and pencils!"

"Yeah, but those drawings are amazing," Benjamin offered.

"I like to copy from the masters. John Singer Sargent. Caravaggio. You can learn so much from these old artists," Rembrandt said.

Old letters and regrets

It wasn't long before Benjamin and Rembrandt struck up a friendship. Rembrandt was sort of a father to Benjamin. Besides, Benjamin never heard from his deadbeat Dad.

"I told you about my robbery, but I don't think you told me your story?" Benjamin cautiously asked Rembrandt one day in the exercise yard.

"Murder. I caught my wife having an affair with a coworker. I suspected it for some time. But then one day I found her car parked at a motel." Rembrandt shook his head.

"That's terrible. I'm sorry." It was all Benjamin could think to say.

"Back then I was an alcoholic. I was drunk. I kicked in the motel door and lunged at the dude. We fought. He fell, I grabbed this marble statuette in the room and bashed it on the guy's skull. Killed him instantly."

Rembrandt looked at Benjamin and added, "And that was that. The prosecution said it was premeditated. I got 30 years. My wife left me. I had a grown daughter, Sarah, but I lost her too." Rembrandt swallowed hard.

"I'm sorry. What happened to Sarah?" Benjamin asked.

"Oh, mostly aging and disappointment, I guess. She used to visit every other month and tell me about life back home. But then it was just letters. For a while, anyway. Now she's down to Christmas cards."

Rembrandt sat on the yard bench beside Benjamin and looked him directly in the eyes. "Benjamin, it's okay. I'm at peace with it all now. I may only have old letters and regrets left of my family, but they have their own lives. I have my art and faith in God."

"I wish I could get where you are, Rembrandt. I used to have dreams, but I'm stuck here for three more years," Benjamin said.

"Well, Benjamin, if you'd like, I'll share with you some hard-earned prison wisdom. I've come up with five life strategies that work both inside and outside prison. I think they can help you." Rembrandt smiled at Benjamin.

"I can use all the help I can get," Benjamin said.

Prison wisdom

The next day in the prison library Rembrandt opened up a notebook in front of Benjamin. On the page, Rembrandt wrote his five life strategies:

1. Let go

2. Forgive yourself

3. Own it

4. Emotional maturity

5. Give thanks

As Benjamin gazed at the list, Rembrandt spoke. "When I got to prison I started to notice something. All the newbies were tense, nervous, and angry. You could see it on their faces. They were grappling with fear, but more than that. They realized all the things they lost on the outside. Affection, status, approval."

"Yeah, that hit me too," Benjamin said.

"What happens in prison is that we build mental toughness to survive. Our worlds shrink to television, exercise, reading, and maybe chess. But over time we realize we never had much control over our lives, even on the outside. We learn to let go. The guys in here that learn to let go, they're relaxed. They smile more. Acceptance can be freeing."

Rembrandt pointed at his list and said, "Number two is forgiveness, of yourself and others. If we keep blaming ourselves and others, it's like emotional quicksand. It will consume us. Forgiveness opens the door to personal growth."

"Third is learning to own your own life. Too many people blame everyone else. Most of our lives reflect our own choices. Yet people constantly deny this. They blame their spouses, children, parents, bosses."

"Yeah, I'm guilty of that one," Benjamin said. "I still blame my Dad."

"Your father has his own demons," Rembrandt said. "You know why I love the library? It's not just art books. I like to read the classics. All the stuff I should have read when I was young. Greater minds than ours have left wisdom on how to live, but we're too busy being petty and superficial to go deeper."

Rembrandt returned to the list. "Fourth on the list is emotional maturity. I wish I understood this years ago. Emotional maturity means not making excuses for yourself, taking responsibility, and avoiding shortcuts in life."

"And last but not least," Benjamin said as he read number five, "Give thanks."

Rembrandt closed the notebook and said, "Yep, gratitude is frequently forgotten. We grouse about everything. The food. Traffic. Our lousy bosses. We complain with such indignation. How would your petty complaints sound to some guy in a terminal cancer ward? Or to a couple who just lost a child in an accident? Learn to give thanks for your health, your family, your life, and your talents."

Benjamin put his hand on Rembrandt's shoulder and said, "Thank you, my friend."

The angels closed their eyes

In his remaining years at Barstow Correctional Center, Benjamin adopted Rembrandt's five life strategies. He studied daily in the library, consuming classic books. He began a course of study in computer science and design.

Rembrandt passed away six months before Benjamin's release from prison. Benjamin mourned his friend's death but felt a deep sense of gratitude for all Rembrandt taught him. Benjamin wrote letters to people he hurt in his life. He wrote to his father to forgive him. He wrote to Sid and shared Rembrandt's wisdom. He even wrote to Sarah, Rembrandt's daughter, to tell her who her father became.

As Benjamin signed the forms and changed into civilian clothing, he said a quiet prayer of thanks to Rembrandt.

In the prison parking lot, Benjamin's mother said a prayer of her own. A prayer of hope, that Benjamin had changed. A prayer for the future.

As Benjamin and his mother drove out of the parking lot,

the angels closed their eyes. They said a prayer of thanks and redemption for the prisoner, Rembrandt. For in saving the life of Benjamin, Rembrandt saved his own soul.

Chapter Six

It's Not in the Stars to Hold Our Destiny but in Ourselves

Jimmy slipped off his sandals to bask his feet in the morning sunlight.

"Dude, check out this video on my Insta feed," Jimmy said, holding up his phone. "It's some dude playing ping pong with his cat."

"No offense, Jimmy, but how about we just talk," Mark said with a smile, adding, "I'm kind of sick of screens."

"Oh, okay...sure." Jimmy slipped the phone into his jacket pocket.

The morning air was crisp, and the sun warmed them both. Few people were in the plaza, and a stillness filled the air. Mark took a bite of his pastry and Jimmy sipped his latte.

"So, I have some news," Mark said.

"I quit working for Awaken.ai and I'm leaving California," Mark said softly.

"Are you kidding me? Awaken is like the primo startup, and you and I grew up here in California. What's going on, Mark? What are you thinking?"

"I'm thinking about reinvention, Jimmy. I want to dive into photography full-time. I want a life, not just a paycheck. And I'm sort of sick of technology. I feel like it gets in the way too much. It distracts from real life. It just keeps growing until we forget who we are."

"I thought your photography and the weddings you shoot were a side hustle? Mark, you can make way more money at Awaken. Don't get me wrong, you're an awesome photographer, but money matters, dude. It's security. And don't you want to be at the forefront of the AI revolution? It's the future."

"Yeah, Jimmy, I know. It scares me a little, to walk away. Artificial intelligence is the biggest thing in the industry right now. But it's...artificial. It's not real. Sure, it could change the world, but it's not what I want my life to be about."

"What did your boss say?" Jimmy asked.

"My boss thinks I lost it. She said to take some time and think about it. But I've been thinking about it for a long time. I mean, look around, Jimmy. Everywhere we go, people have their heads lost in their devices. Me too. If I'm not checking emails, I'm scrolling through feeds. I want to spend more time with my head up, looking at the real world, not a bunch of artificial crap. I mean, ninety percent of the stuff online is a waste of time."

As a full-stack developer, Jimmy could relate. "Yeah, there are days I want to shoot my laptop and live a simpler life," Jimmy said.

Mark slipped out a notebook wrapped in a soft leather cover.

"Uh-oh, here comes the notebook," Jimmy said, knowing Mark was a consummate reader and life-long journaler.

Mark began flipping through pages of dense notes, and then put his finger on a specific paragraph. He looked up at Jimmy with a grin.

"I sense words of wisdom are about to commence," Jimmy said, taking another sip of his latte.

***

"People are a lot like cameras," Mark began. "We let the outside world in, and we reflect it. But how much we let in, and how well we see it, depends on the lenses we wear. Some people have a wide-angle lens, and they see a lot, but miss the details. Others have a fast lens, and their field of view is tighter. Still, others have filters, that skew their view one way or another. We have to be careful because lenses affect reality. In the end, what matters is the subject. What we're looking at."

"What inspired all this?" Jimmy asked.

"I've been reading a book our project manager at work recommended. It's by Aidan McCullen. The title is Undisruptable: A Mindset of Permanent Reinvention for Individuals, Organisations and Life."

Mark glanced at his notebook and said, "Here, listen to this. I copied it down from the book."

Mark began reading:

"Every time we add a lens, it modifies how we experience the world. The difference between that contraption and a worldview is that each time a new lens is added to our worldview, the lenses remain in place. We must be vigilant about the lenses we admit, because they color our view of the world, sometimes to our disadvantage. They can limit us, encourage us to confirm evidence, and make us hold on to mental models, business models, and convictions even when they no longer serve us."

"Okay, what's this got to do with you quitting your job and moving away?" Jimmy said.

"Well, I feel like I've had a lens cap on all this time. I couldn't see anything. I was blind to reality. But then, last summer, I took a backpacking trip in Montana. Remember?"

"Yeah, you showed me the photos. They were amazing," Jimmy said.

"So when I returned from that trip, something changed in me. Work felt wrong. I hated being stuck inside with the computer all day. All I saw were my colleagues, their faces lit up by computer screens. And I couldn't stop thinking about the guy in the jeep."

"The guy in the jeep?" Jimmy said, confused.

***

"I was on my way to Glacier National Park last summer, and I stopped at this local brewery in Flathead Valley," Mark began. "And there was this rugged-looking dude parked in a red jeep with mud all over it in the parking lot. Sitting next to him in the front seat was a huge Husky. The dude was probably sixty years old, with a beard, and not a care in the world. He pointed at my license plate and said 'What part of California?'"

"Uh-oh, was he one of those locals who hate Californians moving into his state?" Jimmy asked.

"No, he was totally cool. Turns out he grew up in California, not far from our hometown. So we end up going into the brewery together, with his dog. We ordered a few pints and sat outside in the beer garden."

"Nice," Jimmy said.

"It was more than nice. It was life-changing," Mark said. "The guy's name is Clint, which is funny because he reminds me a little of Clint Eastwood. He used to work in finance, but then his wife was diagnosed with ovarian cancer."

"That's hard," Jimmy said.

"Yeah, it devastated him. Just before her diagnosis, she found this beat-up little puppy, a Husky, abandoned in a field. They tried to find the owner without luck, adopted her, and named her Zara. I guess the name has Arabic origins. It means 'blooming flower' or 'radiance.' Anyway, Clint told me that his wife declined quickly, and was gone within six months."

"I can't imagine," Jimmy said.

"After Clint's wife died, he questioned everything," Mark said. "Including his work. He came to realize what a selfish prick he was. His whole life was about winning. Getting ahead, stepping on people, and making money. He told me he wasn't a literary guy, but after his wife died, he escaped into Dean Koontz's novels. One of those books, 'The Darkest Evening of the Year,' contained a line that struck him like a thunderbolt. He memorized it and recited it for me. Wait, I wrote it down in my notebook."

Mark flipped through several pages.

"Ah, here it is," Mark said.

And then he read the following:

"Because God is never cruel, there is a reason for all things. We must know the pain of loss; because if we never knew it, we would have no compassion for others, and we would become monsters of self-regard, creatures of unalloyed self-interest. The terrible pain of loss teaches humility to our prideful kind, has the power to soften uncaring hearts, to make a better person of a good one."

"Wow, that's pretty powerful," Jimmy said.

***

Mark leaned forward in his chair and continued. "So, what does Clint do? He up and quits his high-paying finance job, sells his mansion and moves with Zara to Montana. I guess he and his wife used to vacation there, and he always loved hiking in Glacier National Park."

"But what did he do to make a living?" Jimmy asked.

"Clint said his wife loved animals, which is why she rescued and adopted Zara. So Clint ends up volunteering at the Flathead County Animal Shelter. Over time the county officials found out about Clint's finance background, and he eventually became the director of the whole operation. He said he loves the job. The hours are flexible, the work is fulfilling, and he has more free time for hiking and camping." With that, Mark leaned back in his chair, smiling.

"He can't possibly be making the kind of money he used to make," Jimmy said.

"Of course not. But with the sale of his home in California, he found a beautiful ranch house in Montana, not far from the shelter. And his definition of 'wealth' means free time and doing something meaningful. He even quoted that line from Ralph Waldo Emerson...what was it?" Mark began flipping pages in his notebook.

"There he goes again, looking up quotes," Jimmy said with a laugh.

"Ah, here it is." Mark held up his notebook and read verbatim the following:

"The purpose of life is not to be happy. It is to be useful, to be honorable, to be compassionate, to have it make some difference that you have lived and lived well."

"I guess Clint had an impact on you," Jimmy said.

"No doubt, Clint made an impression. But honestly, even before I met him that little creative muse in my head has been whispering in my ear. Telling me to listen to my heart and chase my photography dream."

"So, when do you leave for Montana?" Jimmy said with a slight frown.

"In two weeks," Mark said.

True to his word, two weeks later Mark packed up his Toyota 4Runner and left for Montana. For a new life. A simpler life of photography, the outdoors, and less technology.

***

Jimmy and Mark stayed in touch over the next few years.

Once, Mark sent Jimmy a copy of Outside Magazine, featuring Mark's photography on the cover. Other times, Mark sent Jimmy prints of his best photography. Scenes of camping trips, wildlife, artful shots of the local breweries, Clint in his Jeep, and a few selfies. Mark's hair was long in the pictures, and he had a beard. He was always smiling. He was happy.

And then one day everything changed.

"You've got a phone call on line two," Jimmy's work manager, Doris, shouted to him.

"Who is it, I'm working on a tight deadline," Jimmy said.

"Some guy named Clint," Doris said.

It was the worst phone call Jimmy ever received. Clint's voice was raspy, his tone somber.

"Jimmy, this is Clint. I'm so sorry to have to tell you this. We lost him. We lost Mark. We were hiking. Mark, me, and a few other buddies. We set up camp, drank beers, told stories, and hit the sack. In the morning we couldn't wake Mark up. We used our satellite phone and had to medevac him out by helicopter."

"What the hell happened to him?" Jimmy said, in a state of

shock.

"The doctors think it was his heart. Something congenital and undiagnosed. We don't know for sure. He just passed in his sleep. I'm so sorry, Jimmy. I know you two were close. That's all I got right now. But I'll be in touch."

The writer Walter de la Mare wrote that "God has mercifully ordered that the human brain works slowly; first the blow, hours afterward the bruise." But this wasn't the case for Jimmy. He immediately felt the blow, his heart felt crushed, and his soul felt bruised.

Jimmy slipped out of his chair onto his knees on the floor and wept, to the shock and astonishment of his coworkers.

***

Jimmy's flight touched down two days later at Glacial Park International Airport in Kalispell city.

Jimmy traveled light, with only a carry-on backpack. He made his way to the passenger pickup area and texted Clint. Clint drove up in his red jeep a few minutes later with his huge husky Zara. Clint hopped out of the jeep, walked up to Jimmy, and immediately gave him a huge bear hug.

"I'm so sorry about everything, Jimmy, but I'm glad you're here," Clint said. "The funeral starts at 4 PM, and there's a reception afterward at the brewery. So we've got a little time. I thought maybe you'd like to see Mark's cabin?"

"Absolutely," Jimmy said.

They drove for 45 minutes, and Jimmy mostly stared out the window at the rugged beauty of the countryside. Clint must have sensed and respected Jimmy's mood, saying little. Zara, however, took to licking Jimmy's ear as if soothing him.

Clint drove down a treelined dirt road, past a mailbox affixed to a wooden beam, and parked in the gravel driveway beside a small cabin.

"Here we are," Clint said. "The door's unlocked. Why don't you go inside, take your time, and Zara and I will go for a walk."

"Thanks, Clint, I appreciate this," Jimmy said.

***

Jimmy opened the door to the cabin and walked into what was left of his friend Mark's world. It was a small but tidy cabin.

Mark's camping gear, boots, and a few jackets were all by the front door in an open closet. There was a neatly made twin bed in the corner, with a shelf full of books and a reading light beside the bed.

All around the cabin there were collected items from Mark's travels as a professional photographer. On Mark's desk lay his flip phone, yet another one of his stands against what he called "the tyranny of technology." Beside the flip phone was Mark's Leica M6 film camera. "Digital can never replace the analog beauty of film," Mark often said.

On a nearby shelf sat a beautiful Chimayo pot, a gift from a few Pueblo Indians in the Chimayo region of New Mexico. Pueblo Indians have inhabited that area since the 12th century.

Mark had been hiking through the area a few years ago and happened upon a wedding reception. One of the Indians spotted Mark's camera and mistakenly thought he was one of the photographers. And true to Mark's giving nature, he went along with it and gave away all the photos. As thanks, he was gifted the lovely Chimayo pot.

Mark may be gone, but the cabin was filled with the spirit of

Mark. The photography prints pinned to the walls. The many collectibles from Mark's travels. And just when Jimmy thought it was all too overwhelming, he spotted the edge of a small object jutting out of the bookshelf.

Jimmy pulled it out in disbelief and then sank into the desk chair laughing.

***

Jimmy always believed that the little red 1984 Hot Wheels Pontiac Fiero toy car sitting in his hand had been confiscated years ago by his grade school principal.

Turns out, Mark pulled a fast one on Jimmy.

When Mark and Jimmy were in grade school they found the toy car in the grass during recess. Mark grabbed it first and claimed "Finders keepers," but Jimmy lunged at him and yelled, "Not fair, we both saw it!"

The two began fighting and rolling in the grass before the school custodian separated them and hauled them off to the principal's office. Mark told Jimmy that the principal confiscated the toy car.

"Oh Mark, you sly devil," Jimmy said, still laughing to himself.

There was a knock on the cabin door, and Clint stepped inside and said, "Is everything alright? I thought I heard a shout or something."

"I'm fine, Clint. I just found out what a conniver Mark could be." And with that, Jimmy told the story of the Hot Wheels toy car.

Clint found himself laughing too. And then he leaned against the desk, put his arm on Jimmy's shoulder, and said, "I don't know if Mark ever told you, but I'm a Dean Koontz fan. I used to read his books after my wife died to get my mind off the grief. Anyway, in his book 'Fear Nothing' he wrote something kind of cool: 'Never leave a friend behind. Friends are all we have to get us through this life—and they are the only things from this world that we could hope to see in the next.'"

"Yeah, but don't you feel like Mark left us behind?" Jimmy said.

"No, I don't see it that way, Jimmy. It feels more like he's gone on ahead, to scout out the trail for us. To find the best campsite. I feel like when we get there, he'll have a fire going and ask what took us so long."

***

Mark's parents flew in for the funeral, which was held in a local church. Jimmy was amazed by the turnout of so many different people from all walks of life.

And what struck Jimmy most was how down-to-earth, authentic, and real everyone was.

A reception was held after the funeral at the local brewery. The same one that Mark originally met Clint at. There was music and laughter and Zara was having fun chasing the bar cat around the beer garden. The air was crisp and clean, and the beer garden lights sparkled against the evening sky.

"When do you head back home?" Clint said to Jimmy as he handed him another pint of IPA.

"I don't know, Clint. My boss left a voicemail that she needs me back the day after tomorrow. We've got a big project due. But...I don't know." Jimmy stared at his beer.

"But?" Clint said.

"I used to think Mark was crazy to walk away from his job in AI. But I think I get it now. He longed for something real. It's like he figured out his destiny, in this beautiful place." Jimmy looked up at the stars.

"You know, Mark loved to write down all these quotes. He drove me crazy with them sometimes. There was one he said, I think it was Shakespeare, and I never forgot it." And with that, Clint recited the following:

"It is not in the stars to hold our destiny but in ourselves."

Jimmy smiled, then began typing a text message on his phone. It was only four words. Before he hit send, he looked at Clint.

"Can I ask you a favor, Clint?"

"Sure, anything," Clint said.

"Would you be free to take me hiking and camping the rest of this week? I could use some time out there. You know, to work on my destiny and all that," Jimmy said with a smile.

"It would be an honor, Jimmy. And I have this feeling that Mark will be with us."

Jimmy looked up at the stars in the night sky, then glanced down at his phone and the text message he had typed. Zara was sitting next to Jimmy, and let out an unexpected woof. It was like she was encouraging Jimmy.

"Why not?" Jimmy said, and he hit send on his phone.

The next morning in California Jimmy's boss, Doris, poured coffee into her travel mug. She was running late, and she knew there would be traffic. Another day in the rat race, she thought to herself.

Carol slid into her car, and before she backed out of the driveway, she opened her phone to check messages. There was a text from Jimmy.

She clicked on the text message and read the following:

"I won't be back."

She sat in the driveway staring at the text for a long time.

She thought about Jimmy, and how his buddy Mark had fled this life of commutes and deadlines and blinking screens for something real. She envied Jimmy, and lamented the fact that she was too old now to run away to a simpler life.

And before she put her BMW in gear, she typed the following reply:

"Good for you, Jimmy. Don't ever stop chasing your dreams."

Chapter Seven

The Nobility of Compassion

Sergeant Peter Jensen had been with the Rockport Police Department for sixteen years, but he'd never seen a case like this. For the last two weeks, the calls came in from all over town.

Always the same thing. An angry homeowner or gardener. Insisting the police get to the bottom of it. After all, the spree of thefts had merited several newspaper articles. The theft of flowers, to these victims, was a serious crime.

There was Mr. Jacobs and his dahlias. He was a meticulous gardener. He didn't know who snipped off so many of his prized possessions, but he wanted blood.

And of course, Mrs. Idleberg, whose beautiful roses vanished in the middle of the day. "You must investigate this," she said in her Latvian accent, "because those roses...they were my babies."

Sergeant Jensen couldn't believe his luck. Of all the crazy cases to get stuck with. Really? Flower thefts? The other cops on his shift did what cops do. Teased him relentlessly. Sergeant Jensen found flowers in his locker and on his desk. One day he even found some rose petals in his uniform pockets.

Don't send me flowers when I'm dead

Walter Higgins' long career as an English butler prepared him well for Essex House, the Rockport bed and breakfast he and his wife Mary bought eight years ago.

Walter's mother had passed away and left him a sizable inheritance, which he used to leave Britain and begin a new life as owner and operator of Essex House. Mary was an excellent chef, and Essex House became known as one of the finest B&Bs in town.

Having been a professional butler, Walter was a stickler for details. Beyond the immaculate rooms, hallways, linens, and fine dinner wines, Walter knew the power of color. He hired a top gardener to encircle Essex House with magnificent flower beds.

Walter's eye for details led to a break in Sgt. Jensen's case. "Last night around 6 pm, there was an elderly bloke with a backpack outside," Walter told Sgt. Jensen. "I went and asked him if he needed any help. The man looked at me and said, 'Don't send me flowers when I'm dead. If you like me, send them while I'm alive.' And then he walked off."

"Okay," said Sgt. Jensen. "Anything else?"

"I recognized the line he quoted. It's from Brian Clough. An English football player and manager. And one more thing. When he walked away, I saw one of our roses dangling from his backpack." Walter's eyes twinkled, clearly pleased with himself. "Do you think this is your flower thief?" Walter asked.

"Let's get our composite sketch guy to come and work on a drawing from your description. He's self-taught but pretty good. Once done, we'll post it around town. And thanks for all your help," Sgt. Jensen said.

The free soul is rare

Maria Contreras liked working at the Oceanview Residential Community. She had a soft spot for the elderly and a reverence for the grace and dignity of the greatest generation.

One resident, in particular, had broken Maria's heart. Esther Steinberg. Esther had been an art teacher who specialized in working with developmentally delayed children.

Esther could have been a notable artist, but she relinquished that path to help disabled children. How sad, Maria often thought, that Esther became disabled herself. All because of a crippling stroke.

One evening shift Maria saw the Rockport Police Department's "wanted man" flyer in the break room. She immediately recognized the face in the composite sketch. It was Morrie Steinberg, Esther's husband. He was a retired English professor.

Morrie was a fixture at Oceanview Residential Community. He visited Esther every day and placed fresh flowers all around her room. Even though Esther could no longer talk, the tears of joy in her eyes said everything. Morrie would hold her hand and often tell her that since she could no longer paint, he would paint her room for her. With colorful flowers.

End of the journey

Morrie once told Maria that his wife Esther was unique. He said, "Few of us ever attain what Esther has. Through her art and working with children, she found a life of peace and grace. Charles Bukowski once wrote, 'The free soul is rare, but you know it when you see it—basically because you feel good, very good, when you are near or with them.' And that's how I've always felt with my Esther. So very good."

Maybe Maria suspected all along that Morrie was the flower thief. After all, the thefts had been in the papers for a few weeks. And who could miss the abundance of fresh flowers around Esther's room? But Maria knew that Morrie was on a fixed income and used most of his pension to pay for Esther's care.

With tears in her eyes, Maria finally made the call. It was the right thing to do. Sergeant Jensen arrived within the hour and Maria told him everything about Morrie, Esther, and the daily flowers he brought.

That afternoon Sgt. Jensen sat in the lobby and waited for Morrie to arrive. Sure enough, Morrie strolled in with a large backpack on his shoulder.

Sergeant Jensen immediately recognized Morrie's likeness from the composite sketch. Morrie gazed over at Sgt. Jensen. He stopped walking and looked down toward Esther's room, then back at Sgt. Jensen. "I suppose you're here for me," Morrie said.

For the next hour, Sgt. Jensen interviewed Morrie and got a full confession. "I used to buy her flowers. They made her so happy," Morrie explained. "But money got tight, so I 'liberated' some local color to make a disabled woman happy."

Sergeant Jensen couldn't help but think of his wife, Jennifer. They'd been struggling lately with the mortgage and in their relationship. Maybe if he adopted the same sacrifice and love for Jennifer that Morrie had for Esther, life would be better.

Sergeant Jensen said he admired Morrie. Stealing was wrong, but his heart was in the right place.

There is a nobility of compassion

Morrie was quiet for a moment and then said, "Esther always said that we don't live in a coincidental universe. Things happen for a reason. As the author Wally Lamb wrote, 'The seeker embarks on a journey to find what he wants and discovers, along the way, what he needs.' Maybe we were meant to meet? Either way, I take full responsibility for my actions. Will you at least let me say goodbye to Esther before you take me in?"

In the days that followed Morrie's arrest, the town was abuzz with gossip and letters to the editor. Some were unsympathetic and congratulated the Rockport Police Department for solving the case. Others felt sorry for Morrie but acknowledged that he shouldn't have stolen all those flowers. And then the following letter to the editor was printed in the Rockport Herald:

Dear Editor,

I'm a grade school English teacher. I couldn't help but notice that Mr. Morrie Steinberg was once an english professor. It seems to me that Mr. Steinberg's actions, while illegal, were motivated by love. If I marry someday, I pray it's to someone like Mr. Steinberg. In John Connolly's book 'The Killing Kind,' he wrote, 'The nature of humanity, its essence, is to feel another's pain as one's own and to act to take that pain away. There is a nobility in compassion, a beauty in empathy, a grace in forgiveness.' Perhaps Mr. Steinberg can repay his debt to this community by volunteering his time in our local elementary school, teaching English? I for one would be honored to have him in my classroom.

-Beth Melrose

As luck would have it, District Attorney Edward Stansfield was reading the Rockport Herald the day Beth Melrose's letter appeared. He couldn't help but be moved. In short order, he spoke to the assistant district attorney assigned to Morrie Steinberg's prosecution.

The various victims were contacted about Morrie's case. Once everyone learned of the motivation behind the thefts, a different tone emerged. One of forgiveness more than retribution.

Walter Higgins' wife, Mary, had taken a watercolor class from Esther Steinberg a few years before her stroke. Other victims had seen Beth Melrose's letter to the editor and liked the idea of community service.

A new beginning

Eventually, all the victims agreed not to seek prosecution if Morrie Steinberg agreed to volunteer as an English teacher in the local elementary schools. Morrie was deeply moved by their forgiveness. He readily agreed to volunteer in the local schools and teach English for the rest of his days.

Morrie began teaching English as an assistant instructor in Beth Melrose's classroom. He'd forgotten how much he loved teaching and felt that he found a new lease on life.

> *"Forgiveness says you are given another chance to make a new beginning."* —Desmond Tutu

More than the teaching, it's what happened next that warmed Morrie's soul and brought tears to his eyes.

Maria Contreras called Morrie and told him to rush over to Oceanview Residential Community. There was something he just had to see. People from all over town had brought some things for Esther.

Morrie made his way from the school across town and ran up the steps to Oceanview Residential Community. "Is Esther alright?" he called out to the nurses and Maria. "Yes, Morrie, she's fine. Go to her room and see her!" Maria said.

Morrie ran into her room and found Esther sitting up in bed, a broad smile on her face. The entire room was completely full of flowers. Freshly cut flowers adorned the shelves, windowsills, her bed, the desk, and pots and containers all around the floors. Flowers from the people of a forgiving, kind community.

"What is this?" Morrie asked as he sat down beside Esther, holding her hand. And for the first time since her stroke, Esther looked Morrie in the eyes and slowly said, "It's love."

Chapter Eight

My Piano in the Woods

The hardest part of our move was donating the piano.

I grew up with that baby grand, and it held countless memories. Like all the Fridays after school when I wanted to be with my friends but instead sat for ninety minutes with Mrs. Irma Hincenburg as I labored over scales and pieces like Debussy's Clair de Lune.

Mrs. Hincenburg fled Latvia when the Soviets invaded her country in 1940 after signing a secret protocol in 1939 with Nazi Germany. She and her husband abandoned their home and possessions before emigrating to the United States to start over in Northern California.

Mrs. Hincenburg's husband had been a successful banking president in Latvia and managed to return to the profession, albeit in a less prestigious position. Mrs. Hincenburg returned to her work as a piano teacher after they saved enough money to purchase a used baby grand.

Mrs. Hincenburg has been dead for many years now. Donating my piano called up all those memories.

Or maybe Mrs. Hincenburg's spirit sensed my melancholy and, through memories, reminded me that donating a piano is far easier than abandoning your home, your old way of life, and emigrating to a foreign land to start over.

I can still hear her firm but kind Latvian accent saying, "No, Jack, relax your fingers and press softly on the keys," as her incredibly soft fingers repositioned mine. Her stout body sat beside me on the piano bench, and the cadence of her voice and soft fingers often seemed to anesthetize me into a sleepy state.

I was beginning to feel sleepy when the Principal of Bayshore Christian School, Mike Patterson, interrupted my somnolent memoryscape.

"Jack, are you sure you don't want to sell this nice piano?"

I focused, looked around Mike's office briefly, and said, "I thought about selling it, but that takes time, and we're moving this Saturday. Steven loved his elementary school days here at Bayshore Christian School, so what better place to donate the piano? I grew up playing that piano, so I want it to land in a good home. I figure you could use it in the music program."

"Your son Steven was a joy to have. And your timing is perfect, Jack. Our piano is ancient. We could use a newer one. I can't tell you how generous a gift this is."

"It's my pleasure, Mike. I'll pay for the movers—we'll have to act quickly because I've got a million other things to do before our move this weekend," I said.

"Of course, I can have my facilities guy, Joe, meet the movers anytime this week. And Jack, we're going to miss you in town."

"Yeah, I'm going to miss this town and all of you. But my company is moving to Nevada, and I can't afford to give up my position and look for something else," I said.

"No worries. I'll call Joe and give him a heads-up. Just text or call once you have a day and time to deliver the piano," Mike said. He must have caught a sad look in my eyes because he said, "Didn't you say you grew up playing that piano?"

"Yeah, I spent years as a kid playing it. It's kind of like an old friend. But there's no room for it in the new house in Nevada."

"Well, your old friend will soon be surrounded by our school kids in the music class, making beautiful music and inspiring young souls." Mike always had a way with words.

"Thanks, Mike, I appreciate that," I said as we shook hands.

***

The night before the movers came to take the piano, I sat down on the bench and played Beethoven's Für Elise, which was my sister Lilly's favorite piece.

She was two years older than me, and when we were kids and I practiced on the piano, she kept me company in the living room reading her books and scribbling in her journals.

She was a voracious reader and avid writer.

She loved to leave me little notes in my school lunch bags or under my pillow. Silly notes like, "What if hamsters had long legs like giraffes? Think about it." And, "You have a runny nose and you think it's funny but it's snot."

I was an asthmatic and often sickly kid, and whenever I had the flu or a virus, Lilly always sat beside my bed and read stories to me. Jack London's "White Fang" was my favorite.

Lilly was sweet, loving, and kind. She always made me feel better.

The priest at her funeral told us that sometimes God calls home the sweet, loving, and kind souls. I never understood this because if people are perfect in heaven, then wouldn't it make more sense to leave the sweet, loving, and kind souls here on

Earth where they can do more good?

Anyway, Lilly did a lot of good while she was with us.

She was loving and funny and used to bake these little cakes in her Kenner Easy Bake Mini Wave oven that our parents gave her one Christmas. I'd beg her to make me a tiny cake and she'd say, "I am Princess Cupcake, and you must bow before me if you desire a cake."

I always bowed immediately, and that's how she got the nickname "Cupcake."

Everyone loved Lilly, but in high school she discovered boys and for some reason, the bad boys intrigued her. Before long she was going to parties, and drinking, and then one night she fell intoxicated off an embankment. The head injury put her in a coma and she never woke up. Her death was devastating, and my parents never really recovered from it. I don't think I recovered, either.

I played Für Elise a bit longer but then I had to stop.

***

I remained stoic the morning the movers came and took away the piano.

My wife Claire and I finished boxing the last of our things and that weekend we drove to Nevada. To our new life in a new town.

A few days after we settled in, our son Steven called.

"So, Dad, how's the new house?"

"It's full of boxes. How's my favorite Lieutenant?" I asked.

Steven was already out of college and serving in the Air Force in Colorado. He worked in cyber security.

"Oh, you know, Dad, busy as ever keeping us safe from all enemies, foreign and domestic." The reality was that much of his work was top secret and he couldn't share much.

But that didn't matter. Hearing his voice, knowing he was happy and thriving in his career. That's all that mattered.

I handed the phone to Claire, and as the two of them conversed, I looked out the window, at the Nevada mountains in the distance, and then began unpacking more boxes.

The years unfurled and there were parties and laughter and some tears in our house. The most tears came the day we learned of Claire's cancer diagnosis.

Aggressive cancer.

Near the end, Steven was granted leave and spent two weeks with me. We visited Claire every day in hospice and were blessed to be with her when she slipped away peacefully. I'll never forget Steven afterward, hugging me so tightly as we both wept.

At Claire's funeral, I read the following poem by John P. Read:

Still I hear those voices
From a time so long ago.
I see so many faces
But not the one I love and know.
I walk the same old streets,
Hear your footsteps just the same.
How I'd love to wake tomorrow
And walk with you once again.
Just to look into your eyes
And tell you about my day.
It's those little things I miss
Since the day you went away.
I now pray to God in heaven
To keep you in his care,
To comfort you and heal this hurt
Until the day I meet you there.

Steven was a great help to me, but eventually, he had to return to work, and then I found myself alone in a house deprived of Claire's love, energy, and presence.

My dear father used to tell me, "Don't grow old, Jack," but then what's the alternative? Dying young? I know Dad meant "Don't let age and loss get to you," but I don't think any one of us is immune.

Life brings love and joy. But it also brings loss and pain.

And all we can do is soldier on.

***

A few more years passed, and I sold the house in Nevada.

It's hard to leave a place where so many fond memories reside, but since Claire's death, the house held no joy. I moved to Colorado to be closer to Steven, who was married now with a beautiful wife, Allison, and their lovely little boy, Brian.

I found a spacious condo near Colorado Springs, where Steven teaches at the Air Force Academy.

Now retired, I had more time for books and hiking and enjoying visits with Steven, Allison, and my grandson Brian. Sometimes my past life would find me, like when I got a call from my old neighbor Doug, back in California where I lived before Nevada.

"Jack, Mike Patterson passed away," Doug said over the phone, adding, "Remember him, the principal at Bayshore Christian School?"

"Yes, Mike was a good man. I donated my old baby grand piano to his school."

"That's right, I remember you telling me that. Well, they're going to have a memorial service for him at Gateway Bible Church next Saturday at 10 AM. If you'd like to come, stay with Donna and me for the weekend."

"Thank you, Doug, that's very kind of you," I said.

I flew out for the funeral and got a hotel room. I prefer the freedom of hotels. I thanked Doug again and said I didn't want to be an imposition.

Mike was beloved in the community and after the funeral, there was a reception at the church. They had an open mic and folks shared stories about Mike. And one speaker, a local realtor named Carl, mentioned what a pity it was that Bayshore Christian School closed its doors a few years ago.

This was news to me.

I introduced myself to Carl and asked him why the school closed. He set his drink down and said, "Well, enrollment was down, and then this big developer came to town. Mike was ready to retire and with the cost of living here, he struggled to keep teachers. So he decided to sell. He told me it was the hardest decision he ever made. And then not long after he got sick."

"Poor Mike," I said.

"Yeah, and to add insult to injury, the developer tore down most of the school, but then they ran into money problems and halted the project. So now we've got a big chain link fence around the property, and our City Council is trying to lure a new developer to build condos. Something about their 'housing element' and the need for more affordable homes," Carl said.

"So Bayshore Christian School is now just an empty lot with a fence around it?" I said.

"Well, sort of. A few buildings are still standing, but they're full of graffiti and empty beer cans. The cops try to keep an eye on it, but you know, the local riff-raff sneak in. It's a shame, Bayshore Christian was a nice school," Carl said.

"Yeah, my kid went there. I even donated my old baby grand piano to the school."

"Well, there's still an old baby grand in what's left of the music building. Some real estate associates and I toured the property last month for a potential buyer. We were surprised to see that old piano, but then, it's hard for thieves to cart off a baby grand piano," Carl said with a chuckle.

"Do you still have access to the property?" I asked. "I'd love to see that old piano. I grew up playing it."

"Yeah, I've got keys to the lock on the security fence."

"I'd be happy to buy you lunch or dinner, Carl, if you'd be willing to let me visit the property," I said.

"Tell you what, Jack. Why don't you meet me there tomorrow around 11 AM? I'll let you in, show you around, and then we can grab a beer and lunch afterward at the local brewery."

"Perfect, Carl. I appreciate it. And the beers and lunch will be on me," I said.

I surprised myself.

I hadn't thought about Bayshore Christian School much over the years, but now the possibility of seeing my old piano intrigued me. It was more than intrigue.

Something seemed to be beckoning me.

***

Thomas Wolfe might have been right in his novel "You Can't Go Home Again."

We can physically go home again, but often what made it home in the past no longer exists. There were so many familiar haunts in my old town, but my family was no longer there. Just a few aging friends, and the sad remains of Bayshore Christian

School.

Carl was on time.

He unlocked the padlock on the chain link fence, and we strolled onto the property. There were weeds, leaves, broken bottles, beer cans, and graffiti everywhere. The playground asphalt was disintegrating, although I could still make out some faded hopscotch outlines.

The school's administration building and many classrooms were torn down, but the chapel and music buildings were boarded up and still standing. It was depressing to see what had become of the school.

Looking around, I felt a sadness descend upon my spirit.

We don't realize how special some things in our lives are. We take them for granted, like a lovely little Christian school where your child learned, grew, made friends, and was in the safekeeping of dedicated teachers and a fine principal like Mike Patterson.

I thought back to that conversation years ago with Mike about donating my baby grand piano.

What was it he said about the piano? I think it was, "Your old friend will soon be surrounded by our school kids in the music class, making beautiful music and inspiring young souls." But now the students were all grown up, the school was no more, and poor Mike was gone.

The front door to the music building was partly off its hinges and the paint was faded and peeling. Vulgar graffiti and obscene drawings were spray painted all over it.

As if the devil had defiled the place.

We forced the door open, pushed back some dusty cobwebs, and stepped inside. The glass to all the windows was shattered about on the floor, and a six-foot gaping hole in the ceiling allowed daylight to illuminate some of the interior.

Pinned to a corkboard on a wall was a torn piece of paper with "Mark 15:34" printed on it. And I thought to myself, "Forsaken, indeed."

I nearly tripped over some old beer bottles and debris. We stepped around old desks and music stands. Near the back of the building, an entire wall had been demolished, with frayed and forgotten music books littering the floor and grounds outside the building.

"So where's my old piano?" I said to Carl.

"Good question. It was here in the corner a few months ago, but then, that hole in the wall is new. Maybe the hoodlums dragged it off."

"A baby grand? That's a lot of weight to drag off," I said.

"Yeah, you're right. But wasn't it on wheels?" Carl said.

We walked over the old, crumpled music books on the floor, through the huge hole in the wall, and into the grass and wooded area behind the building. We both noticed that there was a kind of trail through the grass.

Something had been dragged off into the woods.

***

"Are you thinking what I'm thinking?" I said.

"Well, the trail is wide enough, and there are three distinct tracks in the dirt areas," Carl said as we ventured deeper into the woods.

The brush got thicker, and the canopy of tree foliage blocked out much of the light. But then we rounded a corner of trees and entered a small, open meadow containing two fallen tree trunks, empty beer bottles, a few chairs taken from the school, and a fire pit.

And in the middle of it all stood my old, baby grand piano and piano bench.

"Well I'll be darned, those little criminals dragged it out here," Carl said.

I barely heard him as I sat on the piano bench, which was wobbly like an old man with bad knees. I rested my hands on the keyboard and said, "Hello, old friend. I'm so sorry, I should never have let you go."

I've often thought that cherished objects have a kind of soul.

Not a soul like human beings, but a magical essence that embodies them. Even when they're no longer in our lives, a part of their magic remains with us. And maybe a part of us remains with them.

"Carl, I have a question for you?"

"What's that?" Carl said.

"Who owns this property? Is there a way I could get my old piano back?"

It was a crazy thought, considering that the piano was in disrepair. It would probably cost thousands less to purchase a new baby grand than to try and refurbish what was left of my old piano.

"Well, the piano and all the contents on the old school site belong to a development company that bought the site. So even though the piano was dragged off the site, it still belongs to the development company. We need to report this to the police, and then I can make some calls for you."

"That would be great, Carl," I said.

"You're seriously interested in refurbishing this old baby grand?" Carl asked.

"Yeah, I am. Because doing so might refurbish some broken things in me," I said.

***

A week later Carl phoned me with some good news.

The development company said I could have the old baby grand as long as I paid to remove it, which I did. The first two piano restoration companies were not interested in fixing up the old baby grand, but the third company was a small father-and-son operation. I explained the backstory, and the father said, "Sir, I wish more people felt like you do about your piano. It'll be expensive, but my son and I are happy to take on this project."

I think I about cried.

Part of me thought I was crazy going through all this trouble and expense, but something inexplicable continued to guide me like a dream trying to tell you something.

It took many months and a small fortune, but my old baby grand was rebuilt and refurbished. The day the movers expertly carried it into my large condominium and uncovered it in the living room, I felt elated.

And if pianos could speak, I'd swear it would have said, "Thank you for rescuing me and saving my life."

I tipped the movers and later sat down at the keyboard. I let my fingers slide gently over the beautiful new ivory keys.

And I softly played Für Elise, for Lilly.

***

One morning Steven called and asked if I'd be willing to babysit Brian for the evening. Steven and Allison had an event to attend, and I told Steven I was happy to spend time with my grandson.

That evening I ordered pizza and Brian and I played on the

floor with some of his toy cars. He pushed one of the cars and it rolled underneath the piano bench. As he reached for the car, he bumped into the piano bench and discovered that the bench lid could be lifted, which he did.

"What's this, Grandpa?" Brian said as he held up a collection of papers and a flimsy booklet.

"Oh, that's just some old sheet music and songs stored inside the piano bench. They've been there since I was a boy," I said.

Brian flipped through the music, and a folded-up piece of paper fell out onto the floor. As I walked over to help him, he picked up the paper and handed it to me. "Here, Grandpa," he said with a smile.

I realized by the paper's size that it was not sheet music. I sat down on the piano bench next to Brian and unfolded the paper.

My pulse picked up as I recognized the precise cursive. And then I read the note aloud:

"Dear Jack,
Every time you play Für Elise, it reminds me what a wonderful brother
you are. So I'm leaving this little note in your music book, and
someday you'll find it and hopefully, it will inspire you to keep playing
your music. And hopefully, it will remind you that whatever happens
in life, I think you're the best.
Love,
Cupcake"

I was in tears when I finished reading Lilly's note, and little Brian hugged me and said, "Don't cry, Grandpa. Who's Cupcake?"

I told Brian about Lilly, my beloved sister, lost to me so long ago, and that her nickname was Cupcake. And how she used to leave me little notes, and how this one was almost lost forever. I told Brian that I donated my baby grand piano years ago, but then found it abandoned, and how I paid some men to restore the piano so that I could bring it home with me where it always belonged.

And as I sat next to my grandson, I realized that we do not live in a coincidental universe. Some things happen for a reason.

It must have been Lilly's spirit, across space and time, beckoning me to find my old baby grand and rescue it from the woods. So I'd discover the note she left me so long ago. It was almost like she knew that someday, I'd need that note. To rescue me from the loss of losing Lilly, and Claire. To encourage me to keep playing the piano.

To reassure me that everything will be okay.

***

Steven and Allison arrived at my condo around ten o'clock, and as I invited them in I softly said that Brian was asleep in the guest room.

We sat down on the couch and Steven thanked me for babysitting Brian and told me all about their enjoyable evening out. And then Steven noticed the small glass of scotch in my right hand.

"You're not much of a drinker Dad, I hope Brian didn't wear you out," Steven said.

"Oh, no, Brian was wonderful," I said with a chuckle, adding, "In fact, he found something precious and hidden, and I guess I needed a Scotch to relax and celebrate." And then I told Steven and Allison the whole story, about Lilly's note hidden in the songbook. Allison hugged me and Steven said, "Looks like Lilly brought you and your piano back together again, Dad. You used to say that some things in life are pure magic."

"Well," Allison said with a smile, "You might want to refresh your Scotch because we have some news for you."

"Dear Lord, it's already been quite a night," I said.

"Dad, we're pregnant. Allison is 18 weeks along, and we just got the ultrasound results. Brian is going to have a little sister," Steven said, grinning broadly.

"Oh my, that's wonderful!" I said as I stood up and gave them both a hug, nearly spilling my Scotch.

"And we'd like to ask your permission," Allison said.

"Permission for what?" I said.

"We'd like to name her Lilly Claire. If it's okay with you, Dad?" Steven said.

And for the second time that evening, the tears streamed down this old man's face, and I collapsed on the couch, wiping my eyes as Steven poured me another Scotch and Allison hugged me again.

"Of course, it's alright with me," I said to both of them. "It's more than alright. It's wonderful."

And as Allison went to wake up Brian, and Steven poured himself a celebratory Scotch, I strolled over to my baby grand, lifted the fallboard, sat down, and softly began playing Für Elise.

And I swear, as Steven, Allison, and little Brian gathered around me, I felt the loving presence of Claire and Lilly.

And I thanked God that I rescued my piano in the woods.

Chapter Nine

To Dance With the Barn Owl

O ne wrong turn can change the entire trajectory of your life.

Exhausted, sipping a bitter cup of gas station coffee, I was determined to get home by daybreak. I don't like driving through the night, but the writer's conference I attended for the last three days ate up most of my accrued vacation time. I needed to get home, leaving just one day to unpack, do laundry, and sleep before work the following day.

Not that I love my work.

Being a copywriter for a digital company is a means to an end. A bridge to the future, when my novels hopefully reach a broader audience and financial success.

GPS is a wonderful thing when it works. But sometimes high mountains, poor cellular range, and the alchemy of fate set you on a different course and a wrong turn.

The turn off the main highway felt astray, but whenever I ignore GPS, I usually regret it. So I kept driving for miles, as the road narrowed and the surrounding countryside disappeared into curtains of pitch black.

"Where the heck am I?" I said to myself. Then the GPS went haywire and its little voice blurted out "Re-calculating...proceed to the nearest route."

"Great."

There was a gravel driveway in the distance, leading to a small house and a dilapidated barn. An old tractor sat in the yard. The house was dark, but a light shined in the barn.

It was nearly 10 PM, and I didn't want to startle whoever lived there. I parked near the barn. I heard classical music (a Waltz) when I opened my car door. It was coming from within the barn.

I walked over to the closed barn door and called out, "Hello? Sorry to bother you, can you help me?"

Nothing.

I knocked loudly on the barn door. "Hello, is anyone here?"I was about to knock again when a deep voice startled me from behind.

"Can I help you?"

I spun around, barely able to make out the dark figure standing in the shadows nearly ten feet from me. His raspy, baritone voice bore a slight Southern accent.

"Yes, hello. I'm so sorry to interrupt you. I'm afraid I'm lost. Made a wrong turn."

"Hard to say if turns are wrong or right. I'll wager they're just turns. It's up to us to decide what to do with them."

I couldn't decide if the man's response was odd or wise. He stepped forward, out of the shadows, into the ambient light from the barn. I felt like I was in an episode of The Twilight Zone.

He was a bear of a man. Bald, bearded, wearing overalls. A large leather glove covered his left hand. Perched on the glove was a magnificent white barn owl.

"Penelope and I were about to dance together, but then the motion detector went off in the barn, and we knew we had company. We don't get company, especially at this hour, so we slipped out into the night. We're both comfortable in the dark."

The owl repositioned slightly on the glove, spinning its head around to look directly at me. The man came closer. Despite his size, he moved silently and gracefully.

"I'm sorry, you and the owl were about to...dance together?"

"Yes," the man said with a half grin. "We've been dancing together for a few years now. The music and movements seem to calm us both. See, we both have a little PTSD. But then I guess no living thing in this world escapes life's slings and arrows."

Part of me wanted to run back to my car, lock the door, and get the hell out of there. But my writer's brain kept screaming, "This is gold! You can't make this up. Maybe you should go dance with the big guy and his owl!"

"Can't say I've ever danced with an owl before," I said, surprising myself.

***

"Jake," he said, extending his meaty right hand.

"Pleased to meet you. I'm Patrick." His rough hand swallowed mine.

We entered the barn, which surprised me. I expected farm equipment, or maybe a woodworking shop. Instead, there was a large painting easel beside a desk holding a palette, brushes, sketchbooks, and various containers for mineral spirits, mediums, and paint tubes.

There was a lovely landscape painting on the easel, depicting a sort of nocturne mountain scene, in muted colors. It was beautiful, haunting, and solemn.

"Wow, is this your work?"

"Yep. Painting relaxes me. And it's a great way to channel what I feel when I'm out there, in God's country."

"Do you sell your work?"

"Here and there. Mostly, I paint for myself. Galleries are about commerce, and collectors are sometimes about vanity. Neither helps an artist in pursuit of truth and authentic expression."

Jake walked over to a large record player on a table next to a stack of old vinyls. He slipped a record off the player and placed a new one on it.

"I like Tchaikovsky, but Penelope prefers Strauss. Whenever I play 'The Blue Danube,' I swear her eyes get bigger," Jake said.

I pointed to the record player and said, "You're an old-school guy. Do you prefer vinyl music?"

"Vinyl records have grooves that allow for an open, resonant quality. Digital compresses sound. It lacks open space. And you need open space to hear the warmth, richness, and depth of the music. Especially the divine music of Tchaikovsky and Strauss."

"Who is this guy?" I thought to myself.

***

There were some pops and cracks as the record began spinning, and then the music opened up and filled the barn.

Jake ran his right hand across Penelope's neck and back, looked tenderly into her eyes and said, "Are you ready, my dear?"

And the two of them began a slow waltz to the music. Jake hummed slightly, and the owl twirled and swayed on the glove as they gracefully crossed the dusty barn floorboards.

It all felt so surreal.

Jake worked his way over to me. He slid the glove off his hand and said, "Give me your left hand." I reluctantly held out my hand, and he slid the glove on it, with the owl repositioning along the way. Her weight on my hand and forearm felt solid and strangely satisfying.

"Now, hold her close, and feel the music," Jake said. "Feel her presence, her spirit. And when you're ready, do your best to sway, step, and waltz to the rhythms of the music."

I closed my eyes for a moment and felt the owl move slightly. As if she were saying, "Go on now."

Before long, I was swaying and moving to the music. My self-consciousness gave way to the moment, the music, and the presence of this magnificent owl riding across the barn floor to my waltzing.

I felt a twinge of emotion, fullness, and joy.

"Yes, now you've got it," Jake said. "You feel it, don't you? It's like a divine peace. I think it's good for the soul."

***

We took turns for another half hour, waltzing with Penelope. And finally, Jake strolled over to the record player, switched it off, and said, "Well, let's make you some coffee for the journey home."

We walked across the yard. The cloud cover gave way and the gibbous moon illuminated the pathway to the house.

For the first time, I noticed a sign above the front door to the house. It said, "Jake's Backcountry Tours, Birdwatching & Restoration."

"So you give tours," I said, pointing to the sign.

"Yep. After my military service, I retired out here to paint and heal. I went hiking and birdwatching. It's how I found Penelope, injured and stuck in a barbed wire fence. She was little back then, and I mended her wing as best I could, but she doesn't fly very well, so she lives with me now. We give tours for out-of-town folks. Teach them about the birds, and help them heal a bit too."

"Heal from what?" I asked.

"Life's injuries. The noise and blinking screens and keeping up with the Joneses. The people we see are all a bit broken inside. They're searching for some peace. Some hope. Nature has all of that, in spades," Jake said.

We stepped inside the house. I noticed rows of bookcases, a huge leather reading chair, and notebooks. Jake said, "Make yourself comfortable," before disappearing into the kitchen to brew coffee.

I picked up a leather journal on Jake's reading chair and opened it to a random page. The handwriting was immaculate. There were random notes, thoughts, poems, and quotations. I read one in the middle of the page:

> *"Every night the owl with his wild monkey-face calls through the black branches, and the mice freeze and the rabbits shiver in the snowy fields-and then there is the long, deep trough of silence when he stops singing, and steps into the air."-Mary Oliver, New and Selected Poems, Volume One*

Jake poked his head around the kitchen doorway. "Want anything in your coffee?"

"A little milk or cream, if you have it."

He disappeared and I flipped to a different page in the journal, feeling guilty for snooping. Another quote was penned neatly at the top of the page:

> *"We are healed of a suffering only by experiencing it to*

the full."-Marcel Proust

"Ah, Proust. Have you read him?" Jake startled me. He was in front of me, holding two mugs of steaming coffee. He handed me one, nodded at his journal, and said, "It takes a lot of patience to get through 'In Search of Lost Time.' Talk about a guy preoccupied with the minutia of experience."

"I read a bit of Proust at University...Swann's Way, I think. All I remember were Proust's long sentences," I said.

"The German Jewish philosopher and essayist Walter Benjamin called Proust's writing 'the Nile of language' which 'overflows and fructifies the regions of truth.' I found Proust a bit long-winded. Hemingway suits me better," Jake said.

We sat in Jake's living room library. I told him I was an aspiring writer stuck working as a copywriter. I talked about the writing conference I spent the last three days at.

"I wouldn't spend much time at those conferences," Jake said. "They're all marketing sessions, commercialization, and genre piffle, platform discussions, ethics and artificial intelligence talks, cultural appropriation handwringing, book cover design strategy, and agents and publishers bloviating about what they think the reading public, shrinking though it is, actually want to consume. You'd be far better reading great literature, letting it percolate in your creative brain, and then channel the results into your prose."

"How do you know so much about all this?" I asked.

"Well, I read...and I dated a woman who was a novelist," Jake said. "She was disgusted with the industry, where publishing is going. Best-sellers today are mostly celebrity tell-alls, shallow political rants, insipid self-help twaddle, chic-lit soft porn, and formulaic thrillers by the same established authors. People lost their attention span for great literature. They're too busy watching cat videos on YouTube to tackle Dostoevsky or Kafka. And the schools, God help us. They don't teach kids how to read and write. They're too busy exploring gender, race, class, and political indoctrination. Talk to a university graduate today and ask what they've read. They know ibram x kendi, but never heard of the Brontë Sisters."

"Well, it's important that young people read today's thinkers. Contemporary thought. Not just the old, white, dead guys. Right?" I said.

"Sure, a broad perspective is good, but not at the exclusion of the Western Canon. So many of today's writers are all wrapped up in dogmatic politics. Eloquence, elegance, and artful prose are fading. As well as deep thought, about life and purpose and meaning. A lot of today's writers omit what they don't know." Jake sipped his coffee and stroked Penelope, who was perched next to him on a stand.

"Omit what they don't know?" I asked.

***

Jake reached and grabbed another of his notebooks. Scraps of paper with handwritten notes fell out of it as he opened the pages. "Ah, here we are," he said, clearing his throat. "Ernest Hemingway." And then Jake began reading:

"If a writer of prose knows enough about what he is writing about he may omit things that he knows and the reader, if the writer is writing truly enough, will have a feeling of those things as strongly as though the writer had stated them. The dignity of movement of an ice-berg is due to only one-eighth of it being above water. A writer who omits things because he does not know them only makes hollow

places in his writing. A writer who appreciates the seriousness of writing so little that he is anxious to make people see he is formally educated, cultured or well-bred is merely a popinjay. And this too remember; a serious writer is not to be confounded with a solemn writer. A serious writer may be a hawk or a buzzard or even a popinjay, but a solemn writer is always a bloody owl."

"Forget about all those popinjays at the writing conference, Patrick. Read the best books. Travel. Talk to interesting people. Keep journals. Write it all down. And then, when you think you're ready, publish your stories. If they're good, if they move people and make them think, you'll find an audience," Jake said.

"I hope that's true. I mean, you said yourself, people are losing their attention spans. They're all on social media now," I said.

"Yes, but there's still enough of us left. The ones who crave something more. Something truer, deeper, and life-affirming. The cream rises to the top. Good books still get published. And maybe, just maybe, it's not too late to inspire others to dump the YouTube nonsense and feed their minds and souls with something far better." Jake stood up and motioned to follow him.

I took one last look at his library, and Penelope, who was napping on her perch.

In the kitchen, Jake poured another cup of coffee for me into a travel mug. "Keep the mug, Patrick, I've got several."

Jake drew a little map with his fountain pen on a scrap of paper, walked me to my car, and said, "I'm glad you turned down my driveway and danced with Penelope and me. Fate's a funny thing, isn't it? Also, remember what Hemingway said, 'a serious writer is not to be confounded with a solemn writer' and 'a solemn writer is always a bloody owl.' I think Penelope would concur." And then Jake laughed heartily.

"This has been quite an experience. It was a pleasure meeting you, Jake, and Penelope too."

He patted my shoulder reassuringly as I got in the car. I backed up, drove down the driveway, and saw him waving in my rearview mirror.

***

Jake's map led me back toward civilization, and soon I was on the main roadway. I stopped at a 24-hour gas station to fill up, use the bathroom, and buy some snacks.

At the cashier stand, I noticed a framed wall photo of Jake and Penelope, above brochures with the words, "Jake's Backcountry Tours, Birdwatching & Restoration."

The cashier noticed me and said, "People from all over book weekends with Jake. He used to be one of those special forces dudes in the military. I guess he saw some serious action. It affected him. But now he's a wise philosopher/artist," the cashier said.

"Yeah, I met him. I made a wrong turn, or maybe it was fate. Anyway, he helped me out," I said. "He gave me a lot to think about. Especially about my writing. How to become a solemn writer."

"Did you dance with the barn owl?" the cashier asked.

"You know about the owl? Yeah, I danced with the barn owl. It was...I don't know. It was..." but before I could finish the cashier interrupted.

"It was magical, wasn't it? People who visit Jake always say it's a life-changing experience to dance with the barn owl. My wife says there are angels on this earth. Sometimes they're people, and sometimes they're animals. Maybe even an owl," the cashier said.

"Maybe even an owl," I said with a smile.

I got back in my car, entered the highway, and settled in for the long drive home.

I turned on the radio, spinning the dial to find a station amidst all the crackles and static. Finally, I landed on one, strong and clear, as the announcer said, "That was Tchaikovsky's Piano Concerto No. 1. And now, settle in, relax, and enjoy the classics here at KCBN 89.5 on your FM dial, home of the magic of classical music."

I'm not a religious man, and what some people call magic or fate, I call coincidence.

But that was before Johann Strauss's 'The Blue Danube' waltz began playing on the radio, and I could feel the magical Penelope on my hand again, and that same feeling of peace and quietude filled my heart.

In that instant, I knew I would become a solemn writer, and that sometimes taking a wrong turn is how you find your future.

Chapter Ten

The Morning Fox

The fox started coming every day after Carole died. It was the strangest thing. One minute, we were making buttermilk pancakes in the morning, and then, in an instant, Carole was gone.

She woke me at 3 AM and said she was having trouble breathing. I fumbled for my cell phone and called. People came, and in a blur, I was at the hospital. Bright lights. Noise. Confusion. No one could tell me anything. Finally, they let me in to see her.

"How're you doing, babe?" I held her hand.

"Oh, John. I'm so sorry. I thought we'd have more time. Now, you promise me. Water the flowers in the patio garden. Keep up with your art. It'll keep you sane. And make sure you feed her."

"Feed who?" I asked my beautiful wife. My love. My everything, who was slipping away before my eyes.

"You know who. I named her Eloise, after my grandmother." She leaned back on her pillow, fighting to breathe.

God, I loved her. No one ever prepared me for this. How do you say goodbye to the love of your life?

"Babe, who are you talking about?" I caressed her face.

"The fox, honey. I named her Eloise. Don't you remember? She used to play with Troy." Troy was our German shepherd. He passed away last year. The most gentle dog you'd ever meet. He'd play with all the wildlife. It's like they knew he was harmless, a gentle soul.

"Oh yeah, I forgot you named her Eloise. That's perfect. She's a beautiful fox. Very elegant and athletic." I looked deeply into Carole's eyes. "This is so hard. I love you so much."

She closed her eyes and grabbed my hand. "Oh, John, this is life. We've had quite a journey. We were blessed. I'm so sorry we don't have more time. Promise me you'll stick with your art. You do beautiful work. Promise me you'll keep moving people with your creativity. And remember to feed Eloise."

And then she looked at me and said, "Feed her, John. She's special to me. Feed my little fox."

I told her I would, even though I didn't understand.

***

Carole fell asleep after that and never woke up. She seemed fine but then cancer is deceiving. We had a beautiful service and at the reception, many people talked about my Carole. So many nice things were said. I did my best to be gracious, but I was dying inside.

Death takes a part of us when it steals the ones we love.

I awoke the next day, early. My sleep was fitful and I felt tired.

Brewed and poured a cup of coffee. I strolled to the back deck and settled into one of the Adirondacks. The air was crisp and a breeze washed over my face. It was peaceful.

There was a light dusting of snow on the ground. Everything was pristine and crisp and fresh. And that's when I saw her. She crept out of the brush like a Kabuki theater actor. Stealthily, silently, and with elegant grace in each footstep. Her tail was full and her eyes were bright.

She was beautiful, just like my Carole.

I remember asking Carole why the fox was so important to her. I mean, there had been other wildlife that visited our home over the years. Rabbits, coyotes, birds, deer. But for some reason, the fox touched Carole.

She told me: "I read once about a fox cub trapped in a snare for two weeks. He should have died, but he didn't. Do you know why? Because his mother brought him food every day. When he was rescued he was injured and in pain. But he was also chubby."

I held her hand. "Wow, that's amazing." I smiled at her. She reached out with her other hand and said, "John, when you go to bed at night you're going to dream. You're going to be sad and lonely and maybe scared. Just like that fox cub in the trap. But here's the deal. I'm going to visit you in your dreams. I'll be there for you, just like that mother fox. I'll take care of you, honey. In your dreams. Don't ever forget that."

I never forgot that.

The morning after Carole's fox visited, I started leaving little treats in the backyard. I dragged the Adirondack chair out to the rear yard. I'd make coffee in the morning and get up early. I'd cook sausage and bacon and take it out with me.

Soon, Carole's fox started coming every morning. Over time, the fox became more comfortable with me. She'd come closer and closer. Sometimes, I could hold the bacon in my hand and she'd eat it.

Yesterday was Carole's birthday. I got up early and cooked some bacon and sausage for our little fox. But then I fell asleep in the backyard. I was feeling sorry for myself the night before and drank too much wine. So I was a bit hungover and fell asleep in the Adirondack chair.

I've never been a superstitious man or given to religion. But I always sensed that maybe, just maybe, there was more to life than met the eyes. Still, I never dwelled on it.

That early morning of my wife's birthday, as I lay asleep in the rear yard Adirondack, something amazing happened. I was dreaming and Carole was facing me. She held my face in her hands, and she told me that everything would be okay. And then she leaned in to kiss me. I felt her soft kiss on my lips.

When I awoke there she was. Eloise, the little red fox. Licking my face. She had eaten the bacon and sausage I left. I guess she wanted to thank me.

Or maybe it was Carole. Maybe she found a way, through the fox, to reach out and reassure me.

Just like that mother fox who took care of her pup, when he was trapped.

Because I was trapped, too. Trapped in an ocean of grief. Until I awoke with that fox licking my face.

And I knew that everything would be alright.

Now, whenever Eloise visits, I feed her and we hang out. She's as beautiful as my wife. She brings me peace.

She taught me to be thankful. She helps me understand that Carole will always be with me, and that love is the most powerful thing in the universe.

Chapter Eleven

He Who Is Without Sin Among You

Of course, there is the filth. It was the first thing Charlie adjusted to. The stench of urine wafts up from the pavement and dark alleys where rats and cockroaches forage in rotting tents and abandoned cardboard structures.

This is where hope goes to die.

Sex offenders and ex-convicts abound. Addicts slump in prolonged stupors amidst discarded syringes, feces, and empty bottles. Strewn garbage, awakened by gusts of traffic, skips down the street and contorts around Charlie's hiking boots. He picks at the frayed duct tape holding together his left boot sole and surveys the neighborhood.

Skid Row is his home now, among the lost and broken souls.

The name "skid row" originates from the construction of railroads in the mid-19th century, beginning in the Pacific Northwest. Harvested logs were sent to construction sites along greased tracks known as "skid roads." Mostly transient and immigrant men worked these sites, often spending their meager wages on alcohol and prostitutes. When employment evaporated, out-of-work men camped and slept on the seedy streets, known as "skid rows."

Charlie knew all this because he was once a history professor. But that was before his little girl succumbed to brain cancer, and a year later his despondent wife took her life. His world collapsed, and alcohol became a refuge until it became a prison of sickness and anguish.

Friends tried to rescue him.

There were earnest rehab stints. But grief, loss, and hopelessness are potent adversaries, and Charlie's will collapsed. He lost his career, his home, and his aspirations. Nothing mattered anymore. Life deteriorated, and soon he joined the denizens of despair along the makeshift tents and filthy sidewalks of skid row.

Charlie knew where it would end, and he made peace with it because death meant crossing the vale between this world and the next—taking flight to wherever his wife and daughter awaited him.

But not this day, and probably not the next. So he did what he could to subsist.

***

James C. Thomas hated going downtown, but that's where a few of his business warehouses were. He inherited his father's vast company holdings, making him wealthy. He drove expensive cars and wore fine Italian suits.

James spent plenty of time with a personal trainer in his home gym. Looking good was important to him. He loathed the lazy employees in his businesses who complained about their weight and health problems but stuffed their faces with donuts and calorie-dense coffee drinks. "Losers," he often thought to himself. "No wonder this country has an obesity and diabetes epidemic."

On this day, James was still hungover from last night's house party. The usual friends and sycophants were there, but at least someone brought along an attractive real estate professional named Faye. She had been up for a good time, and he tried not to wake her when he dressed and left the house that morning.

It was early. The downtown streets, in their slumber, were devoid of the usual traffic snarl. James navigated his Mercedes past a large street sweeper, scrubbing away the residue of food, drink, debris, and human waste.

James surveyed the rows of tents and garbage. "Derelicts," he said to himself. "They're destroying the city, turning it into a cesspool."

He grabbed the garage remote, clicked it, and listened to his Mercedes engine purr as the parking gate opened. He clicked the gate closed behind him. No sense in leaving an opening for the predators and criminals outside.

***

Charlie found a discarded fast food bag with a half-eaten burger and leftover fries. The burger was cold, and the fries solidified, but deep hunger is seldom capricious. As he wolfed down the food, he noticed the closing gate where the rich dude with the Mercedes always parked.

Unlike many of his neighbors, Charlie had no issues with the success of others. There are spoiled family scions who have their wealth handed to them. But it's a free country, and there are lucky, fortunate people in almost all societies. Enough opportunities exist for anyone who wants to achieve. Even with the racism, sexism, xenophobia, and homophobia that exist in society, Charlie believed anyone with enough ambition could navigate these obstacles and get ahead.

Charlie knew of immigrant families who came here with nothing, only speaking their native tongue. Yet they worked hard, building unsexy, utilitarian businesses like laundry mats, dry cleaners, and liquor stores. They saved their money. And soon, one store became two. Down the line, small empires were made, along with generational wealth.

But the rich dude with the Mercedes annoyed Charlie. Not because he was rich but because he was cruel. Sometimes, dark hearts hide beneath fine clothing.

Often, the rich dude told Charlie to get a job or clean himself up. Once, the rich dude pulled cash out of his wallet, waved it in front of him, and said, "You want this? Do you want this? Then get off your soggy butt and get a job."

Sometimes, the rich dude brought friends to his warehouse. They'd stand out front and talk, pointing at Charlie, laughing. They were ugly and heartless, but there were many ugly and heartless Skid Row residents, too.

Maybe the whole world is hurtling down the road to perdition.

***

Charlie belched and slid into a recessed doorway, to shelter from the morning chill. Across the street from the warehouse stood a dilapidated gas mart. Whenever Charlie and others scrounged money, they'd get liquor at the gas mart.

Across the street, Charlie noticed Father Kelly, from Our Lady of Fatima Catholic Church. Father Kelly often ministered to the forgotten souls of Skid Row.

Charlie felt sad for Father Kelly. Church sex scandals and declining mass attendance often make the news, unlike saintly outreach to the poor. But then, Father Kelly is one of the good ones. He's not doing this for the news or popularity, Charlie thought.

An hour passed and just as Charlie began to nod off, a metal warehouse door swung open, banging against the building. The rich dude ambled out, talking loudly on his smartphone.

It was hard not to eavesdrop.

"Look, Faye, all I'm saying is I have things to do. Last night was great. Maybe we'll have dinner sometime. No, I'm not blowing you off. I'm just not commitment material, you know? Now don't be like that. You knew the arrangement. No strings, right? Hello? Hello?"

The rich dude screamed several expletives. They echoed down the street, and a few heads popped out of tents to see the commotion.

The rich dude crossed the street, entering the gas mart, where he often got coffee. Charlie was glad to be hidden in the shadows of the doorway, where the rich dude wouldn't see and harass him.

Someone was unzipping a tent. Looking to his left, Charlie saw Big Joe emerge from his tattered, sagging shelter. He must have heard the rich dude swearing.

This wasn't good.

Big Joe, despite his meth habit, was still a bear of a man and known to be violent, opportunistic, and unpredictable. Charlie tried to sink further into the darkened doorway entrance.

Big Joe mumbled incoherently, scratched the dirty, matted

hair on his scalp, and kicked empty beer bottles away from his tent.

Then he crossed the street.

***

"Dude, that's a nice watch. Rolex?" the gas mart attendant asked James.

"Breitling Chronomat 44," James said.

"I never heard of that one. Is it expensive?"

"Very."

"Wow, my Dad once had a Rolex, but I think it was a knockoff. He..."

"I'm sorry, but can you move this along? I've got work to do."

"Uh, yeah, whatever...sorry dude. Here's your coffee." The attendant remembered this guy...he was always a jerk.

The gas mart door chimed as it swung open. Cold morning air whooshed in. James and the attendant smelled the stench of the big man filling the doorway.

"Hey Big Joe, what's up?" the attendant said. Big Joe said nothing. He was staring at James, looking him up and down.

"What are you looking at?" James said.

"The jerk that woke me up," Big Joe said with a menacing scowl. He walked over to James and violently shoved him with both hands. James stumbled back into the candy rack, knocking Hershey bars to the floor.

James was a formidable man and never backed down from a fight. He steadied himself and charged into Big Joe, knocking him to the floor. Big Joe leaned forward to get up, but James threw a powerful haymaker, connecting with a loud snap into Big Joe's left ear.

Big Joe went down. A trickle of warm blood threaded past his earlobe, down his neck, and vanished into Big Joe's stained brown T-shirt.

"Why don't you lie there and bleed," James said with a smirk. James turned around, pointed to the ceiling security cameras, and asked the attendant if they worked.

"No, man, the owner won't get them fixed."

"Figures. Well, write down your name and phone number in case this loser tries to sue me or something. I need a witness. You saw he came at me first." James noticed the attendant's eyes got large.

There was a loud click.

James spun around to face Big Joe, standing now, waving a razor-sharp switchblade. "I'm going to fillet you," Big Joe said in a demonic voice.

James stepped back, consumed by fear, as Big Joe advanced. The attendant's shaking hands fumbled with the phone, trying to punch 9-1-1.

The front door chimed, but no one heard it.

James knocked over a display of sunglasses. Big Joe continued to advance, the switchblade raised, glinting off the fluorescent ceiling lights. Big Joe lunged, but someone crashed into him, like a determined linebacker. They both crashed to the floor.

Big Joe scrambled to his feet. He spun around, and facing him was Charlie, clearly out of breath. Big Joe tried to shove Charlie out of the way and attack James, but Charlie grabbed his knife hand and struggled to control the blade. They became a tangle of thrashing limbs and crashed again to the floor, this time with Big Joe on top of Charlie.

Sirens wailed in the distance.

Big Joe sat up, straddling Charlie. And then anguished sounds poured out of Big Joe. His large shoulders heaved up and down to the rhythm of gut-wrenching sobs.

"Why, Charlie? Why did you make me do that? Oh God, Charlie...why?"

"Because we're not animals, Big Joe," Charlie wheezed in a raspy voice.

Only the handle of the switchblade was visible above Charlie's chest. The rest was plunged deep inside him. The handle trembled as Charlie struggled to breathe.

Big Joe collapsed into a fetal position, bawling uncontrollably, repeating over and over, "I'm sorry Charlie, I'm so sorry."

James surprised himself and kneeled beside Charlie. He reached out, held Charlie's hand, and looked into his eyes. "Hang in there, buddy. Help is on the way."

James felt funny. A wave of emotions filled him, and his eyes grew moist. He squeezed Charlie's hand. "I've been so awful to you. So terrible. I'm...so sorry."

"It's okay. We're all broken," Charlie whispered.

"Hold on, buddy. I'm gonna make this right. I'm gonna help you. Don't go anywhere."

"But...I...have...to...go," Charlie said softly.

***

The front door burst open. It was Father Kelly and a few locals pointing and yelling, "Over there, Father, on the floor."

Father Kelly knelt beside James and Charlie.

"Oh, Charlie, what have you gotten yourself into?" Father Kelly said.

"My...escape...plan. Time, Father. It's...time."

"Time for what, Charlie?"

"See...them. Be...with...them...again." Charlie's pupils lost their twinkle to a dull sheen.

Father Kelly motioned the sign of the cross and put his hand gently on Charlie's shoulder.

"Then you go to them, my son. You go to them."

***

Lives are fragile on Skid Row. Death is never far away.

Addiction, crime, mental illness, and living in the harsh outdoors conspire against street people. And there are individuals like James, whose dark hearts are immune to the plight of the less fortunate.

But sometimes, a flicker of light happens. An unexpected experience penetrates the darkness. A touch of grace rekindles hope and changes lives.

Two years after Charlie's death, the parish secretary of Our Lady of Fatima came to Father Kelly's office.

"Father, there's a gentleman here to see you."

Father Kelly set aside the sermon he was crafting. "Thank you, Darlene. Please lead him back."

Moments later, Darlene returned with James C. Thomas. His hair was a bit more gray. He looked thinner than Father Kelly remembered.

"Ah, Mr. Thomas, please come in. Have a seat. What can I do for you?"

"Thank you for seeing me, Father. And please, call me James. I think the last time I saw you was at Big Joe's trial."

"Yes. I visit Big Joe in prison. He's doing better now with treatment. But something inside of him broke after that terrible day. I keep praying for him."

"That terrible day, yes. Well, that's why I'm here to see you,"

James said, his voice drifting off.

"I'm always happy to help, James."

"It's just that I can't stop thinking about Charlie. About what he did for me. And especially what he said to me."

"What did he say to you, James?"

"I apologized to him for being such a jerk. I told him how sorry I was. And he looked at me. You know? Like, right into my eyes. And he said, 'It's okay, we're all broken.' When he said that, I felt strange."

And James began to cry.

***

Father Kelly rose from his desk, grabbed a tissue box, and sat beside James. "Charlie was right, you know. We're all broken. That's why I minister to folks on Skid Row. I think of the adulterous woman about to be stoned in John 8:7: 'Let him who is without sin among you be the first to throw a stone at her.' We must let go of judgment, see the humanity in others, and learn to forgive. I think Charlie knew that."

James wiped his eyes with the tissue. "I'm sorry Father, I didn't come here to fall apart. It's just that after Charlie forgave me and said we're all broken...something inside me shifted. I can't explain it."

"We priests are fond of saying that the Lord works in mysterious ways."

"Well, I've never been a religious man, Father. All I know is that Charlie changed my life. I started treating people better. I even got married. My wife, Faye, helped me sell my huge house. I downsized. I let go of all the narcissistic crap." James managed a smile.

"Good for you, James. Success is fine, but there's more to life than things."

"I agree, Father. That's why I'm here. I saw one of your church fliers the other day advertising for soup kitchen volunteers. When I saw that flier I could see Charlie's face. The forgiveness in his eyes. It made me realize, I want to be like him. I want to be a better man."

"Charlie may have been a broken man, but sometimes grace is camouflaged in human imperfection," Father Kelly said.

"Well, Father, any grace I have was buried most of my life, beneath layers of selfishness. I was a sinful guy willing to throw stones, and I don't want to be that guy anymore. I owe that to Charlie and myself."

"What are you doing tomorrow morning around six?" Father Kelly asked.

"Sleeping in," James said with a smirk.

"No, that was the old James. The new James will meet our soup kitchen staff, and serve some of Charlie's old friends."

"What if they recognize me, Father? I wasn't a very nice fellow back then."

"You shed your camouflage," Father Kelly said, adding, "All they're going to see is your shining grace. And I can't think of a better way to honor Charlie's life and sacrifice."

Chapter Twelve

Stillness in the Midst of Chaos

Linda dropped Timothy off at the daycare and headed to work. Being a dental hygienist was not her idea of a lifelong career, but it paid the bills and ensured independence for her and Timothy.

At five years old, Timothy was too young to understand divorce. All he knew was that Daddy visited every other weekend and Mommy was his rock. Whenever nightmares came, Mommy was there to soothe him back to sleep. When he was hungry, Mommy had a special way of making pancakes or chicken nuggets. His favorite comfort food.

Linda dated periodically, but her true passion was painting. She studied landscape painting at community college and took a few workshops. The rhythms of work and parenting consumed most of her time, but there were golden windows of creativity. Holidays and weekends off, when Timothy was in daycare and she could immerse herself in her art.

Be a good steward of your gifts

Many evenings, when Timothy was asleep and the pace of

life slowed, Linda would brew a cup of soothing tea and settle into some reading. Her favorite poet was Jane Kenyon and her collection of essays, "A Hundred White Daffodils."

Jane Kenyon was a poet and an American translator. Her work was simple, spare, and emotionally resonant. She penned poems of rural images, haylofts bathed in sunlight, and shorn winter fields. She wrestled with bouts of depression and "having it out with melancholy." For some reason, Linda identified with Jane Kenyon. Kenyon had struggles like Linda, but somehow she conjured beauty through her poetry.

Linda's favorite Jane Kenyon line was this:

> *"Be a good steward of your gifts. Protect your time.*
> *Feed your inner life. Avoid too much noise. Read good*
> *books, have good sentences in your ears. Be by yourself*
> *as often as you can. Walk. Take the phone off the hook.*
> *Work regular hours."*

Linda knew that Kenyon's advice was primarily for writers, but it held value for painters as well. Yes, Linda had a day job as a dental hygienist and responsibilities as a mother. But there were slivers of time that demanded Linda's attention. Slivers of time to hone her craft as a realist painter. She needed to be a "good steward" of her gifts.

There's only now

Linda loved good music and serendipitously discovered the recordings of actor and musician Hugh Laurie. She enjoyed listening to his piano compositions and found inspiration in his music as she painted.

Once she researched Hugh Laurie and found this quote of his:

"It's a terrible thing, I think, in life to wait until you're ready. I have this feeling now that actually no one is ever ready to do anything. There's almost no such thing as ready. There's only now. And you may as well do it now. I mean, I say that confidently as if I'm about to go bungee jumping or something — I'm not. I'm not a crazed risk-taker. But I do think that generally speaking, now is as good a time as any."

Hugh Laurie inspired Linda to put up a website of her paintings. It was scary, exhilarating, and fun. She photographed her best work and signed up with a wonderful online art website service to promote her art. But when she uploaded her work to the world, the response was largely crickets. She loved painting, but clearly, her work needed refinement.

Time passed and despite her best efforts, Linda's work sold irregularly. She dreamed of becoming a successful artist and leaving her day job as a dental hygienist. But try as she might to vary her artistic approach, she seemed incapable of growing her collector base. So she focused on raising Timothy and painted along the margins of her schedule.

Mending the broken

Wikipedia describes the origins of Goodwill Industries as follows:

"In 1902, Reverend Edgar J. Helms of Morgan Methodist Chapel in Boston, started Goodwill as part of his ministry. Helms and his congregation collected used household goods and clothing being discarded in

*wealthier areas of the city, then trained and hired the
unemployed or bereft to mend and repair them. The
products were then redistributed to those in need or
were given to the needy people who helped repair
them."*

Linda liked the mission and work of Goodwill and often
shopped there because so many of their products were affordable. And so much of the Goodwill's mission focused on mending
the broken souls in society.

One weekend, when Timothy was on a playdate, Linda spent
some time at the local Goodwill store, exploring deals and products. She came upon a lovely little tonal painting of a quiet
mountain scene. The work was more restrained than her landscapes. Simple, subdued and yet bursting with vitality and character.

On a whim, she decided to buy the piece and hang it in her
apartment studio. The elegant signature "Delgado" was unfamiliar to her but she liked the piece nonetheless.

Light at the end of the tunnel

The years passed and Linda quietly raised Timothy into a
fine young man. He had an affinity for computer science and
after college secured a promising position as an engineer with
Google.

Timothy found a lovely condo and his career was progressing
nicely. Linda couldn't help but feel a sense of pride and accomplishment. Her years as a dental hygienist made it possible to
pay for Timothy's education. Timothy's father contributed little,
only adding to Linda's sense of accomplishment in raising him.

One day Timothy phoned Linda, confiding that he had struggled somewhat for the past year at work. Fortunately, despite a

few difficult quarters, he prevailed and did well professionally. He was on the cusp of a significant promotion.

He mentioned a small painting of hers that hung in his apartment. "Mom, whenever I doubted myself, I looked at your painting. The one of the haystacks in sunlight. I don't know why, but every time I looked at it, I felt a sense of hope. Kinda like a light at the end of the tunnel. And you know what, it helped me get through this year. It's what led to my promotion."

His words meant so much to her. The idea that her artwork inspired him to succeed. Perhaps she had not attained fame and fortune with her art. But at least it helped her son find greater success. At least it was his "light at the end of the tunnel." Still, she was frustrated by the sense that she failed as an artist. That her lack of commercial success meant her art was insignificant and pedestrian.

The true measure of a life

Linda's cat "Winston" was an inquisitive soul. Unfortunately, his curious nature often led to mishaps. So it was one Saturday evening when Winston was pawing the small painting above the bookcase.

Linda heard a crash and ran into the living room. Winston stared at her, frozen atop the bookcase. There on the floor lay the small tonal painting by Delgado. The one she plucked from obscurity at the Goodwill. As she picked it up, she noticed the backside paper was torn. And much to her surprise, within the paper was a small envelope.

Linda slipped out the envelope and opened it, finding a letter within. She unfolded the letter, revealing a beautiful copperplate cursive. Carrying the letter into the lamplight, she read. And this is what the letter said:

"To the person holding this letter, thank you for purchasing my painting. I am an old man with little life left in me. Artwork and painting have been my passion. I've had to perform other jobs and work to support my family, but painting has been everything to me. As Saul Bellow said, 'I feel that art has something to do with the achievement of stillness in the midst of chaos. A stillness that characterizes prayer, too, and the eye of the storm. I think that art has something to do with an arrest of attention in the midst of distraction.'

Artwork and creative expression are gifts we give ourselves, the ones we love, and others. We might dream of artistic fame and recognition, but this is not the purpose of art. The purpose of art is to touch others. To inspire, move, instigate thought, and remind all that the true measure of a life is love, authenticity, and meaningful contribution.

Do not burden yourself with regrets, unfulfilled dreams, and sad-ness. If you have loved truly; if you have improved the lives of others; if you have raised well-adjusted children; then you have lived a worthwhile life. Your artistic expression, whether widely recognized or obscure, reflects your deepest humanity and spirit.

And that is enough.

- Alphonse Delgado."

This Much I Know is True

The world is awash in opinions. Online gurus and self-help authors dispense formulas and directives on how others should live. The problem is that no two people are exactly alike. What might work for some may not work for others. Linda understood this, and Alphonse Delgado's heartfelt wisdom struck a deep chord in her.

Linda held the letter in her hands, her eyes misty with emo-tional resonance when she was startled by the phone ringing.

She answered, "Hello?"

"Hi, Mom," said Timothy, "You know that girl at work I told you about? Nicole? Well, you won't believe this. She's an artist. An oil painter like you. We've been dating for six months now. She could be the one."

"That's wonderful, honey," Linda said.

"Mom, she was looking at your painting last night, the one of the haystacks. She said it reminds her of her late grandfather's art. He was a real estate broker by day and painter by night. She told me he used to say, 'So much of life is uncertain and hard. But this much I know is true: Art is the best of us. Art reveals our souls. Our deepest truths. It need not fetch fame or fortune to be true and authentic.' Isn't that wonderful, Mom?"

"Why yes, son, that's beautiful. Nicole's grandfather was a wise man. What was his name?"

"Delgado. Alphonse Delgado," Timothy said, unaware of the magical joy filling his mother's heart.

Chapter Thirteen

The Janitor

Late in the afternoon, when the sun hangs low and shadows cast deep across the school quad, a lone figure sits quietly on a wooden bench beside the library, sipping sweet tea and savoring his turkey sandwich.

Finches flit about the trees, searching for food in this golden hour before soft sunshine recedes and timed fluorescent lights flicker on across the school's buildings, their artificial glow attracting disoriented moths.

A finch appears in the quad, pecking an object partially buried in the leaves.

"What is he after?" the man says to himself as he finishes the last of his sandwich and sweet tea. He caps his thermos and places it back in the lunch box, which he slips inside a backpack attached to the janitor's cart.

He brushes crumbs off his pants, rises, and strolls across the quad to the pile of leaves. The finch sees him coming, abandons the object, and takes flight.

A tiny green dinosaur in the leaves seems to gaze up at him as if relieved to be free of the bird's torment. He reaches down and picks up the toy.

"Well, we seem to have an abandoned stegosaurus," he says.

"Someone is missing you. I see a little boy, perhaps with red hair and freckles."

He closes his eyes and conjures the image of a living stegosaurus galloping around the quad in the cool night air. He sees the creature's hot breath and feels the ground shake beneath its feet as the immense dinosaur lumbers past him. It's exhilarating, this hyper-realistic image in his mind. But then, he always had this gift for vivid imaginings and visions. At least, his mother called it a gift, but sometimes he thought it was a curse, as it often distracted him, destroying any focus on school work. Perhaps that's why he barely earned a high school diploma.

He puts the toy in his breast pocket, checks his watch, and returns to his duties.

***

Barbara White was working late again.

She always dreamed of being a grade school teacher. Even after all these years at Skyler Elementary School, her devotion to shaping young minds fills her with joy and purpose. Thank God for that, because the rest of her life had not been kind.

She struggled with obesity, going from one diet and personal trainer to another. Sometimes she lost a few pounds, but she was hopelessly "heavy set," as her indelicate mother often said.

Barbara's love for literature didn't help, since keeping company with books can be a sedentary practice. She tried various apps to listen to books while exercising, but they weren't for her. She needed to nestle into a quiet reading chair and experience an actual book in her hands. She loved the physicality of books, even the way some of them smelled. And she loved to use her Waterman fountain pen to scratch notes in the leather reading journal her husband gave her one Christmas.

She cherished the leather journal, even though her husband left her for a yoga instructor two years ago.

Her parents long dead and without siblings, Barbara resigned herself to a quiet, solitary life of reading and teaching English to 5th-grade students. During the weekdays, Barbara often stayed late after school to grade papers, prepare lesson plans, and avoid the loneliness at home.

A gentle knock outside the classroom window startled her.

She looked up and saw Floyd, the janitor, smiling with a wave. She smiled back at him and motioned to come inside the classroom.

"Hello Floyd, how are you?"

"I'm fine, Ms. Barbara, how are you?"

"Just peachy, Floyd. I'm grading papers. Say, how do you like the little book of William Blake poetry I gave you?"

"I like it, Ms. Barbara. Mr. Blake writes nice poems. I don't understand all of them, but I still like them. Especially, his poem about the little boy lost in something called a fen and God leads the boy back to his mother," Floyd said.

Barbara sat back in her chair and recited the poem from memory:

> *"The little boy lost in the lonely fen,*
> *Led by the wand'ring light,*
> *Began to cry; but God, ever nigh,*
> *Appear'd like his father in white.*
> *He kissed the child & by the hand led*
> *And to his mother brought,*
> *Who in sorrow pale, thro' the lonely dale,*
> *Her little boy weeping sought."*

"I wish I could remember books and poems like you, Ms. Barbara. But I'm just not smart that way," Floyd said.

"Oh Floyd, that's nonsense. You're plenty smart. Even when I had you in my class so many years ago, I could see that you had a unique gift. William Blake had it too. It's called eidetic sight."

"What's eidetic sight?" Floyd asked.

"It's the ability to recall and see images vividly. Sort of like a photographic memory. I remember how you could describe things you saw. And you were able to predict things, like that time you predicted 'feathers in the classroom,' and we all thought you were silly, but then later that day a scrub jay flew into the classroom. Do you remember that, Floyd?"

"I remember. The janitor, Mr. Swanson, had to come with a broom and nudge the bird out of the classroom," Floyd said, adding, "Still, I wish I had been better with my schoolwork. Maybe I could have become a teacher like you?"

"It's not your fault, Floyd. You had a learning disability. You were dyslexic. And I'm grateful that you're now our school janitor. The staff and students love you, and you take such good care of our school."

"I love this school, Ms. Barbara. I didn't always, back when the bullies teased me because I was different. But I love it now. I love keeping it clean and happy for the kids and teachers and even the birds."

"We appreciate you, Floyd. And keep reading your William Blake. Tell me what other poems you like next time."

"I will, Ms. Barbara. I will," Floyd said with a smile as he strolled out of the classroom and back to his cart.

Barbara watched him, with a touch of sadness in her heart. She remembered how the kids used to taunt Floyd at school when he was young, distracted, and sometimes stuttered. They couldn't see that there was something profoundly good and gentle in Floyd. He possessed an expansive imagination and ability to foretell future events.

Barbara gazed up at the exterior lights outside her classroom. The moths flew into the fluorescent bulbs, repeatedly bouncing off in a confused, repetitive dance. It reminded her of people attracted to the shiny things in this world, chasing illusions instead of appreciating the fullness of life.

And she thought again about Floyd, how despite his outward simplicity he possessed a balanced inner equilibrium. He took life as it was, and he saw and absorbed everyday beauty in ways that most people miss.

Barbara taught many students in her career who became entrepreneurs, doctors, attorneys, and successful people. But in a way, none of them made her smile as much as Floyd.

He was special.

***

Floyd pushed his janitor cart past Ms. Barbara's classroom. Then he stopped and looked back. Ms. Barbara was reclined in her chair, motionless, with her eyes shut.

He didn't know exactly what she was thinking, but a feeling of longing leaked out of her presence like a lonely ghost. It reached the outer door of her classroom and watched Floyd with amorphous, pleading eyes.

Such visions sometimes disturbed and perplexed Floyd, but he learned over the years not to fight it. Their meaning, sooner or later, often came into focus.

Floyd returned to his work.

He mopped classroom floors, cleaned bathrooms, collected forgotten clothing and lunch pales for the lost and found box, and wiped marks and smudges off the classroom windows.

He took pride in restoring order and cleanliness to the school.

Order and cleanliness were important to Floyd. They were a way to feel safe and secure after a childhood of family dysfunction, fights, fear, and abandonment. His unemployed, alcoholic father left the family when Floyd was five years old. His mother was seldom home, working two jobs to cover rent and expenses. His mom's sister, who lived in the same apartment complex, helped look after Floyd. But she drank too much, was often distracted by unsavory men, and thus was less than reliable.

Fortunately, Skyler Elementary School was only a short walk from the apartment complex. And despite the school bullies who sometimes taunted Floyd, he mostly found school to be a refuge from the disorder and dysfunction of his home life.

Also, school is where he first experienced the visions. Maybe because he could relax at school. Stress evaporated, and mystical portals in his mind opened and received dreamlike images.

Unfortunately, experiencing such visions put Floyd in a temporary kind of trance which teachers and students mistook for mindless daydreaming. Teachers scolded him to pay attention, and he was often teased and bullied by some of the boys at school.

Eventually, the teachers realized Floyd indeed experienced unusual visions and could even predict future events. Like the Scrub Jay incident in the classroom. Or the time he said the principal's head would get chilly, and an hour later a strong gust of wind absconded with the principal's hairpiece.

The janitor back then, Mr. Swanson, was an elderly man with a kind disposition. He befriended Floyd, sometimes joining him in the library after school to help with his homework.

Mr. Swanson had no family.

Floyd once asked him about his family, and all Mr. Swanson

said was, "I lost them in the war. But I'll see them again, soon enough."

Little Floyd lay his hand on Mr. Swanson's shoulder, the way children sometimes console an adult. And Floyd saw a vision of Mr. Swanson collapsing, alone, in the quad beside his janitor cart.

Then Floyd saw shadowy figures appear from behind trees, and they lifted Mr. Swanson. They hugged Mr. Swanson, one by one, and Mr. Swanson's shadow disappeared with the other shadows, even though his body lay in the quad beside the janitor's cart.

Six months after Floyd's vision, Mr. Swanson died of a heart attack.

They found him in the morning, in the school quad, beside his janitor cart. The principal then, Mr. Jensen, was nearly in tears when he said one day after class to Floyd's teacher, Mrs. White, "Poor Mr. Swanson, it's so awful."

Little Floyd overheard this and said, "It's okay, Mr. Jensen. Mr. Swanson went home with his family. I saw it."

Mr. Jensen looked at Floyd like he was a freak, but Mrs. White merely stroked the back of Floyd's head and said, "You're right, Floyd. Mr. Swanson is with his family now."

***

As much as Floyd enjoyed the energy of children during school hours, he cherished this time of day when quietude descended upon the campus, breezes danced through the tree leaves, and serenity embraced the quad and empty corridors. It felt like, after another busy week, the school was finally able to yawn and take a nap.

Floyd's day was almost done, and soon he'd lock up his equipment and stroll home to the small guest house he rented from an elderly couple barely a mile away.

Floyd sat on a bench, closed his eyes, and random thoughts of family drifted into his mind.

His mother died a few years ago, and his aunt moved away to another state. Then two years ago a police officer showed up at his door to inform him that his long-lost father had died.

"How did you find me?" Floyd asked them.

"Your father had your name and address on a piece of paper in his wallet. Maybe he kept track of you?" the police officer said. The officer added that Floyd's father lived on the streets and was frequently taken to the drunk tank to sleep off his benders.

"Men become lost sometimes. Old demons, regrets, addictions. But that doesn't mean that somewhere, inside them, they stop loving. I'm sorry for your loss," the kind officer said.

"Thank you, I'm sorry too," Floyd said.

Floyd keenly understood that loss and hardships are part of life. And yet, as he sat on a bench in the stillness of the evening air, Floyd felt gratitude for the beauty of the world and for the good people he encountered daily. Especially the school children. He loved their energy, curiosity, and innocence. His gift for visions revealed a glow that radiates from the children.

Floyd reached into his backpack hanging on the janitor's cart, and he pulled out the William Blake poetry book given to him by Ms. Barbara.

As a student, he addressed her as Ms. White, but in adulthood that sounded too formal. "Barbara" was too familiar, so Floyd took to saying "Ms. Barbara."

He thought for a moment about Ms. Barbara's loneliness. Then he thought of his long-gone parents and kind old Mr. Swanson. He thought of the innocent children in the school, and the sweet little birds who frolic and flit about the quad each day.

Floyd opened the poetry book and selected a random poem, "On Another's Sorrow," and read aloud to himself.

"Can I see another's woe,
And not be in sorrow too?
Can I see another's grief,
And not seek for kind relief?
Can I see a falling tear,
And not feel my sorrow's share?
Can a father see his child
Weep, nor be with sorrow filled?
Can a mother sit and hear
An infant groan, an infant fear?
No, no! never can it be!
Never, never can it be!
And can He who smiles on all
Hear the wren with sorrows small,
Hear the small bird's grief and care,
Hear the woes that infants bear—
And not sit beside the next,
Pouring pity in their breast,
And not sit the cradle near,
Weeping tear on infant's tear?
And not sit both night and day,
Wiping all our tears away?
Oh no! never can it be!
Never, never can it be!
He doth give his joy to all:
He becomes an infant small,
He becomes a man of woe,
He doth feel the sorrow too.

Think not thou canst sigh a sigh,
And thy Maker is not by:
Think not thou canst weep a tear,
And thy Maker is not near.
Oh He gives to us his joy,
That our grief He may destroy:
Till our grief is fled an gone
He doth sit by us and moan."

Floyd considered the poem and said, "There must be a Maker. Maybe that's where my visions come from?" He closed the book and slid it inside his backpack.

The night was very still, and Floyd stood up. It was time to put away his janitor cart, lock up the building, and head home.

As he turned his cart to head toward the facility building, he heard the sound of a branch breaking by the playground.

***

Floyd encountered school prowlers over the years. Usually, kids at night causing mischief.

Floyd was skinny, spry, and could be ghostly quiet as he crept around the buildings. Also, he learned to slip his jangle of keys deep within a pocket, so they wouldn't rattle and betray his presence.

Floyd stealthily crept up to the playground's edge where he hid beside a tree. And there, standing at the edge of the playground, stood a young man in jeans and a blue hoodie.

Floyd stepped into the open and said, "I'm sorry, but you shouldn't be on school property after hours."

This startled the young man, who looked up at Floyd.

"Yeah, well, I'm just out for a walk. I used to go to school here when I was little. Lots of good memories," the young man said.

"And what do you do now?" Floyd asked.

"Well, I was a stringer for the local paper, but they just had budget cuts. I get paid to tutor students sometimes, but mostly I'm between jobs. And since I can't sleep much, I take walks at night."

"What's a stringer?" Floyd asked.

"A part-time or freelance journalist. I love to write. But it feels like journalism is dying these days. So I'm not sure what I'm going to do. By the way, I'm Jed."

"I'm Floyd."

"Yeah, I remember you. The school janitor."

"I'm not a good writer but I like to read stuff. Ms. Barbara gave me a book of poems," Floyd said.

"Yeah? Who are the poems by?" Jed said.

"William Blake. I just read one tonight about sorrow. And I think it's about God, too. I don't know. The only line I remember is 'Never, never can it be!' I'll have to ask Ms. Barbara about it," Floyd said.

"Who's Ms. Barbara?" Jed asked.

"Oh, she's the English teacher here at the school."

"You mean Mrs. White?" Jed said.

"Yeah, but I call her Ms. Barbara because I'm grown up now."

"I had her as my English teacher. She was nice. And she always encouraged my reading and writing. She was my favorite teacher at Skyler Elementary," Jed said.

"Why don't you visit her sometime and tell her that?" Floyd said.

"You know, I really should. People never do that, do they? They never thank their teachers," Jed said.

The two stood quietly for a few moments, and Floyd could

sense that Jed was a good man, even though he was sort of between jobs.

"What you said, about losing your job and not being sure what you're going to do...the old janitor who once worked here, Mr. Swanson, used to say that when one door closes, another opens," Floyd said.

"Yeah, that's what they say, but I don't know. Anyway, sorry about trespassing. It was nice to see you again, Floyd. Maybe I'll see you around," Jed said.

"Oh yes, we'll be seeing a lot more of each other," Floyd said with a smile.

And the two went their separate ways.

***

Floyd ambled into Ms. Barbara's classroom the following week between classes and asked her about the William Blake poem "On Another's Sorrow."

"Is it about God?" Floyd asks.

"Very insightful, Floyd. Yes, the poem is about God's love and about showing compassion for another's sorrow. I'm not religious, but I do find the poem reassuring. We should all show compassion for the sorrows of others," she said.

"That's what Mr. Swanson did for me. When I was little, he used to help me with my homework and tell me that my parents loved me even if they didn't always show it. I really miss him, but at least he's with his family now," Floyd said.

Ms. Barbara stood up and walked around her desk to hug Floyd.

"I know you miss him, Floyd. We all do. But now we have you to carry on his work, and you're doing a wonderful job," she said.

When she returned to her desk, he smiled and said, "Oh, before I forget, I had a vision. You're going to have a visitor this week."

"Oh yeah, who might that be?" she asked.

"A former student. And I think he's going to solve a problem for the school," Floyd said.

"A problem?" Ms. Barbara asked, but Floyd merely grinned, spun around, and strolled off to his janitor cart.

***

Sure enough, a visitor knocked on Barbara's classroom door two days later. It was just after the last class of the day.

"Come in," Barbara said.

The door opened and a young man in jeans and a polo shirt stepped in. He held a small vase with flowers. He strolled over to Barbara, placed the vase on her desk, and reached his hand to shake hers.

"Mrs. White, you probably don't remember me..." but before he could finish she exclaimed, "Jed! Goodness gracious, what a wonderful surprise!"

"Wow, you remember me."

"Of course I do, Jed. You were one of my best students. And I think I've read some of your pieces in the local paper. I'm so happy you're writing."

"Well, I was writing. Unfortunately, the paper is laying off freelancers. So I've been working part-time at the Tutoring Club here in town to make ends meet."

"Oh, it's so good to see you. I missed our little discussions about books. Not many students love literature the way you did," she said.

"Yeah, you helped me. I remember all the books you recommended. When I got to high school my English teacher said I was advanced."

"So what did you do after high school?" Barbara asked.

"I got a degree in English literature. Then I was accepted into the Iowa Writer's Workshop MFA program, but halfway into the first year, I had to quit when my Mom got sick. After she died, well, I was adrift for a while. I earned a teaching credential, but around the same time, I started freelancing with the county paper," Jed said.

"Wow, Jed. Not many applicants get into the Iowa Writer's Workshop. It's too bad you weren't able to continue."

"Yeah, I know. But it's okay. I used to think I would write the great American novel, but now I don't know. I enjoy working with the kids at the Tutoring Club."

"You know, our other English teacher, Mrs. Janson got married last year and now she's pregnant with her first child. She's taking maternity leave in a few months. You should apply with the school district and maybe become a substitute teacher. With your background, you'd make a wonderful English teacher," Barbara said.

"Maybe I should. You know, it's so weird. I was out walking one night and I ended up near the playground here at the school. I bumped into the janitor, Floyd. Man, he's like a benevolent ghost around here. Anyway, he said something strange to me," Jed said.

"What was that?" Barbara asked.

"He said he and I would see a lot more of each other."

"You know, he always had visions and could predict things," Barbara said.

"Well, I don't believe in all that hocus pocus stuff, but I like your suggestion about teaching. Is there someone I should talk to about it?" Jed said.

"Yes, let's go to the principal's office and discuss this more," Barbara said.

***

Floyd's last day came unexpectedly, much like it did so many years ago for Mr. Swanson. Such is the fleeting nature of life. One day we are engaged with the world, and the next day we are lost to the ages.

The morning rain receded and by lunchtime, bright sunlight reflected off the slick cement surface of the school quad. Floyd spotted Mr. Jed jogging to his classroom and yelled, "Be careful, Mr. Jed, it's slick and you don't want to fall."

"Thanks, Floyd, you're right! I'll be more careful," Jed yelled back with a smile.

It had been two years since the school district hired Jed. At first, he worked as a part-time English teacher. But then, Mrs. Janson extended her maternity leave and eventually resigned, deciding that she wanted to be a full-time mother.

Thus, Jed was hired full-time and discovered his true calling was in education. He loved being an English teacher. Also, having Jed among the teaching staff breathed new enthusiasm and life into Barbara, who suddenly had a colleague to discuss books and literature.

It felt like Skyler Elementary School found a new rhythm and focus on academic excellence.

Floyd finished mopping a large rain puddle on the walkway outside the cafeteria when he felt a stab of pain in his left temple. He pushed his cart over to a bench and sat down, massaging the side of his head.

"Must be getting old," Floyd said, but then another pain shot through his temple and it took his breath away.

A young student noticed Floyd rubbing his head and walked over to him. He placed his hand on Floyd's shoulder and said, "Are you okay, Mr. Floyd?"

Floyd felt the boy's hand on his shoulder and suddenly, randomly, the silly name "Mr. Pickles" entered his mind. Floyd turned around and studied the concerned face of the young boy.

A boy with red hair and freckles.

"I'm fine, young man. Just a little headache. But the question is, how are you?" Floyd said.

"I'm okay, I guess," the boy said. He didn't want to tell Floyd that sometimes the kids tease him over his red hair and freckles. But then, Floyd's visions could intuit these things.

"Young man, when I was your age, I used to stutter. And the kids teased me. Kids always find something to tease other kids about. Don't let it bother you. Besides, if you're sad, you might make your little friend sad," Floyd said.

"My little friend?" the boy said.

"Yes, your long-lost little friend, Mr. Pickles."

With this the boy's eyes began to well up with tears as he said, "I lost Mr. Pickles. I lost him."

Floyd reached inside his breast pocket and pulled out the little green stegosaurus. He handed Mr. Pickles to the boy and said, "It's okay, young man, Mr. Pickles has found you."

Adults sometimes forget how important toys can be to children. Toys provide a kind of unconditional love and comfort. Floyd understood this, and seeing the boy and Mr. Pickles reunited gave Floyd a deep sense of happiness.

With tear-stained cheeks, the boy hugged Floyd and said, "Thank you, Mr. Floyd. Thank you."

"You're welcome, young man, you're welcome. Now you and

Mr. Pickles run along."

Floyd took a deep breath, reached inside his backpack on the janitor cart, and pulled out his book of William Blake's poetry. He turned to a random page and read the first poem he landed on.

A short poem titled, "Eternity."

> *"He who binds to himself a joy*
> *Does the winged life destroy;*
> *But he who kisses the joy as it flies*
> *Lives in eternity's sunrise."*

Floyd remembered this one. Ms. Barbara told him it was about embracing life's fleeting moments and then learning to let them go.

It's nice to stay with what's familiar and what brings us joy, but at some point, we must let go. We have to continue our journey. Move toward the next thing.

Even if the next thing is eternity.

Floyd felt another bolt of pain in his temple, and then a kind of strange warmth. He stretched out on the bench, holding the book of poetry across his chest, like a literary rosary.

"He who kisses the joy as it flies..." Floyd whispered to himself as he gazed up at his beloved finches, crisscrossing the sky above him like angels. And he felt a wonderful kind of peace. His head gently eased to one side, and he could see the trees along the edge of the quad.

And there, emerging from the trees, three shadow-like figures emerged. They glided across the quad and gently settled around Floyd. They began lifting him, high above the school, where the finches danced in the sky. And they continued upwards.

Floyd blinked tears from his eyes, and the smiling shadow faces of his parents and Mr. Swanson came into focus.

And he wasn't afraid.

Chapter Fourteen

Of Things Forgotten and Things Remembered

S arah was in the kitchen cleaning dishes when she heard a faint knocking sound. She turned off the faucet and listened.

There it was again. Two gentle knocks on the front door.

Sarah's thirteen-year-old daughter Ava said, "I'll get it," as she ran from her bedroom.

"Wait for me, honey," Sarah said, but Ava already opened the door. Ava seldom listened, often lost in her world of books.

Sarah joined Ava at the front door. Outside, an elderly woman dressed in impeccable attire smiled at them both.

"I'm so sorry to disturb you," the woman said. "I knocked instead of ringing the bell. Bells are so startling. My name is Francis Blum. I used to live here when I was a young girl."

It was an old house. When Sarah and her husband bought it,

they spent a good deal of money on repairs and upgrades.

"Hello Francis, my name is Sarah and this is my daughter, Ava." Francis smiled and shook hands with them.

"It's a pleasure to meet you both," Francis said. "Again, I'm sorry to bother you. I was hoping you'd take pity on an old woman and do me a favor?"

"Of course, Francis, how can we help?" Sarah said.

"When I was a girl my father was killed in an automobile accident. It was a difficult time. My mother couldn't afford to stay here, and she quickly sold the house and moved us closer to relatives." Francis furrowed her brow slightly as she spoke.

"It was a tough time. I had to say goodbye to all my friends at school, pack my things, and move across the country. It all happened so fast," Francis said. "But I've moved back, now."

"I'm sorry, that must have been difficult," Sarah said. "Do you want to come inside? I'm sure it looks different now, but you're welcome to take it all in. Maybe revisit some memories?"

"That's so kind of you, dear," Francis said. "But what I'd really like to do is find the lockbox."

"The lockbox?" Ava said.

"Yes, darling, the lockbox. I hid it before we moved. I wanted to leave a part of me behind, in case my Dad's spirit came back to the house, and he was lonely. Little girls can be silly that way."

***

Sarah and Ava led Francis into the house.

"Oh, everything is so lovely. I remember the rooms, but it looked nothing like it does now," Francis said.

"This is my room," Ava said.

"Well, my dear, this is where we need to go." And with that,

Francis strolled over to the closet and slowly knelt.

Francis slid open the closet door and asked Ava if she would mind removing all the shoes from the floor. "You see, we need to pull back the carpet if that's alright?"

Curious, Sarah knelt beside her daughter, and the two of them moved the shoes and peeled back the carpet, revealing the floorboards.

"You see the seam there," Francis said. "If you slip your fingers between those two boards, you can lift them."

Sarah wedged her fingers between the two boards, and sure enough, she was able to lift them. The space below was dark, and little dust particles floated about as if released from a long slumber.

"Here Mom," Ava said, as she used the flashlight from her smartphone.

And there, nestled like a coffin in the dark and dust, was a metal lockbox. It was wedged snugly, but with a little effort, Sarah was able to free it and placed it on the floor next to Francis.

Francis began to weep.

***

"I'm sorry, you two have been so kind. And now you have an old woman blubbering in your home," Francis said as Sarah handed her a tissue.

"Don't be silly, I'm sure it's difficult to revisit the past," Sarah said.

"My father was such a good man. He didn't deserve to die young, and so senselessly. I wrote a lot about it, in my diary. And I wrote letters to him. I hid it all away in the lockbox. And I left it here, for my father. For his spirit. So he'd know how much I loved him. I didn't want to leave him behind."

Francis wiped her eyes.

Sarah glanced down at the lockbox, noticing that it was unsecured.

"I found the lockbox by the creek," Francis said. "The clasp was broken, but I thought it would be a good place to keep my diary safe. And then I found the floor space in my closet."

Sarah held the lid to the lockbox, looked at Francis, and said, "May I?"

Francis nodded yes, and Sarah opened the box. She looked inside and then glanced back at Francis.

"So what did you keep in the lockbox?" Sarah asked.

"Just my diary."

"Well, that's strange," Sarah said.

"Why is that?" Francis looked perplexed.

Sarah reached into the lockbox and pulled out a girl's pink diary. She handed it to Francis, whose wrinkled hands held it tenderly like a baby.

And then Sarah reached back into the lockbox and retrieved a leather journal with the monogrammed letters RJB.

"Oh my God," Francis said. "That's my father's old journal!"

Sarah and Ava sat quietly as Francis flipped through her diary, and then turned her attention to her father's journal.

***

"How on earth did his journal end up here?" Francis said. She ran her fingers over the monogrammed letters. "His name was Robert James Blum. He was a journalist for the county paper. He inspired my love of reading and writing."

"I love to write, too," Ava said. "English is my favorite subject in school."

"That's wonderful, dear. Keep at it, and maybe someday, you can become a novelist like me." Francis smiled at Ava.

Suddenly Sarah made the connection.

She thought the name Blum sounded familiar. Specifically, F. Blum, the renowned novelist, and poet. She was nearly as famous as Margaret Atwood.

"Oh my, you're F. Blum! The author," Sarah blurted out.

"That's me. Publishers were biased against lady writers when I started out. That's why I use my first initial," Francis said.

Francis began flipping through her diary. "There's so much here I've forgotten. How I felt back then. My hopes. Dreams. Fears. And so much I remember. The books I read. My ambitions. Notes on writing. Plans for the future."

And then Francis flipped open her father's leather journal. All of the entries began with "Dear Francis."

"I had no idea he kept a journal for me. My mother must have found my lockbox and left the journal for me after Dad died. And with all the stress of moving, and then later on her illness, she probably didn't know I left the lockbox behind... for Dad." Francis took a deep breath and exhaled.

"I'm so happy for you," Sarah said.

"Me too," Ava said with a smile.

Francis flipped a few more pages in her father's journal. "My goodness, so much wisdom and advice he left me. About books. Writing. What it means to be a good person. This journal is like a masterclass in writing and life. I wish I'd found this years ago!"

"Well, even without his advice, you've done well for yourself. You became an amazing writer," Sarah said.

"Thank you, dear, you're so kind. But I've taken enough of your time. When your husband comes home, he's going to wonder who this old, crying woman is in your house."

"Oh Francis, I'm afraid we lost my husband three years ago. Cancer," Sarah said, as she glanced at Ava.

"You would have loved my Dad," Ava said. "He was a police officer, and super funny. And he used to read to me every night. He always told me to dream big."

Francis leaned over and hugged Ava, holding her for a long time. "Oh my dear, I'm afraid life has been cruel to both of us. But thank God we both had fathers who loved us so completely."

And now Sarah was the one tearing up.

***

It had been an extraordinary afternoon, and Sarah still couldn't believe that the author F. Blum's childhood diary, and her father's journal, were hidden away in the floorboards of Ava's bedroom.

Sarah and Ava hugged Francis one more time and then said their goodbyes.

As the days passed, Ava turned to her reading and writing with great gusto, inspired by her encounter with the novelist F. Blum. And she started to keep her own diary, which she stowed in the lockbox that Francis graciously left for her.

At the end of the week, on a lovely Sunday afternoon, Sarah and Ava took a stroll in the park. Much to their surprise, they spotted Francis sitting on a park bench. And in her hands were both her diary and her father's journal.

"Well hello again," Sarah said.

"Oh my, how serendipitous!" Francis exclaimed.

"That means a happy discovery," Ava offered.

"Exactly, Ava. Come, sit next to me, I've been thinking about you. How is your writing coming along?" Francis slid over to make room on the park bench.

"I've been reading Ray Bradbury's Fahrenheit 451. It's all about the future, and books being outlawed," Ava said.

"Oh, that's a good book," Francis said, adding, "There's a line in the book about friendship I never forgot: 'We cannot tell the precise moment when friendship is formed. As in filling a vessel drop by drop, there is at last a drop which makes it run over; so in a series of kindnesses there is at last one which makes the heart run over.'"

Ava smiled, and Francis held up her old diary and her father's journal.

"Ava, I spent this week reading my diary and my Dad's journal. They brought back so many wonderful things forgotten and things remembered. But most of all, they made me smile, and inspired me to write more books."

And then Francis handed the diary and journal to Ava.

"Ava, darling, I want you to have these. I am an old woman who lost her Daddy, but somehow I found the words and was able to become a writer. So I don't need these anymore. You are a young girl who also lost her Daddy, and you are on your way to becoming a writer. And I think you could use these, to help you along your way." Francis smiled at Ava and Sarah.

"Oh Francis, that's so generous and kind of you, but we can't possibly accept these. They're so special and personal to you," Sarah said.

"Thank you, Sarah, but I really must insist. I feel like, strangely, my father's spirit did come back. He found me. His journal found me. I only wish I discovered it years ago. But I've read it now, and maybe my father's wisdom, and my youthful diary notes, can help Ava. We novelists have to stick together!"

Ava held the diary and journal, looking intently at her mother. Ava's eyes were gently pleading.

"Well thank you, Francis. You're so very kind. Ava can keep them both in the lockbox, and you're welcome to visit them, and us, anytime," Sarah said.

"Thank you, thank you so much! I'll take really good care of them!" Ava said excitedly.

"What's buried in the past can sometimes change the future," Francis said, as the three leaned in for an embrace.

And then Francis held Ava's shoulders and said, "Go change the future, Ava! Go write some books! Make your father, mother, and me proud!"

Chapter Fifteen

The Treasure Map

I'd been hiking for an hour in the arid landscape of Patagonia when I came upon an old cabin. It appeared to be a little guest house.

A well-worn dirt path traced from the cabin to a large home in the distance. Just then, a grizzled-looking man spoke to me from the cabin window.

"Can I help ya?"

"Yeah, sorry. Kinda got lost. I'm visiting friends in town." With that, I set my backpack down. The old man opened the weathered cabin door and ambled out.

"Visitors sometimes get turned around out here. Or maybe it's the spirits. The woods and rocks. They have their ways," he said, drawing on a Camel cigarette. Then he coughed. A smoker's cough. Harsh and rattling with phlegm.

"Is this your place?" I asked.

"Nope. The whole spread belongs to Bob and Patty. They let me stay here. To write. Artists need their patrons, by God." His voice was gravel and silt. His face and hands were tan, wrinkled, and as worn as an old leather bag.

"Come inside, son. Have something cold to drink. I'll draw you a little map to find your way back to town." He exhaled, the smoke trailing as he turned towards the cabin.

"Much obliged," I said. Walking inside the cabin, I noticed shelves of books and a small writing desk with notepads and journals strewn about.

If you want different results, become a different person

He told me his name was Jim and that he divided his time between Montana and Arizona. I was unfamiliar with his work, but apparently, he was a writer of some acclaim. I told him I was a landscape painter. I slid a few canvas panels out of my backpack to show him.

"Nice work. You've captured a bit of the dryness and solitude here," he said.

"Well, thanks. I'm in a few galleries but sales are slow. Honestly, I came to Arizona to explore some new landscape themes. Maybe figure out why my art's not selling better. My friends were kind enough to put me up."

"Tell you what," Jim said, "You give me one of those landscapes of yours and I'll give you some advice. What do you say?" He smiled and took another drag on his cigarette.

"What the heck, why not," I said. With that, he surveyed a few of my studies and selected one. "I like this one, it captures the arid feel around here," Jim said. And then he pulled his chair close, squinted, and began.

"Son, if you want different results, you need to become a different person."

"Come again," I said.

"People always talk about finding themselves but what they should be doing is creating themselves. Experimenting, changing things up."

He looked around the cabin. "When I quit my job years ago as an accountant, I began writing with a computer. The early stuff was okay but I realized I relied too much on the Internet. And on copying other writers I liked. I wasn't capturing enough truth. My truth."

Jim pointed at his writing desk. "I don't use a laptop to write. I do it longhand. My editor hates it but the work is more organic. More honest. The long walks with the dogs help, too. Honestly, the problem with all those internet gurus dispensing advice is that one size doesn't fit all. What works for you may not for me."

Jim held up a ballpoint pen. "This is all I need. And some paper. You can read, troll the Internet, and travel. But then you got to shut all that out. Tap the truth inside you. Become the person you need to be to create the work that's inside you."

You have to pay your debts

I looked around the spare cabin. Lots of books, a writing desk. "Why do you come here to work? I mean, I hear what you're saying about the solitude. But it sounds like you're successful enough to afford your own place."

"Because you have to pay your debts," Jim said. "Bob and Patty helped me when I was starting out. They're literary agents and they took a gamble on an unknown writer from Montana. So I come and stay for a few months. Do readings in town at the bookshop they own."

Jim flicked his cigarette in an ashtray, looked down, and said, "You got to pay your debts. It's not always easy or pretty. But it's how you can get up each day and look in the mirror. You can't become the best version of yourself until you pay your debts. Maybe even learn to forgive yourself for past mistakes."

Improve your art by letting go

The sun hung low and I knew I had to get back. But somehow this old writer in a cabin touched me. So much wisdom. So I asked him, "Jim, you've had a look at my art. What can I do to sell more?"

"You'll find your way to that answer," Jim said, "but one thing that might help is learning to let go."

"What do you mean?" I asked.

"Well, we all start by learning the basics. Then we try to emu-late our idols. It's natural. We look at what works for others and chase that. Except it seldom works. We have to find the courage to let go of all that. When we do, we start to listen to what's inside of us. All the greats reached that place. Where they tapped into their brilliant authenticity."

I smiled at the truth of what Jim said.

"You're a tonalist painter," Jim noted. "But I see a touch of Russell Chatham in your work. Maybe a bit of George Inness, too."

I dropped my head. He nailed it. Two of my favorite painters.

"Don't feel bad. I used to think I disguised my affection for Hemingway. Until my editor called me on it. Which was good. Because it got me past that. Helped me dig deeper. When I did, my work started to take off."

The treasure map

I thanked Jim for his hospitality and promised to check out his books. We shook hands and armed with his little map drawing, I made my way back to town.

A few years passed and I'd read some of Jim's splendid novels and poetry. I adopted his advice and my paintings indeed began to improve and sell well.

Jim's wisdom changed my life. And then one day my wife found me sobbing. I had just read that Jim passed away. She held me, without saying a word.

The next day, my wife took the little map Jim had drawn and

had it framed. Beneath the frame, she added an inscription: "Jim's treasure map." I love her for that.

The map hangs to this day in the studio cabin I built in the woods. Where I go to commune with the spirits of nature, let go, and remember the old man who gave me the map to a better future.

Chapter Sixteen

The Old Man on the Scooter

They met in a quaint coffee shop near the edge of town.

Mary liked the location because it was less noisy than the crowded, bustling Starbucks downtown. Here, at the Frothy Mug, she could always find a quiet corner by the window, where she read her books and felt a certain sadness that much of life had passed by.

The old man showed up every Friday afternoon, his silly little scooter always sputtering and stalling. He'd fiddle with this or that and get the thing running again, eventually parking the scooter outside the Frothy Mug. The gentleman had close-cropped white hair, a shaven, well-lined face, and a slender build. He always carried a small leather journal and a rangefinder-style camera.

"Hello, Walter," the servers would say familiarly.

On this day, Walter ordered a cappuccino and raisin scone, settled into a booth adjacent to Mary, and placed his camera and journal on the table. He pulled a large fountain pen out of his inner jacket pocket and jotted notes in his journal. Then he picked up his camera, eyed the electronic viewfinder, toggled through images, and returned to making notes in his journal.

"On assignment for National Geographic?" Mary said to him, surprising herself. She seldom conversed with other customers.

"Heavens, no. I'd be broke. They killed the National Geographic newsstand magazines in 2023. Laid everyone off. Now it's just a shell of itself, with freelance contributors. Folks can still get digital and print subscriptions, but somehow it's not quite the same. So, I'm afraid my photography and journal musings only serve my own entertainment," Walter said.

"I didn't know that about National Geographic. I used to love the articles and photography. I guess this is what's left of the world we live in," Mary said.

"It's a digital world now. But I refuse to succumb. Give me a good fountain pen, leather journal, and a rangefinder-style camera any day over the ocean of piffle and smartphone images glutting the Internet," Walter said.

"Yes, but does anyone see your words and images? I'm told that if you're not online, you don't exist," Mary said.

"I'm a happy reader, scribbler of musings, and obscure photographer. By the way, I'm Walter."

"Nice to meet you, Walter, I'm Mary."

And this was how it all began.

***

Every Friday, Mary would settle into her favorite window booth at the Frothy Mug, and before long Walter would roll up on his temperamental scooter. He'd stroll in, order, and ease into a nearby booth.

Often Walter and Mary shared a booth and talked about life.

Walter was nearly ten years older than Mary, and both were well into their retirement years, hovering in a liminal space between reasonable independence and full-blown dotage.

Mary was a widow. Her husband, Douglas, died five years ago of a sudden heart attack. And in a way, Mary died too. Retirement without the one you planned it with becomes a lonely journey. The condo they shared was so silent now. Even the sweetest memories of their life together sour with the reality of Douglas's loss.

And then there are the health challenges.

Mary navigated a few serious illnesses, which left her feeling old and less vigorous. And since she and Douglas never had children, and her relatives lived out of state, Mary felt increasingly isolated and alone. She had some girlfriends, but they were married and talked mostly about grandchildren and superficial things.

Mary had been an English teacher and missed those classroom days of engaging young minds with the likes of Emily Dickinson and Jack London. But after retirement, she and Douglas moved to a more affordable state, and thus Mary lost contact with her students, coworkers, and friends.

The only place Mary found refuge was books.

One Friday afternoon, Mary and Walter claimed a corner booth in the back of the Frothy Mug, to enjoy their coffee and chat.

"Looks like you're making healthy choices," Mary said, pointing to the fresh cookies next to Walter's coffee.

"At my age, I decided what the heck. Besides, I've always had a sweet tooth," Walter said.

"Well, you're slender, so you don't have to worry about your weight. You don't have to experience the charms of menopause. I used to be quite svelte, but all of that's gone now," Mary said.

"It's not gone, Mary. It's just different," Walter said.

"Oh Walter, look at me. The bloom of youth is gone. My husband is dead. My figure is shot. And the landscape ahead only leads to a dark cul-de-sac of infirmity, irrelevance, and death." With that, Mary looked down at her coffee, and then out the window.

"Do you really believe all that?" Walter asked.

"Yes. The only solace in my life is books, and the conversations we enjoy. Otherwise, I feel like an apparition, wandering unseen. When I was young and walked past men, they'd turn around to look at me. Now they don't even see me."

"I see you, Mary. I see an attractive, intelligent, wise woman who's lost sight of what this stage of life offers us," Walter said.

"That's sweet, Walter, but I don't see that woman in the mirror."

"That's because you only see the superficial reflection, not the spirit within it," Walter said, smiling.

"Perhaps. And tell me, what exactly does 'this stage of life' offer us, apart from decrepitude and loneliness?" Mary said.

"Freedom, Mary. We have abject freedom."

"Freedom to disappear into ourselves?" Mary said sarcastically.

"No, freedom to be ourselves. Freedom to no longer worry about the world's judgments, petty comparisons, needless jealousies, and endless ambitions. We can dress as we please, pursue our passions, and relish the free time our working years never allowed. And we gain the value of wisdom," Walter said, with a glint in his eye.

"Don't you get tired of people ignoring you? Treating you like an irrelevant old person?" Mary asked.

"Sure. I think it was Leon Trotsky who said, 'Old age is the most unexpected of all things that can happen to a man.' I suspect it's equally true for a woman," Walter said.

"Trust me, it's equally true. I hate how invisible I feel. And people treat me like a child sometimes," Mary said.

"Yes, I've experienced that, too. I wrote something down about that. Here in my journal." Walter opened his leather journal and flipped through pages of immaculate, copperplate cursive.

"Ah, here it is. May I read this short poem to you?"

"Of course," Mary said.

Walter sipped his coffee, cleared his throat, and said, "This little poem is from Shel Silverstein. It's called 'The Little Boy and the Old Man.' I think it captures what we're talking about."

And with that, Walter read the following:

"Said the little boy, sometimes I drop my spoon.
Said the little old man, I do that too.
The little boy whispered, I wet my pants.
I do too, laughed the old man.
Said the little boy, I often cry.
The old man nodded. So do I.
But worst of all, said the boy,
it seems grown-ups don't pay attention to me.
And he felt the warmth of a wrinkled old hand.
I know what you mean, said the little old man."

Walter closed his journal and looked up at Mary, whose eyes were misty.

"Exactly my point, Walter. Once we start wetting our pants, what's the point anymore?"

"Well, Shel Silverstein had an answer for old age. It was in a poem of his called 'Growing Down.' I don't have it in my journal, but it's about a crabby old man named Mr. Brown who told all the kids to grow up. To wipe their noses. Be polite. Wash their hands. Stuff like that. Until the kids told Mr. Brown to try 'growing down.' To crawl on your knees. Climb a tree. Eat ice cream. Wish on falling stars," Walter said.

"I don't think this old body wants to risk crawling on my knees or climbing trees," Mary said.

"Well sure, we can't do everything. But ice cream and wishing on falling stars sounds nice," Walter said. "That reminds me of another poem I wrote down."

"I must say, Walter, as a former English teacher, it's a pleasure to speak with a literate man," Mary said.

"Here it is," Walter said, and then he began reading the poem.

"For age is opportunity no less
Than youth itself, though in another dress,
And as the evening twilight fades away
The sky is filled with stars, invisible by day."

"Ah yes, Henry Wadsworth Longfellow. I remember that one," Mary said.

"The thing is, Mary, we live in a youth culture. Especially with all this social media stuff. And I think it's disorienting for seniors like us. It's hard to keep up with all the technology. We no longer recognize the movie stars and music. I think all of that adds to the sense of irrelevancy and loneliness. But we forget, like Longfellow wrote, that there's opportunity in aging. The sky above us may get darker, but we can see the stars better," Walter said.

"What does that mean, Walter? I should take up astronomy?" Mary said with a giggle.

"No, Mary. Embrace everything. Dare to live. People may see our age on the outside, and we might even feel it. But we don't feel that way on the inside. We're all the ages we've ever been. We have to remember how to tap those times and find a way to live them now," Walter said.

They sat together in their little booth at the Frothy Mug, pondering their conversation.

"You know, Walter, I've often thought about starting a book club in my senior condominium complex. I see a few of the other ladies reading books by the pool, and it would be fun to come together and discuss books, literature, and ideas. I think books might save us all from the melancholy of aging. You see, Walter, you're inspiring me," she said.

"I certainly hope so. I belong to a camera club. I'm the oldest person, but it doesn't matter. We all share the same passion for photography, and the younger ones get a kick out of my old school, rangefinder-style camera," Walter said.

Just then, Walter's cell phone buzzed in his jacket pocket.

"Ugh, I almost forgot. I've got an appointment I'm going to be late for," Walter said.

"Leaving me for a hot date?" Mary said.

"My hot date is a rather imperious, middle-aged oncologist with no sense of humor," Walter said.

"Oh, I'm sorry Walter."

"No apology necessary, Mary. You're cracking little jokes. That's progress. And I love your book club idea. Life is meant to be lived, Mary, however we can. Remember Robert Browning and his 'Grow old along with me! The best is yet to be, the last of life, for which the first was made.'"

"Oh Walter, now you're just trying to impress this old English teacher," Mary said with a smile, hoping Walter would not see the concern she felt about his health. Oncology appointments are scary things.

"Start that book club, Mary, and I'll see you next week," Walter said.

***

Mary followed Walter's advice and approached several women where she lived about her book club idea. Everyone loved the idea. It was agreed that they would take turns hosting the weekly meetings, and each would bring an appetizer. For their first book, they settled on Kristin Hannah's new novel "The Women."

That Friday, Mary settled into her favorite booth at the Frothy Mug and waited anxiously for Walter to arrive on his rickety old scooter. She couldn't wait to tell him about the book club. And she was wearing a new outfit, having decided that she was going to stop feeling sorry for herself and update her wardrobe.

A few hours passed, but Walter never came.

She phoned his cell phone, but it went straight to voicemail. "Walter, where are you? It's Mary. I want to tell you all about the book club, and show off my new sundress," she said to the recording.

Mary tried phoning Walter a few days later, but again, it went straight to voicemail. And she didn't know where he lived. She didn't even know Walter's last name. They were coffee shop pals, and they never really deepened their friendship.

Some relationships are like that.

They work best on that narrow landscape between acquaintance and friendship. That place where you know each other in a particular setting, and the gentle distance and mystery about your broader lives keep the relationship fresh and uncomplicated.

The following Friday, she waited for Walter again, but he didn't show.

She continued with her life.

The book club grew, and some of the women became cherished friends. She told them about Walter and how he inspired her to see aging as an opportunity. A chance to gaze at the stars. To grow down instead of up. To eat ice cream.

To live life fully.

***

Mary used to scan the newspapers and online notices to see if there was any news. Any mention of an elderly man named Walter. But there was nothing.

Until one sunny afternoon when a man in a suit and fedora knocked on her door.

"Yes?" Mary said from inside her locked front door.

"Hello, I'm looking for a Ms. Mary Swanson. My name is Marv Steinberg."

"I'm sorry, but what's this regarding?" Mary said, her door open now but with the security chain still attached.

"It's about the estate of Elliot W. Boyd, Ms. Swanson," the man said as he adjusted a leather satchel over his shoulder.

"I don't know anyone by that name. Well, come to think of it, I do know that name. Elliot W. Boyd is a best-selling novelist. But I don't know him, just that he writes poignant fiction. Didn't he win the Man Booker Prize?"

"Yes, Ms. Swanson, I represent Elliot W. Boyd. I'm his agent. May I come in?"

Mary unlatched the chain and led Steinberg into her living room. She offered him something to drink, but he politely declined.

"So, what's this about?" Mary asked.

"I'm afraid Mr. Boyd passed away. He was battling cancer and collapsed rather suddenly. It's still such a shock. I've been working with his estate attorney and tying up loose ends. He never married and had no children. His work, his writing, was his life. Well, he also liked to dabble in photography," Steinberg said.

"Photography?" Mary said, feeling like a puzzle in her mind was beginning to come together.

"Yes, street photography. He liked to wander the streets taking candid pictures. They helped him create characters and narratives for his novels."

"My coffee shop friend, Walter, liked to shoot street photography. Oh dear, Walter is Elliot W. Boyd, isn't he," Mary said, her voice a bit shaky.

"Yes, he preferred to use his middle name with close friends."

"I wondered what happened to Walter. I didn't know where he lived, and I never saw any obituaries with his name. Now I know why. Oh, poor Walter. He was such a splendid, kind, wonderful man. He helped me come to terms with aging. He quoted poems and told me to grow down," Mary said.

"Grow down?" Steinberg said.

"Yes, it's from Shel Silverstein. Walter was always sharing poems and quotes from literature. I was always amazed by how well-read he was. Now it all makes sense. My Lord, Walter was Elliot W. Boyd. I can't believe it. He never said anything about being a famous author."

"Walter was a humble guy," Steinberg said, adding, "He even rode around on a pathetic old scooter."

"Yes, I remember that scooter. Thank you for coming and telling me about Walter. This is a lot to take in. By the way, how did you know about me? How did you find me?" Mary said.

"After Walter passed away, we started to go through his things. In his leather travel journal, he wrote about you. About his friendship with you, and how impressed he was with your plans to form a book club. I have what he wrote here in my satchel." Steinberg pulled out Walter's familiar old journal. He flipped to a page filled with immaculate handwriting.

"May I read it to you?" Steinberg asked.

"Of course, yes, please," Mary said.

Steinberg read the following:

"I met a wonderful, radiant, intelligent woman at the coffee shop. Her name is Mary and she lives nearby in a condominium retirement community. She was once an English teacher, but retired now and feeling a bit adrift. Lost her husband, and her zest for life. But she loves books. We enjoy coffee, have become friends, and I encourage her. She encourages me, too. Today she said she wants to start a book club where she lives. I think my heart nearly stopped when she said that. Especially in light of what I've been finishing up. And she said something profound: 'I think books might save us all from the melancholy of aging.' It's like she read my manuscript and summed up the message. And so I know what I have to do now."

Tears edged out of Mary's eyes and Steinberg offered her his handkerchief.

"I'm so sorry, Mr. Steinberg, but this is a lot to take in. And I'm confused. What did Walter mean about his heart nearly stopping and something he was finishing up? And he knows what he has to do now?"

"Walter had just completed a brand new novel. It's about a group of widows who form a book club in a small coffee shop and discover the salvation of literature," Steinberg said.

"Good Lord, I had no idea," Mary said.

"Of course you didn't. When you told Walter about your desire to form a book club for the ladies where you live...well, it must have felt like a divine coincidence to Walter. I remember when he began the novel, he wasn't sure if it would work. But I guess all his coffee dates with you inspired him. Especially what you said about books saving us all from the melancholy of aging," Steinberg said.

He reached inside his satchel and said, "There's something else."

"Mr. Steinberg, I don't think I can take something else. I'll have to skip the coffee shop and find a stiff drink somewhere."

Steinberg pulled a book out of his satchel and held it up. The title on the cover read, "The Coffee Shop Book Club."

"The book comes out next week. This is an advance copy. I know Walter would have wanted you to have a copy. Had he lived, he surely would have inscribed it for you. But in a way, he already did," Steinberg said.

"What do you mean?" Mary asked.

"Take a look inside," Steinberg said as he handed Mary the book.

She opened the cover and found the following dedication a few pages inside:

"For Mary, and all the souls who form book clubs and never give up on life, even when it feels like life has given up on them."

Once again, the tears flowed, and Steinberg smiled and told Mary she could keep his handkerchief.

***

The following month Mary's book club gathered at her condo, and everyone settled in with their hors d'oeuvres, drinks, and book bags. It was a Friday night.

One of the ladies, Tracy, reached into her book bag and said, "Hey everybody, I have a suggestion for this month's book. I just bought it in the bookstore, and the owner told me this book is already a New York Times bestseller. The book's title is, 'The Coffee Shop Book Club.' Is that perfect for our group, or what?"

"That does sound perfect," Mary said, never divulging the connection between Walter and Elliot W. Boyd.

Tracy passed the book around and everyone inspected it, approvingly. "Then it's settled, this will be our next book," Tracy announced. And everyone was talking about literature and Mary's home was full of friends and books and life. All because a humble old man named Walter encouraged her to live again.

She opened the curtain and gazed at the stars blinking brightly in the night sky.

And quietly, to herself, she recited the lines:

"For age is opportunity no less
Than youth itself, though in another dress,
And as the evening twilight fades away
The sky is filled with stars, invisible by day."

Chapter Seventeen

Why Didn't You Fight for It?

S usan stared at the dessert display case, and then quietly cursed her mother.

Even here, on vacation in Italy, her past refused to loosen its grip. The painful grade school memories, the cruelty of children, and the tears that frequently followed her years of weight gain and loss.

She had been the little fat girl in school. She always felt excluded, mocked, and alone. And so she found solace in the very thing that ensured her misery.

Food.

Specifically, the rich desserts and baked goods that her mother loved to make. Susan never understood why her mother was always baking. Always tempting her with delicious cookies, cakes, and pastries.

It was almost like her mother wanted Susan fat. Like she wanted to ruin her life.

It took a lot of time, focus, and hard work for Susan to undo the damage of her youth.

She found a therapist, a nutritionist, and a personal trainer.

She explored her dysfunctional mother-daughter relationship. She changed her diet. Became a CrossFit junkie.

But Susan didn't stop there.

Physical fitness often sparks other achievements, and she doubled down at the law firm. She stayed late and accepted the toughest cases.

But most of all, Susan's knack for generating business and understanding the firm's economics helped catapult her from an associate to partner in an unheard-of six years.

By all measures, Susan was successful.

And yet, she was unhappy.

***

Susan looked away from the dessert case and gazed at her watch.

Ten in the morning.

"Good," she said to herself, "It's before 11 AM, so I can order a cappuccino." She knew Italians frowned on drinking cappuccinos after 11 AM. She liked to embrace the local customs, and not stand out as a tourist.

Sipping her cappuccino on the outside patio, she gazed at the Tower of Pisa, and all the people filling Pisa's cathedral square (Piazza del Duomo).

She was proud of the fact that she came to Italy by herself, to escape life for a while and try to figure out why she was so unhappy. She'd been all over Tuscany, and despite her fitness addiction, the thought of fighting the crowds and hiking to the top of Pisa Tower didn't excite her.

And that's when she noticed the nearby horses and carriages.

Susan usually liked to explore on her own and avoid the tourist stuff. But for some reason, a carriage ride around the town and square sounded relaxing. She finished her cappuccino and strolled over to the first horse and carriage.

"Buongiorno," Susan said to the stout-looking man sitting beside the carriage.

The man looked up from his smartphone and said, "Buongiorno, signora, vuole un passaggio?"

Susan smiled, unsure of what he said.

"Good morning, madam, would you like a ride?" He stood up and motioned towards the carriage.

"Why yes, that would be lovely," Susan said.

"My name is Aldo, and my horse is Leonardo, but he's not as smart as his namesake."

"Your English is very good. By the way, I'm Susan."

"Nice to meet you, Susan. I meet a lot of American tourists, so my English has improved over the years."

Aldo held Susan's hand as she stepped into the carriage, noticing that she wore no rings.

"Welcome to Pisa, Susan. Allow Leonardo and me to show you around," Aldo said with a smile, and then the carriage rocked gently forward, and they were off.

***

Aldo was friendly and his eyes sparkled with sincere kindness. As they rode along, Aldo spoke about the town's history.

Susan asked a few questions, but then sat back and quietly took it all in. She couldn't help but wonder why, despite being in the beauty of Tuscany, her unhappiness seemed to follow her.

Aldo noticed her silence and said, "Is everything alright?"

"Oh yes, it's lovely here, Aldo. I guess I'm just distracted. I'm sorry. Have you been a carriage operator for long?"

"Yes, Leonardo and I have been together ten years."

"So I guess you enjoy it?" Susan asked.

"Oh yes. I love people, and it beats working the olive trees like my father did."

With that, Aldo began telling Susan how his father was a farmer, and how hard he used to work. "Papa was a good man, but his life was not my life. So I came to the city and began my own business. Our parents mean well, but we must chart our own path."

"Some parents mean well. But others...well, let's just say not all parents have their kids' best interests in mind," Susan said.

"Your parents were not good to you?" Aldo asked.

"My father meant well, but he owned a hardware store and worked a lot. And my mother was a homemaker who loved to bake all the time. She was always in the kitchen, but she was kind of remote."

"Remote?" Aldo asked.

"Well, she wasn't overly affectionate. She had trouble express-ing her feelings. So she escaped into food, which she constantly pushed on us. I became a fat kid, and it took a long time to overcome it."

Susan looked away, surprised that she shared all that. But then, sometimes it's easier to talk to strangers.

Aldo looked back at Susan. His kind eyes seemed to smile as he rubbed his protruding belly. "I have not overcome it. I have a gelato problem!"

Susan couldn't help but laugh out loud.

***

They eventually ended up back at the Piazza del Duomo.

"Leonardo needs a break, and so do I," Aldo said as he held out his hand and helped Susan step down. Susan paid Aldo and was going to apologize for bringing up her personal life, but Aldo smiled and said, "Susan, would you do me a favor?"

"Of course," Susan said.

"I'm meeting my son, Antonio, in a little while. Would you join me for an espresso, I'd like to tell you something. Of course, if you have to go, I understand."

Susan had no plans, and since Aldo was so friendly and kind, she agreed. They strolled to a nearby cafe, ordered, and sat beneath a covered patio.

Aldo took a sip of his espresso, set it down, and pulled out an old pocket watch from his jacket.

"This used to belong to my father," Aldo said as his beefy hands held the silver pocket watch. "It was lying in the dirt beside him, the day I found Papa. His heart, you see. It just gave out."

"I'm sorry, Aldo," Susan said.

"Thank you. Of course, that was years ago. I keep the pocket watch to remind me how precious time is. Sometimes we run out of time, and we never get to say the things we need to say. Papa and I sometimes argued. We didn't agree on much. But I loved him. I just wish I could have told him."

Aldo gazed at the pocket watch, then he looked back at Susan. "Before you came to my carriage, Susan, I was on my phone reading on the Internet, looking for new books. I came across a quote from an author named Shannon L. Alder. I think maybe it was fate that I share the quote with you."

Susan was far from superstitious, but her curiosity got the best of her. "Please, I'd be happy to hear it."

Aldo held up his phone, swiped a few times, and said, "Ah, here it is, are you ready?"

"Yes," Susan said.

Aldo cleared his throat and began reading:

> *"When you loved someone and had to let them go, there will always be that small part of yourself that whispers, 'What was it that you wanted and why didn't you fight for it?'"*

Susan sat back, a little stunned. Aldo put his phone down.

"Forgive me, Susan, for we have just met, and we are talking of personal things. You are such a lovely person, but...C'è una tristezza in te. There is a sadness in you."

"I guess it has to do with my Mom. Like you loved your father, I love my mother. But she was baking all the time, hiding in the kitchen. Making me fat."

Susan's eyes began to well with tears.

"Oh Susan, I'm sorry to upset you." Aldo offered her a tissue. "We don't get to choose our families. But we forget that our parents have their own battles. Have you ever wondered what your Mother was hiding from? Why she spent all that time in the kitchen, baking?"

Susan wiped her eyes and sat up a little. It was a good question. What was her mother hiding from? Why was she baking all the time in the kitchen? Susan had focused so much on her own struggles, she hadn't thought about her mother's struggles.

"If you want things to be better with your Mama, Susan, then you must fight for it," Aldo said. And then he stood up, opened his arms, and shouted, "Antonio!"

Susan looked over and saw Aldo's son, Antonio, approaching them. He wore stylish sunglasses and a light sports coat over a white tee shirt. He was ridiculously handsome.

"Antonio, this is my new friend, Susan. She is an American on holiday here in Tuscany," Aldo said.

"Ciao, Susan...it is beautiful to meet you," Antonio said in his best English as he removed his sunglasses. "My padre and I are going to lunch. You join us?"

Antonio had a big, beautiful smile and warm eyes like his father. It was tempting to join them, but Susan knew she had something more pressing to do.

"I would love to join you both, but I have to make a phone call. I'm staying near here. Perhaps tomorrow, around the same time?" Susan couldn't believe she suggested meeting again, but Antonio was like an irresistible magnet, and Aldo was such a gentleman.

Aldo leaned closer to Susan and handed her his pocket watch. "It's a date, Susan. Until tomorrow, please borrow my pocket watch. To remind you how important time is. How important that phone call is."

"Oh, no, Aldo, I couldn't possibly take your pocket watch," Susan said.

"It's only a loan, Susan. To give you motivation. To remember what you want and to have the courage to fight for it."

Susan took the pocket watch and gave Aldo a long hug. "Only until tomorrow, Aldo. Thank you."

***

On her way back to the hotel, Susan noticed a woman seated on a doorstep. There was something sad about her. She seemed alone, huddled with her things, frowning, unhappy.

The woman reminded Susan of her mother. Same gray hair. Same frown. Same aloneness. For the first time, Susan felt a pang of sorrow for her mother.

That night, after a glass of chianti for courage, Susan phoned her mother. She set aside an ocean of buried feelings and simply said that she missed her. That she loved her.

They spoke for hours.

Susan learned that her parent's marriage wasn't a happy one. That her mother buried her pain by baking in the kitchen. She baked to make Susan happy, not realizing how much the food complicated Susan's life.

So many misunderstandings. So many unintentional wounds. So much time wasted.

Susan held Aldo's magical pocket watch as she spoke with her mother.

There were tears and pleas from both for forgiveness. And then her mother said, "Oh Susan, I love you so much. I'm so sorry for any pain I caused you. Thank you, thank you for calling me. And when you're done exploring Italy, please come home and see me. We have so much to catch up on."

That night, for the first time in ages, Susan slept deeply and soundly.

The next day around noon Susan returned to the little cafe near the Piazza del Duomo. She sat down and held Aldo's pocket watch in her hands.

Not far away, Susan spied a young bride and groom taking pictures. It was so romantic. She thought about love, and what her future held.

"Buongiorno, Susan." It was Antonio, smiling broadly.

"Buongiorno, Antonio. It's nice to see you again. Where is your father?"

"My father and Leonardo take family around town in carriage. So I lock up fitness gym, and come join you."

"Fitness gym?" Susan asked.

"Yes, I own many fitness gyms in Tuscany. Fitness is my life. It's why I have not sat down and marry yet. I want to, how do you say, expense to the United States."

"I think the word you want is expand," Susan said with a smile, enjoying Antonio's broken English.

"Yes, yes, expand!" Antonio's radiant eyes and smile were intoxicating.

"Oh, before I forget, here is your father's pocket watch. Please tell him thank you. I think it's magical. It helped me reconnect with my mother."

"I'm glad," Antonio said. "Oh...my father write down quote from one of his books. He ask that I give to you."

Antonio rummaged through his pockets and pulled out a piece of paper with beautiful handwriting on it. "May I read to you," Antonio said.

"That would be lovely, Antonio."

Antonio smiled, and read the following:

"Life can only be understood backwards; but it must be lived forwards.-Søren Kierkegaard"

"Your father is a wise man," Susan said as the waiter brought them espressos. "He taught me the importance of fighting for the things that matter. And his pocket watch reminded me that time doesn't last forever. We must live and love, despite our faults, while we can."

Antonio slid his chair closer, raised his espresso, and said, "Verso il futuro. To the future, Susan!"

"To the future," Susan said.

And for the first time in her life, she felt like the chubby little girl living inside her was finally set free.

Chapter Eighteen

No, It's Not Too Late

Maggie set her glass of chardonnay down, smiled at the group, and said, "I can't tell you how much I've enjoyed working with you all. It just doesn't seem real. I've been in this design firm for 25 years. I feel ancient!"

Everyone smiled and then Phillip, her boss, raised a glass. "A toast to Maggie Fuentes! Thank you for your expertise, loyalty, and friendship. May your well-earned retirement open new doors and happiness!" Applause erupted as the festive balloons bounced around them in the wine bar.

"Thanks, Phil. Thanks, everyone," Maggie said. She looked down at her wine glass for a moment. "I just wish Edward could have been here. We used to dream about this moment. About our next chapter."

Maggie's best friend Melissa hugged her, knowing how much Maggie missed Edward, and knowing that husbands are supposed to be there when you retire from a long career. To tell you how proud they are of you. To embrace you and take you home. Make your coffee the next morning and say, "So, what do you want to do today?"

Edward's pancreatic cancer took him too soon, and Maggie was retiring to an unknown future. Still, she put on a brave face, held up her retirement plaque, and said, "Thanks again, you guys!"

The invisible woman

Maggie was unable to have children. She and Edward considered adoption when they were younger but eventually focused on their careers. Over the last few years, Maggie complained to Edward that she was becoming an old woman. Her hair had grayed, her eyes required glasses and despite yoga and walking, it was harder to keep the weight down.

"You're a beautiful woman, inside and out," sweet Edward always said. And while she owned a dynamite smile, big brown eyes, and attractive features, she knew that the passage of time can be unkind.

"I was walking into Starbucks yesterday," Maggie told Melissa a few weeks after her retirement, "and these three good-looking young men strolled out. The three of them walked right past me. Like I was invisible."

Melissa frowned and put her hand on Maggie's shoulder. "Sweetie, you're a beautiful, smart, talented woman." Maggie smiled at the comment and said, "Yeah, but let's face it, when you're in your sixties, fewer men turn around and admire you. It's not that I want to reclaim my youth. I guess I just feel adrift and alone." Melissa gazed at a small painting on the wall of Maggie's living room.

"Didn't you paint that?" Both women gazed at the artwork and Maggie said, "Yeah, I painted that five years ago. The design firm sent several of us to take a few painting workshops, to help us improve our landscape art. It was wonderful. We painted in the foothills of the Sierra Nevadas. Edward and I talked about me getting into fine art, but I never did much with it."

Melissa smiled and said, "Maybe it's time you revisit that."

The wisdom of Christopher Reeves

The following week Maggie was getting her mail when she came across her neighbor, Douglas. Douglas was a paraplegic military veteran, confined to a wheelchair ever since an IED in Iraq altered the trajectory of his life. He was also an accomplished watercolor artist, and Maggie realized he might have some tips to help her dive into fine art.

"Douglas, may I invite you over for some coffee and scones? Now that I'm retired from the design firm, I'm thinking about getting back into fine art. I'd love to get your advice." Douglas grinned and said, "You know, each scone requires about fifteen laps around the neighborhood to work off! But you have a date."

Later, at Maggie's house, she brought a tray with coffee and scones and the two talked. Maggie shared her feelings of uncertainty. "I feel lost, Douglas. Maybe it's too late to start over with a fine art career?"

"You know, Maggie, after Iraq I thought my life was over. Then I remembered how much I loved artwork. I used to enjoy watercolors and started back up. I took workshops, painted like crazy, and now I'm selling work in several galleries."

"That's amazing, Douglas. But I'm in my sixties. Even if I get back into painting, I feel like I'm too old to accomplish much with it." Maggie frowned as she said this.

"Maggie, do you know what the actor Christopher Reeves once said? 'I think a hero is an ordinary individual who finds the strength to persevere and endure despite overwhelming obstacles.' I love that quote. Besides, there are lots of artists who found success later in life." With that, Douglas took a sip of coffee and nibbled on his scone.

"Oh really, name one," Maggie said.

"Millard Kaufman wrote his first novel, 'Bowl of Cherries,' when he was 90 years old. Kathryn Bigelow was nearly 60 when she directed 'The Hurt Locker' and 'Zero Dark Thirty.' She won an Academy Award. The artist Louise Bourgeois created drawings, prints, and sculptures all her life, but only became well known in her early 70s after a 1982 retrospective at the Museum of Modern Art in New York." Douglas took another bite of his scone, pleased with himself.

"Wow, I guess it's never too late to chase your passion and follow your dreams," Maggie said. "All this time, I've been feeling sorry for myself. I guess I should dust off my French easel and get busy painting?" She smiled at Douglas, admiring his spirit and wisdom. And then he leaned forward and said something profound.

"Maggie, we celebrate beauty, youth, and child prodigies. We overlook the determined souls who overcome obstacles and whose stunning accomplishments arrive later in life. To achieve in one's golden years, despite the indignities of aging, is more remarkable to me than the early success of some wunderkind. It's not too late, Maggie. It's not too late to embrace the next chapter of your life!"

No, it's not too late

Inspired by Douglas' wisdom, Maggie found her old French easel in the attic and threw herself back into painting. Much to her surprise, she hadn't forgotten how to craft a pleasing painting. She remembered many of the workshop lessons she took years ago.

With summer just a few weeks away, Maggie decided it was time to take a workshop and update her artistic skills. She always admired the artwork of Scott L. Christensen and decided to travel to Victor, Idaho, and attend one of his workshops. She knew the workshops were popular and filled up fast.

Maggie phoned Christensen's studio and spoke with an assistant about the upcoming workshop. "I'm recently retired and praying that there's still room in the workshop," Maggie pleaded. The assistant was pleasant and kind, stating, "Let me check the roster and see."

Maggie thought of her late husband, Edward, and her friend Melissa's kind support. She remembered the past workshops she'd taken. She reflected on her neighbor Douglas, and his uplifting encouragement. She held her breath as the workshop assistant checked the roster. And then the assistant said, "No, it's not too late. We have one opening left."

"No, it's not too late," Maggie said to the assistant. "Not too late at all. Go ahead and sign me up."

Chapter Nineteen

Nothing You Love Is Lost

Sometimes, if we are lucky, the thing we need finds us before the thing we want.

In William's case, the thing he wanted was defeat. Annihilation. An end to his loneliness, despair, and sadness. Which is why he poured copious amounts of whiskey into his coffee mug.

He lacked the courage to use more immediate solutions.

A pacifist his entire life, he loathed firearms and violence. Thus, guns, knives, fatal plunges, and other violent ends were out of the question. Pills were an option, but he hated pills. Maybe some part of him wanted the process to be slow so that he could observe his decline. Because suffering, he felt, was a kind of atonement. Abusing alcohol daily, over time, would surely produce the result he was after.

And so he drank his coffee and whiskey.

By mid-morning he was on his third cup, sinking into a dilapidated recliner, with an old photo album open across his lap. He thumbed the pages, gazing at wedding pictures, when he and Ruth were young and full of promise.

And then there were the pictures of Timothy, their only son.

Such a sweet and loving boy.

William closed his eyes.

He remembered the day they came to his work. Two uniformed police officers. There had been a terrible accident. "Perhaps you should sit down, sir," the younger officer said. It all felt like a dream. No, a nightmare. Their words became a blur, but their meaning burrowed deep into his mind and would forever haunt his soul.

Ruth and Timothy were dead.

***

So many of life's stories and outcomes come down to chance.

That fateful day, Ruth suggested William skip work and join her and Timothy for a day at the beach. "You work too much, William. What's the point of living this close to the beach if we seldom go?" she said.

But William was an ambitious architect.

"No, you two go. I've got clients to meet today. How do you think we afford all this?" William said. And so William drove to work in his Suburban. Ruth and Timothy slipped into her Miata sports car later that morning and drove to the beach.

Had William taken the day off, they would have driven together in his large Chevy Suburban. The timing might have been different, but even if the speeding pickup truck plowed into them, the Suburban would have absorbed the impact. Tragically, that's not what happened. Ruth's little Miata was no match for a speeding Ford F150 truck.

In an instant, William's life had changed.

He buried his beloved wife and child, and let his career consume him. The architecture firm grew, along with many clients and awards. At night he'd sit at home alone, flipping through architecture books containing the work of Frank Lloyd Wright, Zaha Hadid, Frank Gehry, and others. Sometimes he'd sketch building ideas. Anything to help him escape the loss and pain.

The years clicked by.

He couldn't shake the guilt of going to work that awful day. Increasingly, William's love for architecture waned. He tried to distract himself with social engagements and travel, but everything lost its luster. Not to mention, his health suffered. Headaches, stomach problems, and insomnia tormented him. Doctors prescribed pills and medicines, but they didn't help.

So William decided to give up. Sold his architecture firm. Bought more whiskey.

He eased into a lonely retirement, with an eye to slowly drinking himself to death.

***

One night William opened the door to Timothy's room, left unchanged from the day his beautiful boy left this earth.

William spied the stuffed giraffe on Timothy's bookshelf. Ruth and Timothy loved giraffes. "Giraffes are willing to stick their necks out for you," Ruth used to say, as Timothy giggled and William would reply, "What does that even mean?" which only made Ruth and Timothy laugh more.

Often William would collapse on Timothy's bed, holding the stuffed giraffe close to his chest, and whispering Timothy's name over and over.

William lost his older sister Emily when he was only 18 years old, so he knew something of untimely loss before Ruth and Timothy's accident. Emily fought a rare form of cancer for nearly a year, with bravery and stoicism.

The day before Emily passed she said, "Oh William, don't worry. I've done so much in my life. It's okay, sweetheart. Remember Benjamin Franklin? He once said, 'Some people die at 25 and aren't buried until 75.' It's not the years we're given, it's what we do with them. And I got to do a lot."

Emily always had a divine light about her, something William wished he could channel.

Raised Catholic, William grew away from the church and religion. Virgin births and burning bushes all seemed so silly to him. And yet there were nights, even now, when he'd pick up his mother's old rosary, lay in bed, drink his whiskey, and say a little prayer.

He felt that something was unraveling inside him. So what harm could there be in a little prayer?

"God help me," he whispered to himself.

***

The sun was out the next morning, a welcome change from the previous week of rain and chilly weather.

Hungover, William walked down to the local coffee shop. He ordered a large coffee and sat outside in the sun. Closed his eyes.

"Excuse me, is this seat taken? Do you mind if I join you? This sun is just marvelous."

William opened his eyes and looked up. The woman was middle-aged, with wind-blown hair, wearing a puffy white jacket, athletic pants, and slipper-like high-top shoes with buckles on the sides. She smiled radiantly, and her eyes were kind.

"Please, join me," William said, motioning at the empty chair.

"I'm Emily," she said.

"Beautiful name. My sister's name was Emily. I'm William."

Suddenly a cell phone rang. "Oh shoot," she said, "Let me turn this darn thing off. I have a love/hate relationship with my phone. I need it for work, banking, and when I get lost. But it gets in the way. I need serenity sometimes. And how can you have a decent conversation when the phone keeps ringing and chirping."

Emily shoved the phone into her jacket pocket.

William and Emily talked. It was the kind of easy conversation that strangers sometimes have when there is no common history to measure and no concerns about betrayed secrets.

William learned that Emily and her husband ran a non-profit fundraising organization. One of their biggest clients was a local orphanage, The Hand of Hope. Emily shared that she and her husband were unable to have children, but they found joy in helping orphaned kids. When William told Emily that he was a retired architect, she got excited.

"We need to build a new west wing at the orphanage, but money is tight. Would you ever consider design work like that? We can't pay a lot. A lot of contractors give us a reduced rate," Emily said.

This opened up a broader conversation.

William said he'd lost his passion for architectural work. He shared about the deaths of his wife and son. About how he threw himself into his career, only to burn out and never escape his guilt and sadness. He couldn't believe he was telling Emily all this, but something about her made him feel at ease and trusting.

Emily reached across the table, squeezed his hand, and said, "Oh William, I'm so sorry." And then she reached inside her purse and pulled out a book.

"I found this children's novel at the orphanage, and I just love it," Emily said. "It's called, *Jeremy Thatcher, Dragon Hatcher.* The message of the story is about being a loving caretaker to a creature who needs you, building a strong bond, and then loving the creature enough to let it go. Do you mind if I read you a brief paragraph?"

"Sure," William said, amused and curious.

Emily flipped through a few pages, smiled at William, and then read the following:

"Nothing you love is lost. Not really. Things, people—they always go away, sooner or later. You can't hold them, any more than you can hold moonlight. But if they've touched you, if they're inside you, then they're still yours. The only things you ever really have are the ones you hold inside your heart."

When Emily looked up, William's face was buried in his hands. His shoulders rocked back and forth as he wept.

Emily pushed out of her chair and wrapped William tightly in her arms.

After his emotional breakdown, William said how embarrassed he was.

"Don't be, William," Emily said. "We've all got stuff to work through. When my husband and I found out we couldn't have children, we went through a rough patch. We argued a lot. We even talked about divorce. But then I thought about my wonderful mother, who died years ago. I thought about what she'd want for me. And I realized she would want me and my husband to be happy. I think that's what the ones we lose always want for us. To be happy. And so I pulled myself together, and my husband and I got help. And that's what led to our charity work with the orphanage."

"Thank you, Emily," William said.

***

They exchanged phone numbers, and William said he'd consider her offer to visit the orphanage and evaluate the west wing expansion.

That evening at home, William poured himself a glass of whiskey, ambled into his bedroom, and spied his mother's rosary dangling from a knob on the bureau drawer.

He thought of his little prayer the other night..."God help me." And then he recalled a C. S. Lewis quote he learned in Catholic school:

> "I pray because I can't help myself. I pray because I'm helpless. I pray because the need flows out of me all the time, waking and sleeping. It doesn't change God. It changes me."

He thought of his chance meeting with Emily. Took another sip of his whiskey, and felt its warmth spread inside him.

He laughed.

"Working in mysterious ways, are we Lord?" William said out loud. "And don't you think running into a woman with my sister's name is a bit trite?" He laughed again and took a longer sip of whiskey.

But this time it burned going down.

He walked into Timothy's room, picked up the stuffed giraffe, and lay on the bed. He was tired. The day's events and whiskey settled into him. The glass rolled out of his fingers onto the floor.

And William drifted into a fitful slumber.

When William awoke the next morning, the toy giraffe was lying on the pillow, staring at him with seemingly disappointed eyes.

"I'm sorry, Timothy," William said.

William's cell phone was buzzing on the floor. He picked it up and read the text. It was from Emily:

"Hey William, I'm driving out to the The Hand of Hope today. I know it's short notice, but would you like to join me? I can pick you up at noon, and then you can see whether or not you'd like to help us with the project?"

William gazed at the giraffe, and then back at his phone.

"Alright. See you at noon," William texted.

Emily arrived on time in a white Range Rover.

They chatted amiably the whole way and soon arrived at the long driveway entrance to the orphanage. Above them stood a large archway sign that read, "The Hand of Hope." Cypress trees lined both sides of the winding driveway that climbed up to the scenic main campus of the orphanage.

"Here we are," Emily said.

Children were playing out on the lawns. Emily and William

strolled to the main entrance, where a young priest carrying a newspaper opened the door to greet them.

"Oh, Father Murray," Emily said, "This is my friend, William. He's come to help us with the west wing design."

"Well, I'm just here to have a look," William said, as he and Father Murray shook hands.

"Of course, I understand, William," Father Murray said, "We're just glad you're here. Let me drop this newspaper off in my office, and then I'll show you around."

"I didn't know people still read newspapers," William said. "I thought everyone was online now, or watching that TikTok stuff."

Father Murray chuckled. "Well, I may be young but I love newspapers. Their physicality. The print on my fingers. All the different sections to read."

"What's your favorite section...the sports?" William asked.

"Oh, not sports so much. I read the headlines and opinion page. I'm a bit odd in that I always read the least read section of the newspaper."

"And what's that?" William asked.

"The corrections," Father Murray said. "They're usually tucked down at the bottom of the page, away from the headlines, special features, and interesting stories. They remind me of people."

"How so?" William said.

Father Murray stopped, looked down, and then back at William. "Well, newspaper editors don't like to make mistakes, which is why they hide the corrections at the bottom of the page. People are similar. Our wounds and mistakes are tucked away, too. Hidden beneath our smiles, feigned happiness, and exterior features."

"How true," Emily said.

Father Murray added, "We tuck away our wounds, guilt, and

regrets so that no one will see them. We keep our mistakes hidden, hoping maybe they'll go away. But of course, they're always there. Waiting. Watching. Hoping that one day we'll acknowledge them, accept them, and set them free."

Emily nodded, William cleared his throat, and then Father Murray said, "I'm sorry, listen to me. I sound like a walking Sunday sermon. Shall we tour the campus now?"

And the three of them walked through the grounds and all the buildings.

William could see the need for a west wing, and he knew that the design work would be a simple project. But he wasn't sure he wanted to commit. He felt torn inside. Part of him wanted to continue his slow destruction. His anguished atonement.

But another part of him, something dormant and deep, longed for life. Longed to be free of the past, the pain, the loss, and the sting of guilt and regret.

***

At the end of the tour, Father Murray showed William some of the children's bedrooms.

They spoke to the children, and William couldn't help but feel for these abandoned young souls. Without the orphanage, where would they be?

"Let me introduce you to Steven," Father Murray said. "His room is the last one on the left, and then Emily can take you back home." Father Murray knocked on the door, and the voice of a young boy said, "Come in."

They walked into Steven's tidy room.

The boy wore glasses, and all around his desk were drawings of animals. Father Murray picked up one of the sketches. "This is lovely, Steven. You're becoming a fine artist."

Emily pointed to another drawing and said, "Wow, Steven, I wish I could draw a horse that well. Do you want to be an artist when you grow up?"

"I like drawing animals, but I don't want to be an artist," Steven said. "I want to be an animal doctor. I forgot how to say it..."

"Veterinarian," William offered.

"Yeah, that's it," said Steven. "I want to be a veterinarian."

"Do you have a favorite animal?" Father Murray asked.

"I love giraffes," Steven said without hesitation.

William had to catch his breath. He felt strange, like something was loosening inside of him.

"Did you say giraffes?" William said.

"Yeah, they're my favorite. They can run fast, and they're the tallest animals. And even though they have long necks, they're not long enough to reach the ground. So they have to bend their legs to drink water. And I read that their leg muscles are super tight so that their blood can make it back up their body to their heart."

"Do you mind if I sit down a minute?" William said.

"Of course," Father Murray said, as he pulled out Steven's desk chair. "Are you alright, William?"

"Yes, Father, I'll be fine."

William took a deep breath. He couldn't explain what he was feeling. Like something was lifting. A sorrow and weight deep in his soul seemed to be evaporating, all because a little boy said he loved giraffes.

"Do you like giraffes?" Steven asked William.

"Oh yes, Steven, I like giraffes a great deal."

"What do you like about them?" Steven asked.

"Giraffes are willing to stick their necks out for you," William said.

And with that, Steven burst into laughter.

Emily and Father Murray laughed, too. The late afternoon sun sent shafts of warm light through the bedroom window, and the whole space around them glowed.

"Thank you, Steven, for showing us your drawings. I think you'll make a wonderful animal doctor, and I hope you get to help as many giraffes as possible," William said.

"Do you want to be an animal doctor, too?" Steven asked.

"No, Steven, I'm an architect. I design buildings for people, and I'm going to help Father Murray and Emily design and build a new wing for you and your friends."

Emily let out a cry of delight and hugged William. Father Murray shook William's hand and said, "That's wonderful, William, just wonderful. Bless you."

Later, on the drive home, Emily opened the car windows and they both enjoyed the cool breeze. She could sense that something had changed in William. Something profound.

"What are you thinking about?" she asked as William gazed at the landscape.

"I'm thinking that somewhere out there, beyond space and time, my Ruth and Timothy are smiling. They don't have to worry about me anymore. They're finally free."

"And so are you, William," Emily said, "So are you."

Chapter Twenty

A Note on the Windshield

I blame it all on the evening breeze.

If not for that late afternoon gust of wind, the note beneath my driver's side windshield wiper would never have flicked up, catching my attention.

I would have driven home, and the rainstorm that arrived later that evening would surely have disintegrated the note's flimsy paper. I don't believe in fate and I hope things don't happen for a reason because the note altered my view of life.

Had I not worked late that day, maybe the note would never have found its way to my car's windshield. But what's the point in speculation, we can never really know why life unfolds the way it does.

When the breeze lifted the edge of the note into view, I was annoyed. No doubt another windshield advertisement. I stepped out of the car, lifted the wiper, and grabbed the small piece of paper.

The handwritten note was clearly not an advertisement. The letters were printed in lowercase, and this is what they said:

"I hate you! I never want to see you again! You said you were working late but here you are, parked outside her apartment. Cheater! Don't call me, and don't show up at the Blue Dish. We're through! -C"

What are the odds that some guy who's cheating on his lady would have the same car as me? I chuckled at the thought and stuffed the note in my pocket.

***

My wife Debbie and I have been married for 25 years. Our son and daughter are grown up now, living and working in the city. We've had our ups and downs, like any couple, but remain devoted to one another.

I suppose I have my father to thank for the longevity and joy of my marriage. He once told me, "Find someone who's kind. Looks are great, but they're a terrible predictor of compatibility and happiness. A kind person may have flaws, but kindness reveals character. And strong character can sustain a marriage."

When I got home that evening, I told Debbie about the note and read it to her.

"Oh dear," she said. "Can you imagine her boyfriend's shock? He must have gone to see her, only to be accused of cheating. All because your car, apparently, looks like his."

"Yeah, poor guy," I said, adding, "Lousy luck. Although there must be a backstory. He must know a woman who lives in the apartments next to where I parked. Maybe he cheated in the past?"

"Too bad you don't know who she is," Debbie said. "Then you

could tell her what happened. Maybe her boyfriend is a good guy?"

***

The next day at work, I pulled the crumpled note out of my pocket. I almost threw it away that morning, but something told me to hang onto it. I read it again. The part about not showing up at the "Blue Dish."

I did a Google search for "Blue Dish," figuring it must be some kind of diner or restaurant. Sure enough, there was a Blue Dish diner on 5th Street. On my lunch hour, I decided to swing by there and see what I could find out.

The diner had a 1950s theme, with cozy booths in front and big round-cushioned bar seats in the back. I sat on one of the bar seats and a heavy-set woman behind the bar welcomed me.

"What can I get 'ya?" she said.

"How about your club sandwich and a water," I said. I noticed her name tag, with the name Madge.

"Hey, can I ask you a question?"

"Sure thing, sweetheart," she said.

"Do you have a woman who works here with a first initial of 'C' in her name?"

Madge looked at me warily. "What's this about? Are you a cop or something?" she said.

"No, I'm not a cop. It's just that I found this note on my windshield yesterday, and I think it was meant for someone else."

I told Madge the whole story and handed her the note.

"Yep, that's Cindy's handwriting alright. I'll be darned. I guess you and Steve, her boyfriend, have the same car. Cindy is off today, but she'll be in tomorrow. Why don't you stop by then?"

I thanked Madge, ate my lunch, and headed back to work.

***

I told one of my co-workers, Joe, about the windshield note and all that transpired. Joe was older than me, and I always respected his advice and wisdom.

"Good for you, trying to fix the misunderstanding," Joe told me. "That's all we can really do in life, try to make things better. Sometimes things work out, sometimes they don't. But at least we know we tried. It's the effort more than the outcome, I think, that spreads a little grace in the world."

I wasn't sure if I was spreading grace in the world, but the next day I found myself back at the Blue Dish, nervously seated in a booth. It wasn't long before a pretty young woman entered the diner and disappeared in the back. A moment later she emerged, wearing a "Blue Dish" apron and a name tag with "Cindy" on it.

"What can I get for you?" Cindy said with a cheerful smile.

"Just a coffee, and perhaps a few minutes of your time?" I said.

"For what?" she asked.

I handed her the note she left on my windshield. She stared at it and then back at me.

"Did Steve put you up to this? I don't want to see him!"

"No, no, I don't even know Steve. You put this note on my windshield. Look outside across the street. Do you see the white Infinity? That's my car."

Cindy stared at my car, the note, and then back at me.

"Oh my God!" she said.

***

Cindy asked her manager if she could take her break early. She slid into the booth and I told her the whole story. She shook her head, teared up a little, and confirmed that Steve also had a white Infinity. The same make and model.

"I'm so stupid," Cindy told me. "I guess I was just being insecure."

Cindy explained that Steve's ex-girlfriend lives in the apartments next to where I had parked my car. She assumed he parked there and was having an affair with his ex-girlfriend.

"I don't mean to get personal, but has Steve been unfaithful in the past?" I asked Cindy.

"No, he's always been great. Really sweet and kind. But his ex-girlfriend used to be a model. She's very pretty. When I saw his car, um your car, well, I thought the worst."

"Well, Cindy, you're a beautiful young woman. I wouldn't worry about his ex-girlfriend," I said.

"Thanks, that's sweet. And thank you for taking the time to find me. I really need to phone Steve and clear this whole thing up."

We slid out of the booth. Madge called to Cindy and pointed to her wristwatch.

"Mind your own business, Madge! Can't you see I'm busy!" Cindy said. It surprised me, but then I knew this must have been stressful for her.

Cindy hugged me and thanked me again.

***

That evening Debbie and I sat on the back porch after dinner and enjoyed some coffee. I told her all about Cindy and Steve and the outcome of my visit to the diner. I also told her about my co-worker Joe's advice about "spreading a little grace in the world."

"There's been times when I did the right thing to help people and things didn't work out. And there's been other times when they did," Debbie said. "The times it didn't work out used to discourage me, but not anymore."

"Why is that?" I asked Debbie.

"I'm not sure. I doubt there's any kind of cosmic scorecard that keeps track, but acts of grace just make me feel better, regardless of what happens."

"That sounds like a good philosophy to me," I said.

***

The following week, just for fun, I invited my co-worker Joe to join me for lunch at the Blue Dish diner. I had grown fond of their club sandwich and was curious to see how Cindy was doing.

When we arrived, we spotted Cindy in the parking lot outside the diner. She was passionately kissing and embracing a handsome young man.

"Well look at that," Joe said. "Looks like she patched things up with her fellow." We watched as the young man walked to a motorcycle, slipped on a helmet, and rode off.

"I thought you said her boyfriend had a car like yours?" Joe asked.

"I guess he has a motorcycle too," I said.

Joe and I entered the diner and Madge seated us in a booth. I introduced Madge to Joe and then we ordered our lunch.

"I'm so happy for what you did for Cindy," Madge said. "She and Steve got back together. In fact, you should say hello, he's in the diner right now." Madge pointed to Steve, who was seated across the diner from us.

I noticed Steve was holding a colorful bouquet.

"Isn't that sweet?" Madge said. "He brought flowers to surprise Cindy with."

Just then, Cindy strolled into the diner, with a smile on her face. Madge smiled back at Cindy and pointed to the corner of the diner. Cindy turned around and spotted Steve, who waved to her with the bouquet.

Cindy cheerfully walked over to Steve, giving him a kiss and a hug.

"Ah, young love, isn't it beautiful?" Madge said.

Chapter Twenty-One

Sins of the Father

The day she left I was busy finishing a huge landscape. It was an epic canvas. The pièce de résistance for my upcoming one-man show.

I remember talking to her from my studio. Telling her all about my painting. How thrilled I was with the tension in the piece, and the vibration of colors.

Little did I know, I was talking to an empty house. While I was immersed in myself and my art she had been packing and then quietly left.

Sometimes life makes no sense. Especially the perverse contradictions. Like when one area of your life is blooming beautifully, but at the expense of another part of your life.

It's an old and familiar saga. The collision between love and creative passion. Look no further than Frida Kahlo and Diego Rivera. Art and love can fuel a tortured alchemy.

Having it all

There's a sign hanging in my studio bathroom. This is what it says:

"Having it all doesn't necessarily mean having it all

at once."

I always figured it meant I could piecemeal my happiness. You know, have art success now and work on the love thing later. But it doesn't seem to work that way. There's a longing that remains.

I phoned my father and invited him to join me for a beer at our local brewery. I figured a few IPAs were in order, to help me untangle my relationship mess.

Dad didn't mince words. "It's your own fault, son. I love you, but let's face it, your first love is art. How can she compete with that?"

The short answer? She can't. Who wants to compete with an all-consuming passion? God knows she tried at first. Staying up late until I finished a piece. Going to all those gallery openings. Helping me update my website. But I guess hope doesn't spring eternal and her patience waned.

I can't blame her. After all, what did I contribute? Who was I to think her world should revolve around me? Why didn't I take more of an interest in her passions? The thing about selfishness is that you're the one who gets stung in the end.

I missed her terribly but stayed focused on the upcoming show. Everything was set in place. I finished all the pieces for my one-man show, shipped them to the gallery, and made my travel arrangements.

And then the phone rang.

"Mom had a heart attack!" my sister Heather said. "We're at County General. It's serious. I called Father O'Malley." I could hear the fear in Heather's voice, I grabbed my car keys and raced to the hospital.

Father O'Malley was the local priest in our Catholic church and a family friend for many years.

Sins of the father

Dad and Mom divorced when I was thirteen. I think I cried for a month. Dad was an entrepreneur and completely immersed in his work. Mom was always ushering us kids to school and sports and playdates.

Dad? He was like a kabuki theater actor, flitting around in the shadows of our lives. Periodic appearances but never really present. I was mad at him for many years but in the last few we started to reconnect.

Father O'Malley spotted me at the nurse's station and pulled me aside, saying, "Your Mom is sleeping right now, and your sister went down to the cafeteria. Let's talk."

We strolled over to the chapel and sat down. Father O'Malley faced me, held my hand, and said, "Heather told me the doctors stabilized your mom. She'll require four stents but should be okay." I breathed a sigh of relief. Then Father O'Malley continued.

"You know how close I am to your father and mother. But I must tell you, your father fell victim to his work. It always came first. It's why he's so financially successful. It's why you guys have such a beautiful home on the west side. Let's face it, your Dad thrives on the trappings of success. His BMW, his impressive home. But here's the thing. I don't think he's happy. I think he bypassed the blessed things, like family and small pleasures, for his business success."

I looked at Father O'Malley and said, "Why are you telling me this, Father?"

"Because you're just like your father. Sins of the father and all that. You're consumed by your art. And I worry that you've put all your eggs in one artistic basket. It seems to me you wouldn't be alone right now if you found a bit of balance. A space in your life. A space for her," Father O'Malley said.

Of course, he was right. Father O'Malley was always right. I had driven away the only woman I truly loved because my art was more important to me.

"How did you know about our breakup?" I asked Father O'Malley. He smiled and said, "I'm a priest. It's my job to pay attention to my flock." Then he lowered his head and said, "I just worry that once the gallery openings are over, and after the reviews and adulation, you'll have no one to share it all with. Just like your father can't share his success with your mother anymore."

We are what we do

One of my favorite authors is the late Dr. Gordon Livingston. I feel kind of stupid because I've read all his books but obviously didn't absorb anything.

Dr. Livingston wrote the following:

> *"We are what we do. Not what we think, not what we say, not what we feel. We are what we do."*

What I do is paint. And drive away the people who love me. Maybe Father O'Malley and Dad are right. I've put my art first and everyone else second.

I remember when Dad and Mom got divorced. I was angry and sad. I felt like Dad let us down and hated him for a while. But then Father O'Malley told me this:

> *"There's one thing that evil can't stand. And that's forgiveness."*

Those words hit me deep and began a thaw in my heart. Before long I reached out to Dad and started a new relationship. To my surprise, he admitted his mistakes and regrets.

What is essential is invisible to the eye

My one-man show was quickly approaching and I was excited. I knew some influential art dealers and journalists would be there. A few days before the show I sent an email to my girlfriend. Well, my former girlfriend. And part of what I wrote was this:

"My family priest told me the other day, 'What is essential is invisible to the eye. The things that are center stage are rarely the most important.' I've made my art center stage for a long time. Everything else was second. But I'm beginning to realize that I need more than art. As the poet Robert Browning wrote, 'Without love, our earth is a tomb.' I need love. I need someone to hug when I come home. Someone who knows my history. Someone to care for me when I'm sick, and that I can care for equally. Someone to share our mutual successes and failures.

What I need is you."

Finally, the night of the one-man show arrived. To my great surprise, Mom recovered enough to attend. Heather and Dad helped her into the gallery. "I'm so proud of you, son," Mom told me. I hugged her for a long time.

Father O'Malley was there. He told me my work must be divinely inspired. God bless him.

There were photographs, interviews, and conversations with patrons. It was an amazing night. A night any artist would kill for. Except, something was missing. The woman I most wanted to share it all with.

Near the end of the evening, as the crowd thinned, my agent came over and handed me an envelope. "She asked me to give this to you," he said. I opened it carefully and read the words:

"I need you, too."

My agent smiled and said, "Look above you on the second landing." I looked up and there she was. Clutching a bouquet of roses and smiling broadly.

I bounded up the stairs and wrapped my arms around her. Told her I loved her. Told her I was sorry. As Father O'Malley smiled at us from below, I realized that without love, my art would never be enough.

And I felt like I could breathe again.

Chapter Twenty-Two

The Old Man With the Briefcase

N o one paid much attention when the old man with the tattered leather briefcase and umbrella walked into the bar.

He was dressed in a tweed jacket, slacks, black tie, and matching black fedora. Compared to the casually dressed patrons in the dimly lit bar, he was overdressed. But then, all walks of life could be found in the city's bars.

"What would you like?" the bartender said.

"Coffee, please, with a splash of cream if you have it," the old man replied.

The bartender grunted and said it would take a few minutes, he had to brew a fresh pot. The old man smiled as he slid onto a bar stool, next to a chubby fellow nursing a whisky and beer.

"Pardon me, could I grab one of the napkins next to you?" the old man said to the chubby guy.

"Uh, sure," the guy said as he handed the old man several napkins.

"You see here, on my briefcase, I've got a pigeon poop stain," the old man said as he spit on the napkin and began rubbing out the spot.

"Damn pigeons, they're filthy things," the fellow said as he threw back the last of his whisky.

"I think pigeons are a lot like people," the old man said. "Appearances can be deceiving, and they're often misunderstood. By the way, my name's Francis, but you can call me Frank." He offered his right hand.

"Bob," the fellow replied as he shook Frank's hand.

***

"I think pigeons get a bad rap," Frank said. "Did you know you can find them on every continent except Antarctica? They're actually quite clean, and strong fliers. They sometimes do somersaults in the air, just for fun. They mate for life. Even after they've raised their chicks, they remain together year after year. And they're intelligent."

"Intelligent?" Bob asked.

"Sure, they were among the first birds that mankind domesticated. We've used them to deliver messages. The Coastguard used pigeons to spot people lost at sea."

"Why do you know so much about pigeons?" Bob asked.

"I guess I've always had a soft spot for birds and animals. And for people down on their luck. I grew up in a small town in the province of Perugia, Italy. We had plenty of birds, animals, and some sad souls. So, I try to help them," Frank said.

"Well, you've come to the right place," Bob said. "Bars are full of people down on their luck."

The bartender handed Frank a fresh cup of coffee and cream. Frank thanked him, took a sip, and then said to Bob, "Ralph Waldo Emerson said that shallow men believe in luck or in circumstance, whereas strong men believe in cause and effect."

"Hmm. I wonder if Emerson was ever fired from his job? Or had his old lady walk out on him and demand alimony? Sometimes bad stuff happens," Bob said as he drank more of his beer.

"I gather you've had personal experience with bad luck?" Frank asked.

"Have you got an hour?" Bob said with a laugh.

Frank smiled as he opened his dilapidated old briefcase and pulled out an antique-looking silver pocket watch. He placed it in front of them both on the bar, noted the time, and said, "The next hour is all yours."

***

Bob was reluctant to get into his recent job loss and divorce, but there was something kind and reassuring about Frank. Or maybe the alcohol made Bob more chatty.

"I got laid off from Walmart last month. Some crap about being late and not doing my job. The bills started piling up, and my wife said I was a worthless drunk. She filed for divorce and moved out. Honestly, I think she was just looking for an excuse to leave."

"Why did she think you were a worthless drunk?" Frank asked.

"Look, sure, I like to hit the bar once in a while. Knock a few back, and hang with some friends. And yeah, maybe I was late a few times for work, but that doesn't make me a worthless drunk. I think my wife was just judgmental like my old man used to be."

"Your old man?" Frank said as he sipped his coffee.

"Yeah, my old man was something else. Couldn't hold down a job. Drank too much. Took my mom for granted. But there were days, here and there, when he was really great. I remember one time, he took me to a comic book shop. Bought me a special edition Spiderman. He wrote on the back, 'For my boy Bobby, love Dad.'" Bob looked down at his beer bottle, absorbing his own words and a flood of old memories.

"Men get lost sometimes, Bob. Wounds from the past get in the way of good decisions. But those moments of kindness and thoughtfulness show us the good inside them, trying to find the light."

"Yeah, that day in the comic book shop was special. I remember hugging Dad and showing all my friends the Spiderman comic book. Two years later, Dad passed away. He got sick or something."

"I'm sorry," Frank said.

"Yeah, the worst part was that I lost the special edition Spiderman comic book. I left it in my backpack on a park bench to play basketball. When I came back, it was gone. It was like the last bit of my Dad was taken away. And ever since that day, my life got harder."

***

Frank gazed down at his silver pocket watch, noting a half hour had elapsed. He sipped more of his coffee and then turned to face Bob.

"Sometimes all it takes is one bad event to change the course of our lives. We get stuck on a path, not realizing that we can change course anytime we want to if we're willing to do the opposite," Frank said.

"Do the opposite?" Bob asked.

"Yes, do the opposite of everything that's not working. It's so simple and yet we don't see it. For example, we eat junk food and hardly exercise, yet complain about being overweight. The solution? Do the opposite. Eat healthy food, exercise, and watch the weight come off."

"Yeah, but some things aren't so simple," Bob said.

"Like what?" Frank asked.

"Like how do you stop hating your wife for walking out on you? How do you tell your father how angry you are at him for the way he treated Mom, and for dying too soon? How do you deal with a jerk of a boss that fires you?" Bob slammed back the last of his beer and motioned to the bartender for another.

"All of that sounds like anger, which is understandable. But I still recommend doing the opposite," Frank said.

"And what would that be?" Bob asked.

"Forgive."

Frank let the word hang in the air for a moment. And then he said, "Forgive your wife for ending the marriage. Forgive your Dad for falling short, and for leaving you too soon. And most of all, forgive yourself."

"Forgive myself? For what?" Bob said as he looked over at Frank's kind eyes.

"Forgive yourself for holding onto the anger. The pain. The blame. Forgive yourself for drinking too much. For falling short at work. Forgive yourself, Bob. It's the opposite of what you've been doing."

Frank put his hand on Bob's shoulder. "If you can forgive yourself, Bob, you'll find your way out. Back towards the light of life. To the man you and I both know you can become."

With this, tears came.

Years of pain, regret, anger, and sadness seemed to pour out of Bob as his shoulders heaved and he held his face in the palms of his hands.

***

After a little bit, Bob collected himself and said, "I'm sorry, I guess the beer has me kind of emotional."

"No apology necessary, Bob. You were carrying a lot of pain. And like I said, I have a soft spot for people down on their luck."

"Well, thank you, I don't think I've ever shared all that with anyone before. And I appreciate your advice. About doing the opposite. I think it's time I start doing the opposite of the bad decisions I've been making." Bob stood up and excused himself to use the restroom.

"What the heck did you say to him?" the bartender asked.

"Not much. Sometimes people just need to tell their story and figure out that there's always a better way to move forward."

Frank sipped the last of his coffee. Looking at his pocket watch, he saw that an hour had passed. He opened up his old briefcase, put the pocket watch inside, and pulled out a book-size envelope.

"Would you do me a favor?" Frank said to the bartender. "Would you leave this for Bob when he gets back?"

"Sure thing," the bartender said. "Hey, are you a psychologist or something?"

"Nope, I'm just someone trying to make the world a better place. I started in a little town called Assisi, but now I try to be everywhere." Frank stood up, put on his fedora, grabbed his suitcase and umbrella, and strolled out of the bar and across the street toward a flock of pigeons. The pigeons gathered all around him, like moths to a light.

Later, Bob returned from the men's room and sat on his barstool.

"Here, this is for you," the bartender said. "The old man with the briefcase said to give it to you. Do you want another round while you open it?"

"No thanks, I'm done with the beer," Bob said.

Bob opened the envelope and let the contents slip out. It nearly took his breath away.

He stared at the special edition Spiderman comic book for a few minutes, feeling a sense of awe and disbelief.

And then his trembling hands slowly turned the comic book over, and on the back in his father's cursive were the words, "For my boy Bobby, love Dad."

Chapter Twenty-Three

The Greenhouse

They found them in the greenhouse.

It wasn't much of a greenhouse, but to them, it was a sanctuary. A safe place where she could work with soil and plants while he painted and listened to classical music.

Sometimes they'd take a break and have tea outside, at the edge of the lawn where they buried their old dog, Brownie. His death hit them hard. A harbinger of what they both knew the future held. But then they'd sip their tea and reminisce about the past and New England and their careers and children.

Friends who visited often marveled at how the two had a sort of telepathic connection. Always finishing each other's sentences.

She'd often say, with a twinkle in her eye, "When you've been together as long as we have, well, you just know each other's thoughts." With that, he'd smile and retort, "And you know when not to say anything. I think that's the key to a good marriage. Keep your mouth shut."

The police received a call from their daughter, who lived four hours away in Springtown. "I'm concerned, they always answer the phone or call back. It's been two days now," she told the dispatcher.

And so, patrolmen were sent to their old, craftsman house on a tree-lined cul-de-sac. They parked on the street and strolled down the nicely kept driveway, lined with trimmed hedges.

No response at the doorbell, so they went around to the side gate.

"I see heat coming from the vent," one of the police officers said. "Looks like their furnace is still on."

And then he looked closely at the windows, for flies. A telltale sign of death. But nothing was there, just some small, potted succulents and two, wood-carved figurines.

The officers made their way to the backyard and walked along the footpath beside the lawn. They spied a small cross at the edge of the lawn but had no idea that Brownie, the old collie, was buried there.

"Joe, let's check the greenhouse," said one of the officers. They opened the rickety, red door and slid past some tall, potted ferns.

And there they were, seemingly frozen in time. Curled up on the floor against the wall of the greenhouse, with a wool blanket wrapped around them. The old man had his arms around her. Like he was cradling and protecting her.

The officers found no evidence of foul play but were perplexed by the scene, until they found an envelope sitting atop the old man's French easel.

The names Peter and Ashley were written in elegant cursive on the unsealed envelope. For investigative purposes, the officers opened the note and read it.

Dear Peter and Ashley,

Mom and I had a wonderful Sunday in the greenhouse. We enjoyed our tea and then got busy. I worked on my floral painting and Mom re-potted some lovely peonies. We were reminiscing about the vacation we all took that year to the Grand Canyon, and how Brownie got sick in the car.

And then Mom gave me this strange look and collapsed.

I held her and said I'd call for help but she whispered no, that it was alright. Then she looked up at me and said she was ready. And we both cried. I held her for a long time. I grabbed the old wool blanket in the cabinet and wrapped us up in it. I rocked her for a while but knew she was gone.

And I guess something inside of me gave up. It started to get chilly, but I decided to stay with Mom.

I love you both so much. I hope you'll forgive me, but there comes a time in old age when you hear the whispers of your ancestors. And when the love of your life crosses over the vale, well, you feel left behind.

If I were younger and my body less ravaged, I would have stuck around a bit longer. But most days I don't feel well. I've lived longer than I ever expected. Besides Mom, both of you are the greatest gift a man could ever have. I'm proud of you both and will always be with you. But I don't want Mom to make this journey alone.

So, I'm just going to stay with her now.

All my love, always,

Dad

The officers stood speechless after reading the letter. They had never witnessed a scene like this before. Heart-wrenching, yet beautiful at the same time.

Joe, the officer who read the letter, was married. He couldn't help but think about his wife.

The officers called the coroner and police chaplain. It was determined the old gentleman had succumbed to exposure. The couple's children were notified and when read the letter, they wept and held each other. They later learned that the old couple had their financial affairs in order and both children were provided for.

At the end of his shift, Officer Joe stopped by a florist's shop. When he arrived home he found his wife in the kitchen, slicing bell peppers for the dinner she was preparing.

She asked how his day went, but he didn't answer. She turned around to face him and he handed her the beautiful flower bouquet. "Oh, Joe, how lovely. Thank you, sweetheart." She kissed him and he held her close, whispering, "I love you, honey."

She got a vase from the cupboard and said, "This is the first time you got me peonies. How beautiful."

Then she turned to Joe and looked into his moist, glistening eyes. "Is everything alright, honey?" she asked.

"Everything is perfect," Joe said.

And then he held her tightly, never wanting to let go.

Chapter Twenty-Four

All God's Angels Come to Us Disguised

E dward was an awkward boy and he knew it. Nature had not blessed him with striking features. Chubby, short, and freckled, he struggled to fit in at school.

His protruding ears and pronounced overbite didn't help, nor the fact his father was an alcoholic. His mother loved him dearly, but she was often gone. She had to work at the grocery store because her husband spent more time in local dive bars than in the odd jobs he'd occasionally pick up.

"Hey, freak boy, what's in your lunch bag?" Edward knew the voice well. As he turned around the school bully, Brent, grabbed the lunch bag from Edward and opened it.

"Ah, look what we have here! Peanut butter and jelly." Brent shook it out of the bag and let it fall to the dirt.

"Courage is fire, and bullying is smoke."—Benjamin Disraeli

"Wait, here's a bag of M&M's. Cool! Guess I'll take this and let you live." Brent shoved Edward down and tossed the crumpled bag at him.

Your heart knows how to paint

Edward never told his mother about Brent or the other mean kids at school. He tended to keep to himself and retreat into his imagination.

He loved the library, where he could read about other people and places. The library was safe. But eventually, school would get out, and he'd have to walk home.

One day, as he slid past the park fence on his route home, he noticed an old woman along the edge of the grass. Her clothing was tattered and she wore a beanie cap. Beside her was a shopping cart with black, plastic bags.

> *"All God's angels come to us disguised."* —*James Russell Lowell*

Edward was curious. In front of the woman were a small tripod and some sort of box. He knew to avoid strangers but there was something non-threatening about her. She looked kind.

"Hi." It was all Edward thought to say.

"Hello, young man." She smiled.

"What are you doing?" he asked.

"I'm trying to paint those trees over there. Aren't they lovely?" she said.

Edward could see that she was holding paintbrushes and her paint box held paints inside it and a canvas board attached to the lid. He asked about the box and she told him it was a pochade box.

"Can I watch you paint?" Edward asked, setting his backpack

down.

"Certainly you can. But only if you help me."

"I don't know how to paint."

"Your heart knows how to paint. You just need to let the rest of you catch up."

She handed him a brush and adjusted her tripod to lower the pochade box. He asked what her name was and she said, simply, "Madam Painter."

Children can be cruel

A friendship was born. Each day after school Edward traversed the park and looked for the old woman. Most days she was there and the two would paint.

He began to learn about shapes, values, and colors. She showed him how to sketch and simplify his drawings. And they talked. He told her about his alcoholic Dad.

"Your father loves you, Edward. But sometimes men get lost in themselves. Maybe they're sad or someone hurt them long ago." She looked into his eyes.

"People hurt me, too. Like Brent." He told her about the school bully. How mean other kids could be because he looked funny.

"You look fine, Edward. Children can be cruel. If there's one thing I want you to know, love and kindness are the most powerful things in the world. Love and kindness. Don't ever forget that, even when you're angry at the world."

And then she hugged him.

After that day, Edward never saw the old woman again. He continued to walk through the park and search for her, but she was gone. Like a guardian angel, she had come into his life when he needed a friend and then vanished.

The sense of its necessity

Edward continued to grow up. One Christmas his mother surprised him with a beautiful French easel. It was used, but functional. Later, in high school, he would meet a few students who liked art.

He made some friends. His Mom found a better job and he got braces for his teeth. His Dad surprised him one birthday with a set of oil paints—his way of atoning for the many times his drinking let Edward down.

Edward's art progressed and he won a scholarship to a fine art college. Below his senior picture in the yearbook, his dedication read, "Thanks Mom, Dad, and Madam Painter."

Time marched forward.

Edward's father eventually passed on and his mother retired to a comfortable apartment. Edward's art career took off and he became quite famous, successful, and well-known in his home-town. He married and had two children.

How effective you live

One day Edward's daughter came home from school with a flier. The school had organized a fundraiser for a student fighting leukemia.

"Her name's Susie and she's really sick, Daddy. Can we help?" Edward picked up his daughter and said, "Of course, sweetheart. An old woman once taught me that the most important things in life are love and kindness. I'll donate a painting."

> *"The value of life is not in its duration, but in its dona-tion. You are not important because of how long you live, you are important because of how effective you live."—Myles Munroe*

The night of the school's benefit-auction most of the town

turned out. Edward's painting attracted collectors from New York and a bidding war ensued. The painting sold for a small fortune and everyone applauded and cheered.

The principal tearfully thanked Edward and asked if she could introduce him to Susie's parents. "Of course," Edward said. So they crossed the school auditorium and the principal said, "Edward, this is Susie's mother, Barbara. And this is her father, Brent.

Brent.

He'd aged, his hair thinned, and his eyes softened. No doubt life, and now his little girl's illness, had siphoned the childhood meanness out of him.

Brent's wife thanked Edward for his generosity. For helping her little girl. "I'm happy to help," Edward said. And then Brent stepped forward.

He looked sadly into Edward's eyes. Then he put his arms around Edward, hugged him tightly, and wept.

Chapter Twenty-Five

Letters of Hope

T he first letter arrived in Rose Swanson's mailbox two weeks after the death of her beloved husband, Vern.

Married for forty-one years, Vern and Rose were devoted to one another. They often walked around town holding hands. In today's world of divorce and broken families, it was nice to see two people whose love thrived and deepened over the decades.

But then Vern experienced dizziness.

Tests and scans were taken, and Vern was told the bad news. An aggressive Glioblastoma Multiforme. Near the end, which came quickly, Rose held vigil beside Vern's bed.

With a box of photographs on her lap, Rose reminisced and showed Vern images of their life together. The photos made Vern smile, but eventually, he fell into a coma. The following night, as Rose held Vern's hands, his breathing slowed, and then he slipped away.

The funeral was well attended. In the days that followed, folks dropped off food and made sure Rose was doing okay. Rose put on a brave face and said she was holding up, but she wasn't.

***

How can anyone be okay when the love of their life has departed, and the home they once shared becomes a vessel of memories and daily reminders of loss and loneliness? How can anyone carry on, when all you want to do is escape the pain and find a path back to the one you love?

Rose hid it well.

She told friends and acquaintances around town that she was adjusting, and that time heals all wounds. But she knew such words were only platitudes to appease others.

Platitudes to buy time, until she could summon the courage to finally do it. To finally end her life and begin the journey to Vern. She resolved to do it that weekend. She had it all figured out.

The car in her garage. A hose connected to the tail pipe. A painless end, and a pathway to wherever Vern had gone.

Sometimes, when people decide to end their lives, their mood improves. Relieved, perhaps, to finally have an escape plan from their emotional pain.

On Friday afternoon, Rose went to the mailbox at the edge of the driveway and bumped into her neighbor, Judy Bloom.

"Hello Rose, how are you doing?" Judy said with a smile.

"Pretty well, Judy. Finding my rhythm," Rose said as she opened her mailbox and collected the bills and letters.

"It's good to see you out and about. Let me know if you need anything," Judy offered.

"Thank you, Judy, I appreciate that," Rose said. As she strolled back to the house, Rose imagined Judy telling her friends the following week, "I can't believe it, she seemed fine. I spoke to her Friday at the mailbox."

Back in the house, Rose sat down in the living room and went through her mail. It was the usual bills and belated sympathy cards.

But then there was a cream-colored envelope addressed to her in exquisite handwriting. The envelope had no return address, and the back contained a red wax seal with the stamped letter "H."

"I wonder what this could be?" she said.

***

Rose carefully opened the back of the envelope and pulled out the neatly folded stationery. She unfolded the paper and was struck by the immaculate penmanship.

She read the following:

Dear Rose,

Your beloved husband Vern's obituary ran in the local paper recently, and the accompanying photograph reminded me of a pleasant encounter with him a few years ago.

We both arrived at the barbershop and he held the door for me, with a smile and the words, "After you, dear Sir."

What a kind and thoughtful man.

Inside, I overheard Vern's conversation with one of the barbers. The barber asked him what he loved best about retirement, and Vern said, "I get to spend every day with my wife."

You brought Vern such joy.

And now, I imagine, you are lost in an ocean of grief and uncertainty about the future. This is not unusual, especially when two people have been married as long as you have.

Queen Elizabeth II said, "Grief is the price we pay for love."

Some say that grief lasts forever. But then, the impressionist painter Renoir said, "The pain passes but the beauty remains." Helen Keller noted, "What we have once enjoyed deeply we can never lose.

All that we love deeply becomes a part of us."

The best way to honor the ones we have loved and lost is to continue living our lives fully and completely.

When we dive back into our passions, help others, and continue to grow in our hearts and minds, we send a kind of ethereal love letter. It travels far beyond the shores of this world to our lost loved ones. And when received, it fills our loved ones' souls with eternal joy and peace. Because they know that we're going to be okay.

Send Vern that love letter, Rose.

Tell him about your gardening and the good work you're doing with your church. Show him that you're bigger than death. That you can continue loving and honoring him by living your best life.

I know you can do this, Rose, and I sense that Vern will be cheering you on.

Sincerely yours,

Hope

The letter nearly took Rose's breath away, as tears flowed down her cheeks. She had no idea who Hope was, or how Hope seemed to know so much about Vern and herself.

But it didn't matter, because the letter awakened something inside Rose. For the first time since Vern's death, Rose felt like she could breathe a little. Grief's vise grip on her heart loosened. She sensed the truth of the letter, that Vern would want her to live on.

For the first time since Vern's funeral, Rose felt like maybe she could craft a meaningful future. She could honor Vern by helping others and finding her best self.

For the first time, Rose felt hope.

***

Stanley Carlson had never been to jail before.

There were other low points in Stanley's life like the day his wife left him and filed for divorce. Or the day his boss fired him because Stanley was late to work again and "increasingly unproductive."

But then, Stanley was a survivor.

He wasn't about to let his ex-wife or unforgiving boss ruin his life. He was going to show them all. He found a new job and celebrated. He bought everyone at the bar a round. He even got the phone number of the blonde woman sitting next to him.

It had been a fantastic night until he noticed the emergency lights in his rearview mirror.

The officer was efficient, professional, and quickly noticed Stanley's glassy eyes and slurred speech. She ordered Stanley out of his car and put him through various field sobriety tests.

He failed them all and ended up in a pair of handcuffs.

The back of the patrol car was uncomfortable. "Why are your backseats made of plexiglass? They're totally uncomfortable," Stanley complained to the officer. "It's harder to clean puke out of cloth seats," the officer said.

They parked in an enclosed sally port at the rear of the jail, and the officer led Stanley out of the car and to the jail's locked security doors. She pressed a button, and after a moment, there was a buzzing sound, and the door unlocked.

They entered a hallway, where two uniformed jail staff met them.

"Drunk driver, mostly cooperative," the officer said to the jail personnel as she handed them paperwork.

The jail staff patted Stanley down. They removed his wallet, keys, an empty flask in his left pocket, his belt, and shoes. They told Stanley that all his possessions would be recorded and returned to him upon release.

It was noisy.

There were loud voices, the clanking of doors, buzzers, loud-speakers, and people yelling in holding cells.

And the smell.

The drunk tank they put Stanley in held five other inebriated souls. Two were passed out, and the others were mumbling to themselves. It smelled like a stale brewery mixed with vomit and body odor.

Stanley sunk against the wall in the corner. He held his face in his hands and wept for the marriage he once had. He wept for the jobs he had lost. He wept for the little boy he once was, who dreamed of great things.

He wept for the better man he had failed to become.

***

When Stanley was sober, they released him from jail. His things were returned to him, and he was given a court date for his DUI offense. He arranged an Uber ride home since his car had been towed and impounded.

Back home, Stanley swallowed several Advil and drank lots of water to assuage his hangover. He sunk into bed and slept all day.

When he awoke he found several messages from his new boss, asking where he was. Great, he thought, I'm going to lose another job. Why does this keep happening? But then, he knew the answer.

And for the first time in his life, he said the words, "I'm an alcoholic."

Stanley denied this all his adult life, until now. Stanley's father was a binge-drinking alcoholic, so it seemed to run in the family.

And life did not end well for Stanley's father. He developed liver cirrhosis that led to an early death.

"Ah Dad, I'm so sorry. Looks like your son followed in your footsteps," Stanley said. And then he sank into his living room chair, waiting for the Advil to ease the pounding in his head, and he dozed off.

His father came to him in a dream.

Stanley's father may have struggled with alcoholism, but he was a gentle man who loved his family and son. Yet he carried demons in him from the Vietnam War, and alcohol was the only tool he knew to cope. But in this dream, Stanley's father was sober, and he whispered in Stanley's ears, "Son, you can change. Be the man I wasn't able to be."

And this is how it began, thanks to one dream in the throes of a hangover.

Stanley showed up the next day at his first Alcoholics Anonymous meeting. He was nervous and felt strange sitting in that old church conference room amidst an eclectic mix of locals. He was surprised at some of the people there. For example, the president of the local bank. And a dentist he recognized. But then, alcoholism doesn't discriminate. It afflicts all gender, race, and socioeconomic backgrounds.

Everyone was encouraging, and the dentist ended up being his sponsor.
"Call me anytime, Stanley. We've all been through what you're going through. You can do this," the dentist said.

Stanley threw out all the booze in his house. He joined the local health club. He sat down with his new boss and told her everything. About his drinking problem. The DUI arrest. And the meetings he was attending. Much to his surprise, his boss didn't fire him. Turns out she was in recovery, too. Twelve years sober, she said.

The letter arrived one month into Stanley's recovery.

He came home one afternoon from the gym and checked his mailbox. Amongst the bills and junk mail sat an elegant, cream-colored envelope, bearing Stanley's name and address in exquisite penmanship. On the back of the envelope, a red wax seal was affixed, with the letter H stamped in the middle.

"What the heck is this?" Stanley asked himself as he sat in his kitchen and tore into the envelope. He slipped on his reading glasses, and read the letter.

Dear Stanley,

We don't know one another and I hope you'll forgive my forwardness in sending this note. I have been a writer all my life, which means I have also been a close observer of people, places, and things. I see the comings and goings of people, especially in this little town we live in.

My mother struggled with alcoholism her entire life.

I loved her dearly, and I always prayed that she would find a path to recovery. Sadly, she never did, and I mourn the better life she could have had.

The late author and poet Charles Bukowski, crude as he could be sometimes, was a keen observer of people. Especially people on the margins of society. An alcoholic, he spent much time with prostitutes and drinking in bars, so he deeply understood how souls can lose their way.

Bukowski wrote the following:

"I was drawn to all the wrong things: I liked to drink, I was lazy, I didn't have a god, politics, ideas, ideals. I was settled into nothingness; a kind of non-being, and I accepted it. I didn't make for an interesting person. I didn't want to be interesting, it was too hard. What I really wanted was only a soft, hazy space to live in, and to be left alone. On the other hand, when I got drunk I screamed, went

crazy, and got all out of hand. One kind of behavior didn't fit the other. I didn't care."

When we stop caring, something inside us dies.

To your great credit, you decided to care. So did the late author Caroline Knapp, whose book, "Drinking: A Love Story," I recommend.

Here's a snippet from the book:

"When you quit drinking you stop waiting."

I love that line because of its truth. When you quit drinking, you stop waiting for the other shoe to drop. You stop waiting for five o'clock when you can escape work and get a drink. You stop waiting for the hangover to recede. You stop waiting for the cop behind you to drive past. You stop waiting for your spouse to find the hidden bottle.

In short, you stop waiting for your better self to come out of the shadows. When you quit drinking, hard as it can be, you suddenly find the promised life. A better life. A sober life. You sleep better. You feel better. You remember more.

The wait is over, Stanley. Welcome to your new life.

Sincerely yours,

Hope

Stanley was so moved by this letter from a stranger that he shared it with everyone at AA. He asked, "Does anyone know someone in town named Hope? Is she involved with AA?"

But no one knew who Hope was.

"Maybe she's an angel?" someone in the group said.

"Yeah, maybe she is. Because man, the letter just blew me away. It uplifted me, you know?" Stanley said.

Everyone nodded in agreement.

***

The mysterious letters showed up all over town.

Tommy Johnson's dog, Duke, was struck and killed by a car, and a few days later, Tommy received a cream-colored envelope in the mail with that same immaculate cursive and the encouraging words:

When our beloved animal companions leave us, they go to a place where they live forever. It's a peaceful place where all their needs are met, they are free, and they can visit us in our dreams and memories. To remind us how much we are loved and that everything will be okay. And one way we can honor their lives when the time is right is to adopt a new furry friend. Because every time we rescue an animal in need, we bring joy to all the animal companions we loved and lost.

When Army Sergeant Brianna Jackson returned to town after a training accident that ended her military career, she decided to study and take the state exam to become a grade school teacher. She wanted to begin a new career in education and inspire young minds.

After she was certified and began her new position as a third-grade teacher at Fairmont Elementary School, a mysterious letter arrived in her mailbox. The copperplate penmanship beautifully expressed the following words:

Dearest Brianna,

Kudos to you for serving your country and demonstrating such leadership and courage. Your injury may have ended your military career, but now a new chapter has begun in your life. You have entered one of the noblest professions.

Nelson Mandela wrote, "Education is the most powerful weapon which you can use to change the world."

Keep inspiring those wonderful children in your classroom, Brian-

na, and may you continue to change the world.

Sincerely,

Hope

The town's newspaper published an article about the letters, followed by a story in the local television news.

Opinions varied.

Some felt that the letter writer was creepy like a voyeur spying on folks and then sending letters about their lives. But most people in town thought the letters were benevolent and beautiful.

As one local said to the news reporter, "Don't you think, with all the bad things going on in the world, we deserve a little encouragement and love? Imagine if we all started writing each other letters like that?"

And so that's the way it was for some time.

The letters kept coming to those who seemed to need them the most. And always with words of encouragement and hope. Some felt the letter writer's name wasn't Hope, but rather a pseudonym that captured the purpose of the letters.

A few town sleuths tried to figure out who the letter writer was. "Probably an old person, because young people don't know how to write cursive like that," one local said. According to a few postal workers, the letters were dropped off in various outgoing mail slots around town, so no one knew who the author was.

And then one day, a few years later, the letters stopped coming.

***

"Mayor Carlson, I have a phone call for you on line one. It's Dan Miller, the Producer at the local news station," Wendy, the

Mayor's executive assistant, said over the phone intercom.

"What's it regarding?" Mayor Carlson asked.

"They found out who the letter writer was," Wendy said.

"Put him through."

"Hi, Dan. Wendy tells me you know who the mysterious letter writer is?" Mayor Carlson said.

"Well, Mayor, we know who he was. I'm afraid he passed away last week. We might never have known, but one of his caretakers stumbled on some things while she was looking for his DNR order," Dan said.

"His DNR order?" Mayor Carlson said.

"Yeah, a 'Do Not Resuscitate' order. A lot of older residents at the assisted living center have them. That way, if they have a stroke or heart attack, the emergency responders don't have to take life-saving measures. I mean, when you are old and in-firmed, sometimes death is a welcome reprieve from suffering," Dan said.

"Yeah, I get it. So what did the caretaker find?"

"She found a wooden box in his closet full of cream-colored stationery, several fountain pens, ink bottles, red sealing wax, a lighter, and a stamp with the letter H on it. And there were some unfinished letters, too. All written in that beautiful, elegant cursive we've seen in the letters around town. Anyway, we're doing a story on it at 5 o'clock, and we wanted to give you a heads-up. And we're sending a reporter and cameraman over to get a statement from you if you don't mind. After all, you were one of the lucky people who received a letter from him."

"I appreciate the heads up, Dan. And sure, I'm happy to talk to your reporter. But I'm curious, who was he? Why did he send out all those letters? How did he know about so many people in town?"

"Well, turns out he was a retired literature professor. He used to teach at the University. He lost his wife to cancer years ago. His caretakers said he never quite got over her death. For a lot of years, he was mobile and used to take the bus all over town. And I guess he was adept online, and followed the local news and even social media closely. I think that's how he learned so much about folks here in town."

"I wonder why he stopped writing his letters?" Mayor Carlson asked.

"He had a stroke and was no longer able to write. He did leave behind a diary, and one of the caretakers peeked at it, even though she wasn't supposed to. Apparently, he started writing all those letters to honor the memory of his wife, who he wrote was a Saint on Earth. And she was. She used to work at the County orphanage and volunteered on weekends at the animal shelter. Really, they were quite a couple," Dan said.

"Wow, I'll say. Okay, Dan, send over your reporter, and thanks again for the heads up," Mayor Carlson said.

***

Rose Swanson and her neighbor Judy Bloom enjoyed tea at Rose's house that afternoon. They had become close friends over the years, ever since Rose received that mysterious, beautiful letter and shared it with Judy the next day, crying together.

They enjoyed gardening and often sold the squash they grew at the local weekend farmer's market.

"Hey, can you switch on the 5 o'clock news, Rose, I want to see if it's going to rain tomorrow," Judy said.

Rose clicked on her television, and the two sat back on the couch to watch the news. A handsome young anchor opened the broadcast with the following:

"I'm Phil Carter, and this is your five o'clock news. Now, our lead story. For years, locals received mysterious, beautifully handwritten letters in the mail. Letters of encouragement, wisdom, and advice. And they were always signed, 'Sincerely yours, Hope.'"

Rose and Judy looked silently at one another and leaned forward to watch the rest.

The anchor continued:

"His name was Professor Theodore H. Flannery. He taught English literature for many years at the county university. A few years after he retired, Professor Flannery's wife, Helen, known locally for her work at the orphanage and animal rescue, passed away. The couple had no children, so Professor Flannery spent the years reading, walking about town, and writing. We take you now to the University, where our reporter, Juan Sanchez, spoke with one of Professor Flannery's colleagues, Professor Emeritus of Biology, Eleanor Foster."

"This is unbelievable," Rose said. "I can't believe I was one of the people who received one of his letters."

The news segment cut to reporter Juan Sanchez, standing next to Professor Eleanor Foster on an expansive front lawn of the University.

"Professor Foster, what can you tell us about Professor Flannery?"

"He was a wonderful, kind, gentle man. Devoted to his wife and his students. He was an amazing literature professor. But you know, he did have a touch of sadness in his eyes. He wanted to become a novelist and inspire people with words, but somehow his manuscripts never found a willing publisher. That happens, you know. Sometimes we're better teaching a subject," Professor Foster said.

"Why do you think he wrote all those letters to total

strangers?" Juan Sanchez asked, holding the microphone up for Professor Foster.

"I think he wanted to honor his wife's memory. Helen was such a splendid woman. A true humanitarian. She believed the highest calling we can have is to help others and improve the world around us. So I think Teddy, that's what his colleagues called him...Teddy wanted to follow his wife's lead and use his writing ability to help inspire others. In a way, his letters are better than a novel. They're his magnum opus. His love letters to humanity," Professor Foster said.

"Love letters to humanity. Well said, Professor. Thank you. Back to you in the studio, Phil."

Rose and Judy weren't the only ones watching the five o'clock news. A few miles away, Tommy Johnson and his rescue dog Skip had the news on.

"Mom, come quick," Tommy yelled.

"What is it?" his mother said.

"You won't believe it. Remember the letter I got after Duke died? Well, they figured out who wrote the letter. He was a retired English professor. And get this, his wife used to work at the animal rescue where I adopted Skip after Duke died."

"That's amazing," Tommy's mother said, as she sat down to join him and watch. The news anchor, Phil Carter, said, "Thanks again, Juan. Let's go now to reporter Elizabeth Traynor at City Hall."

"Thanks, Phil, I'm here at City Hall with Mayor Stanley Carlson. Mayor Carlson, you were one of the people who received a letter a few years ago from our mystery letter writer, Professor Flannery. Your reaction?"

"Well, Elizabeth, all I can say is that Professor Flannery's letter changed my life. Back then I was down on my luck. I was divorced. I had a drinking problem. As most people know from my opponent's smear campaign during the Mayoral election, I was arrested for DUI. After I started attending AA meetings and cleaning up my act, that mysterious letter arrived. I keep it framed in my office."

"That's amazing," the reporter said.

"Yeah, I'll never forget one line in the letter. He wrote, 'When we stop caring, something inside us dies.' And I decided right then and there that I did care. I cared about my life. About becoming a better person. So I got sober. I volunteered. I got into local politics. And, well, here I am today. But the weird thing is that I always thought the letter writer was a woman because it was signed 'Hope,'" Mayor Carlson said.

"Well, Mayor, our sources tell us that the Professor's middle name was Hope. According to a University associate of his, Professor Flannery's late mother struggled with alcoholism. She gave her son the middle name of Hope because he seemed to radiate a kind of loving grace. A kind of hopefulness," the reporter said.

"Well, his mother's instincts were spot on. Because Professor Flannery gave hope to so many of us in this town. Hope to overcome our struggles and live better lives," Mayor Carlson said.

"Thank you, Mayor Carlson. Back to you, Phil."

"Thanks, Elizabeth," Phil Carter said, adding, "And thank you, Dr. Theodore Hope Flannery. You may not have realized your dream of becoming a novelist, but your letters gave hope to many in this small town, and your legacy will never be forgotten."

The station cut to a commercial break.

***

Another person watching the 5 o'clock news that afternoon was Brianna Foley, who excitedly called out to her husband, Draymond.

"Draymond, you won't believe it!" she yelled.

Draymond came into the room. "What is it? Is everything alright?"

"Yes! Remember that letter I showed you years ago? After I got discharged from the army because of my injury. Before we got married, when I was just starting my teaching career," Brianna said.

"Yeah, someone named Hope sent you a handwritten letter of encouragement."

"Exactly. Well, it was from a retired literature Professor named Theodore H. Flannery. And his middle name was Hope. After his wife died, he wanted to honor her kindness and legacy by encouraging others. How cool is that?" Brianna said.

"You know, that name sounds familiar. I've heard it before. At work, I think," Draymond said.

"You work in a publishing house in the city, miles from here. Why would his name be familiar?" Brianna asked.

"I don't know. Let me call Jill in the office. I know I heard that name recently, and Jill has the memory of an elephant," Draymond said.

He phoned Jill, the senior editor at the publishing house, and told her the entire story about Dr. Theodore Hope Flannery and that he remembered hearing the name somewhere.

"That's because I mentioned him two weeks ago, Draymond. Don't you remember? We found a few of his old manuscript submissions in the backroom slush pile closet. Remember, Douglas discovered them, and he thought the writing was pretty good.

"Good Lord, you're right, I remember now. Brianna won't believe the coincidence. It's all pretty remarkable. This guy touched a lot of lives with his letters.

"Hey, I have a crazy idea," Jill said. "What if we were able to collect all the letters he wrote? You know, put out press releases and invite people to send us copies of his letters. It would make an amazing book."

"You know what, Jill, you might be on to something. Let's float the idea with Douglas at tomorrow's staff meeting."

***

Douglas was the new head editor at Little House Publishing, a mid-level publishing house with several best-selling titles already under their belt.

Douglas had a discerning eye for great literature, but he also understood the publishing world and how unique and uplifting titles can sometimes catapult to best-seller status.

When Draymond and Jill floated their idea about Dr. Theodore Hope Flannery's collected letters, something stirred in him. Call it an intuition, a spiritual vibration.

"I like it. I like it a lot. Okay, let's explore how we can collect copies of all those letters," Douglas said in the staff meeting, adding, "We'll have to get legal involved to obtain permissions and sign-offs. And once we comb through all the letters, we'll need a book title for the collection. Something concise that captures the impact and essence of his letters."

"How about 'Letters of Hope?'" Draymond volunteered.

Everyone in the room grew quiet.

It was the kind of moment when something profound was happening. And something profound was happening. The kindness, love, and legacy of an old literature professor swirled around in that publishing house conference room. Dr. Theodore

Hope Flannery's spirit was with them. Everyone could feel it and loved Draymond's suggestion for the book's title.

It took a little over a year.

Nearly all the letters were collected, except one lost to a house fire and another buried with its owner. Douglas told the publishing staff he'd give a raise to anyone who could convince the family to sign off on an exhumation order, but he was only joking.

The book was titled "Letters of Hope" with the subtitle, "A Literature Professor's Gift to Those In Need."

News of the book and its story spread far and wide, catapulting it to The New York Times Best Seller status. Suddenly, Little House Publishing grew in stature, and many fine authors and writers began working with Douglas and his expanding staff.

***

Dr. Theodore Hope Flannery had left behind a modest living trust. Any proceeds from the sale of his assets were to go to the local orphanage and animal rescue where his beloved wife had worked for so many years.

Dr. Flannery posthumously achieved what he always dreamed of when he was alive. He had become a successful, published author, and through the proceeds from his book sales, the local orphanage and animal shelter received a windfall of much-needed, recurring income.

Dr. Flannery's late wife Helen would have been so proud, just as everyone in the community was proud of Dr. Flannery. Through his elegant, cream-colored stationery and fountain pens, he inspired everyday people through his letters to live better lives.

Lives filled with hope.

Sometimes, at dusk in town, locals swore they saw an old couple walking hand in hand down the street beside the duck pond. Other times, volunteers at the animal shelter reported seeing an old couple walking the dogs around the facility, but they'd always disappear.

Mayor Swanson had a similar experience.

He'd been invited to visit the local orphanage and read to the children for their "literature week" program. Mayor Swanson brought his copy of Dr. Flannery's book to read a few of the moving letters.

The children were all assembled in the orphanage's library, and Mayor Swanson opened the book and read the letter he'd personally received, along with a few others. And he told the kids to never give up in life. That anything is possible.

After the reading, on the way to his car, Mayor Swanson thought he heard a twig break in the distance. When he looked up, he saw what appeared to be an old couple standing by a tree, and the man waved to Mayor Swanson.

Mayor Swanson waived back and said, "Thank you, Dr. Flannery. Thank you for saving my life. God bless you and Helen."

Mayor Swanson stepped forward to get a better look, but lost his footing on a mound of grass, dropping his copy of Dr. Flannery's book.

He reached down, picked up the book, and gazed back at the tree.

But the old couple were gone.

Chapter Twenty-Six

How Old Trees Speak to Us

We met unceremoniously. I stepped into a clearing, and there she was. Bespectacled and stooped over her dilapidated French easel. She eyed me warily but turned her attention back to the canvas. Despite her grey hair and advanced years, she hurried back and forth gingerly.

"I have to step away from the piece to see the whole. That's how I find the false junctures." Her voice startled me.

"The false junctures?" I asked, confused.

"Yes, the false junctures. The places where things don't connect properly." She squinted, assessing me. Then she put down her brushes and reached into a backpack on the ground. "Care for a drink?" she offered. Much to my surprise, she pulled out a flask.

"Uh, no thanks, I don't drink. I have no talent for it." It was the truth. My father was an alcoholic, and I inherited the same propensity—sins of the father, sins of the son. I lacked a reliable off switch, so I steered clear of booze.

"I admire that," she said just before taking a swig. "What's the line in that Clint Eastwood movie?" she asked. "Oh yes, 'A man's got to know his limitations.' I love Dirty Harry. He says it like it is." She belched and took another sip.

My mouth was agape with incredulity. I'd been hiking these trails on and off for the last three years to get away from people, be alone, think, and figure out the mess of my life. I miss my six-year-old daughter. Divorce and visitation every other weekend was all my ex and the courts allowed.

"Hey, where'd you go just now?" the woman asked.

"Oh, sorry. I'm not used to running into people out here." I gave her a half-smile.

"People can be a distraction when you're sorting out your life," she said as she set down the flask and plopped beside her backpack. "Young man, I'm a widowed and retired old woman. But if you like, I'll share with you a few things." As she spoke, the wind danced through the tree leaves. Everything felt surreal.

"Okay, why not," I said as I sat down with this enigmatic woman in the woods.

Life is a lot like parking lots

She told me that she used to teach creative writing in the English department at the local university. Her husband Alfred passed away nine years ago. Her only daughter was all grown up. The woman said she lived alone now, with just a Siamese cat, her books, and a love of outdoor painting.

I told her I was a sales rep for an athletic clothing company. I went through a nasty divorce and only saw my daughter every other weekend. I told her my drinking was partly why I was divorced, but I've been sober for several years now. I admitted that I don't care much for other people. "I thought I'd be much further along by now with my life," I admitted.

The woman smiled and said, "I heard this Israeli writer on NPR recently. He said, 'We all think we are the star, the one whose name is on the marque, and everyone else are bit players. But everyone else thinks they are the star. Just like parking lots, we are all looking for our space."

She gazed at me and asked, "Do you enjoy your work?" I thought about that and said, "Yeah, I do. It's challenging and fulfilling. But for some reason, I still feel empty. Lonely, maybe. I guess I'm not a happy-go-lucky type."

She took another swig from her flask and said, "Friedrich Nietzsche said, 'There is one thing one has to have: either a soul that is cheerful by nature, or a soul that is cheerful by work, love, art, and knowledge.' Sounds like your career is fine, but your love, art, and knowledge need work."

The hidden life of trees

We sat together silently, watching the trees sway in the wind. Then she spoke. "You know, I just finished a fascinating book titled 'The Hidden Life of Trees.' The forest is a social network. Trees communicate and support one another. They can sense with their leaves and roots and fit into one another's respective ecosystems. Without trees to draw water inland, we'd all be in trouble."

I gazed at her, mesmerized—this amazing sage in the woods. I closed my eyes and listened as she continued.

"When Scots pine trees are attacked by caterpillars, they release a scent from pheromones in their leaves. The pheromones attract wasps who lay eggs in the leaves. The eggs turn into larvae that eat the caterpillars. Some trees send out electric signals via fungal fibers underground that spread out for several miles, informing other trees of conditions. It's sort of like 'tree email.' People don't appreciate how much trees communicate and support one another."

It was fascinating but I had to ask, "Why are you sharing this with me?" She got quiet for a moment. Then she said, "See all those leaves shimmering in the light and dancing in the breeze around us. Can you feel the peace in that? This is how old trees speak to us."

"And what are they saying?" I asked, somewhat amused but curious.

"They're trying to tell us that we are just like them. Both isolated and connected. We must lay down roots and establish our presence. But we must build alliances and connections, too. Trees take a long view, just as we should plan for our future. Trees don't blame. They take responsibility for themselves. And they find peace in their companionship."

"You're making trees sound a tad anthropomorphic, don't you think?" I pointed out.

"No, I'm saying we can learn a lot from trees. Maybe I'm analo-gizing a bit but think about it. Trees are admirably independent. Strong, yet connected to others. Meanwhile, we're such fragile creatures. Always worrying about what others think. Lao Tzu noted, 'Care what other people think and you will always be their prisoner.' We need to get comfortable with our individuality, like trees, yet leverage the power of community, too. Nobody should be lonely in life."

A good life is like a good painting

I asked the woman her name and she said "Betty Ann." I told her that I went on hikes to figure out my unhappiness. My work was fulfilling, I was healthy and enjoyed my hobbies of hiking and camping. But something was missing.

"Remember when you first bumped into me?" she said. "I was talking about finding the 'false junctures' in a painting? The places where things don't connect properly? Well, that's what you need to figure out in your life. You see, a good life is like a good painting. You must smooth out some of those rough edges and have proper values. And to balance out the grayness, you need a little color. Also, a painting is lonely until it finds a frame and at least one person to share its beauty with."

The sun was setting and it was getting chilly. I thanked Betty Ann for her wisdom and advice. From trees to art, my head swirled with everything she told me. I hiked back to my jeep and drove to town, deciding to enjoy a hot latte at the local coffee shop.

As I sipped my latte a pretty woman sat across from me. Our eyes connected. She said I looked familiar and I told her where I worked. Turns out she just began working in the local Patagonia store and she remembered me from a sales meeting.

Recently divorced, she moved to town for a fresh start and to be closer to her mother.

"What does your mother do?" I asked. She smiled and said, "Oh, she's a retired professor. But now she drives me crazy talking about trees and painting."

"Betty Ann?" I said.

"Why yes, do you know her?" she asked.

"Yes, she helped me understand what the 'false junctures' are in my life."

"The false junctures?" she said.

"Yeah, it's the places where things don't connect properly."

"That sounds like my mom. Did she tell you about one of the largest living organisms on earth? It's a grove of quaking aspen trees in Utah called the Pando. It's a forest, but all 47,000 aspen trees come from a single root system spread over 106 acres in Utah." She smiled at me. "Mom is a font of wisdom."

I offered to get her another coffee and she accepted. Maybe old trees do speak to us. Like the Pando in Utah, maybe people are all connected, too. How else to explain meeting Betty Ann in the woods, and now her daughter?

All I knew was that the 'false junctures' in my life seemed to be disappearing. Things were beginning to connect again. And a feeling dormant for so long was resurfacing.

A feeling everyone longs for—a feeling we all deserve in our lives. Maybe old trees feel it too.

It's called happiness.

Chapter Twenty-Seven

But I Guess It Doesn't Matter Anymore

W henever someone entered or left the brewery, rain, and winter chill rushed in like an invading army.

Roger flicked the lapels of his jacket up around his neck, took another sip of his nut brown ale, and eyed the appetizer menu. It had been a long week, but even after fifteen years of long-haul trucking, he still loved the solitude and freedom of his profession.

It wasn't that he didn't like people. It was just that he preferred them in small doses.

The young woman who just entered the brewery pulled up a bar stool next to Roger. She slipped off her large backpack and laid it down by her feet. She motioned to the hipster fellow with tattoos and suspenders behind the bar and said, "Excuse me, bartender."

"I prefer beertender," the young man said with a grin, adding, "What can I get you?"

"I'll have what Mr. Vikings is having," she said, pointing at the logo on Roger's jacket.

Roger held up his glass and said, "Well, this here is a lovely nut brown ale, my favorite."

"Sounds perfect," she said with a smile.

"I'm Rochelle. By the way, is that your Peterbilt outside?"

"How'd you guess?" Roger said.

"Well, the other four guys in this place look in their early twenties and don't seem like truck-driving types," she said as Mr. Beertender slid a pint of nut brown ale in front of her.

"Truck driving types?" Roger said.

"Sure, you know. Rugged, independent, steely-eyed, and able to handle themselves." She smiled and took a sip of her beer.

"Ha, well, I know a petite lady trucker who drives a pink Mack truck," Roger said.

"And I'll bet she's rugged, independent, steely-eyed, and able to handle herself."

"Well, yeah, you've got me there. Oh, I'm Roger," he said, and the two clinked their pints and sipped their beers.

In the corner of the brewery, someone threw more logs into the fireplace as Don Henley sang "New York Minute" over the ceiling speakers, and the low murmur of conversations coalesced with the warmth and music into a kind of serene cocoon of refuge and comfort.

"Why do you think Harry did it?" Rochelle asked.

"Pardon me?" Roger said as he set down his beer and repositioned to face her.

"The Eagles song that's playing. Listen to the opening lyrics."

Rochelle recited them:

> *"Harry got up dressed all in black*
> *Went down to the station*
> *And he never came back*
> *They found his clothing scattered somewhere down the*
> *track*
> *And he won't be down on Wall Street in the morning"*

"The answer is in the next set of verses," Roger said, and then repeated from memory:

> *"He had a home*
> *Love of a girl*
> *But men get lost sometimes as years unfold*
> *One day he crossed some line and he was too much in*
> *this world*
> *But I guess it doesn't matter anymore"*

"See, that's what I disagree with. It always matters. What we do always matters. If we give up and throw ourselves in front of trains, we forfeit the future. And no matter how bad it gets, you never know what's just around the bend." She took another sip of her beer.

"I like your optimism. We truckers sometimes talk like that. No matter how long the shift or how bad things get, you never know what's around the bend. But then, I've known colleagues who hit a string of bad luck, and well, sometimes they fall into a hole and can't climb out. Maybe like that Harry fellow in the song," Roger said.

"Oh, I know all about that. My daddy lived in that hole. It started with alcohol and meth, and then burglaries and robberies to support his habit. His hole turned out to be a prison," Rochelle said.

"I'm sorry, that's a tough thing. Is he still in prison?" Roger asked.

"No, he's dead. Got himself into a prison beef, and some Aryan nation, neo-Nazi dudes beat him to death. Then it was just me and mamma, but she worked all the time at Costco, and when I turned 18, me and my boyfriend Jamal ran away together."

"We had big dreams...you know?" she said.

***

Roger studied Rochelle as she spoke.

She was pretty, looked to be in her early twenties, and her smile could light up a room. She also had a world-weary look in her eyes. A maturity tethered to fatigue that belied her youth.

And yet there was a hopefulness about her.

"Are you and Jamal still together?" Roger asked.

"Nope. He started getting physical, and then he cheated on me. I gave him the boot. I tried to make it on my own, but the rent was too high, and then I lost my job during COVID. They fired most of us. So now I'm just trying to make it home before Christmas. Mamma retired, and she's got some health issues and could use my help. Also, she lined up a job for me back home, at Costco."

"Do you have far to go?" Roger asked.

"Mamma lives on the east coast, in Jamestown, New York. I've got no idea how I'm going to get there. Unless you want to give me a ride?" Rochelle said with a laugh.

"Well, I might be a long-haul trucker, but I stick mostly to

California and Nevada. Why don't you fly home?" Roger said.

"Don't have the money...but I'll figure it out." She took another sip of her beer.

Roger ordered a burger and fries and offered the same for Rochelle, but she declined. "Gotta watch my figure," she said.

While Roger waited for his food, he picked up his camera on the counter and snapped a few shots of the brewery's interior. Photography was his passion, and he took his camera everywhere.

"Wow, that's an old-school camera, with dials and all," Rochelle said. "Why don't you just use your smartphone to take pictures?"

"Smartphones don't provide the same depth of field and dynamic range that I like. And I prefer the feel of a proper camera. I enjoy controlling the ISO, shutter speed, and aperture. My Dad was a newspaper photographer, and he taught me. I did some photography for my high school newspaper, but now I just shoot street and travel stuff for myself. I enjoy documenting life," Roger shared.

"That's cool. What kind of camera is it?"

"It's a Leica M 240 rangefinder. It belonged to my father. And I've got a cheap 35mm lens on it, but I've saved up enough to finally buy a used Leica Summilux lens," Roger said.

"Is the lens expensive?" Rochelle asked.

"I can get a used one for two or three thousand dollars."

"Good Lord! That's crazy. That's so expensive," she said.

"Yeah, I've been saving for a while. But the image quality is amazing. If you get into photography, avoid Leicas. They're remarkable, but you'll go broke. Their latest camera, the M11, will set you back around 11K. And that's just the camera with no lens," Roger said.

"Here, take a picture of me, it's pretty easy to use," Roger said. He showed Rochelle a few settings, and then he stood up for her as she lifted the camera and looked through the viewfinder.

"Smile," she said, before clicking the shutter button.

And Roger smiled. It was the first time he remembered smiling in a long time.

"I'm a professional photographer now," Rochelle said as she handed the camera back to Roger.

He stood up, slung the camera's leather strap around his neck, and announced, "Be right back, the loo is calling." As he strolled off to the men's room, Rochelle motioned to the guy behind the bar.

"Ready for another beer?" he said.

"No thanks, but can I ask you something? Do you know that trucker guy, Roger? Is he a good guy? He seems to be."

"Absolutely. He and his wife live a few miles from here. Every time he comes home from another long-haul trip, he swings by here for a beer and burger. He and his wife had a son named Garret, but they lost him last year. Some dude ran a red light and destroyed Garret's little car. The poor kid was killed instantly. It was terrible. So, Roger kinda keeps to himself, but he's a good man."

"Thanks, I appreciate that. A girl has to be careful these days," Rochelle said.

***

Roger phoned his wife after leaving the men's room.

He told her he was at Willy's brewery, and asked if she wanted a burger, but she'd already eaten. He mentioned the young woman, Rochelle, and that he might offer to give her a lift.

"Well, make sure she's not some scammer or criminal," his wife said.

"Yeah, I know. Don't worry," Roger said, adding, "See you soon, sweetheart."

The only reason that Roger was still alive was because of his wife.

After Garret died, Roger was ready to give up on life. And sometimes he still thought about it. He couldn't bear the thought of leaving his wife behind, but the loss he felt was suffocating, and letting go seemed like a path to relief. Maybe even a path back to Garret, wherever he was now.

Roger returned, sat at the bar, and quietly finished his dinner.

The hipster behind the bar gazed down at the backpack on the floor beside Rochelle and asked where she was headed. She looked at him, and then at Roger.

"I was told there's a Greyhound bus station near here," she said.

"It's about fifteen miles from here," Roger said. "I'm not sure how late they're open. If you catch the bus, where will you go next?"

"I'm not sure. I have to figure it out," she said, looking down at her beer.

Roger noticed a fake Christmas tree propped up in the corner of the brewery, near the fireplace. It wasn't decorated yet, since it was early December, but its presence summoned dark feelings. Christmastime was the hardest for Roger because, without Garret, he and his wife felt a profound and persistent emptiness in their home and lives.

Emptiness is a hard thing to wrestle with.

Roger fiddled with the dials on his camera and then quietly recited the opening lines of an old Pablo Neruda poem.

"There are cemeteries that are lonely,
graves full of bones that do not make a sound,

the heart moving through a tunnel,
in it darkness, darkness, darkness,
like a shipwreck we die going into ourselves,
as though we were drowning inside our hearts,
as though we lived falling out of the skin into the soul."

"It's not the cemeteries that are lonely, it's us. We're the ones who are lonely. Lonely for the people we lost. Lonely for the people we might still be," Rochelle said softly.

Roger looked at her.

How can someone so young be so wise, he thought? Maybe it's the bloom of youth that inoculates young souls from the damage of misfortune and hardship. Years stretch far ahead, so they can brush off the pain and dust of life's indignities and suffering. They have the energy and hope to get up and keep going.

And maybe their resilience is a bit infectious?

"Hold on, I'll be right back," Roger said.

He went outside, where it was still raining and cold. He found an overhang on the side of the brewery and phoned his wife. He had an idea, and he wasn't sure how his wife would feel about it.

"Oh, honey, I trust your judgment," his wife said.

Rochelle said she'd never been in a big rig before.

"Well, this is a Peterbilt 389. I bought it with the money I inherited after my Dad passed away. It has a lot of miles on her now, but she still runs well," Roger said.

"It's a nice truck. And thank you, Roger, for being so kind. I really appreciate the ride to the Greyhound station."

"Rochelle, it's late. I phoned my wife, and she suggested you stay with us tonight, and I can drop you off at the Greyhound station first thing tomorrow morning. We don't have many visitors, and I think it would give my wife a boost to meet you. What do you say?"

"Oh, Roger, I don't want to be an inconvenience," Rochelle said.

"It's no inconvenience. To be honest, what you said back there in the brewery moved me, about being 'lonely for the people we might still be.' See, my wife and I lost a son, and we've been wounded ever since. So we'd benefit from spending a little time with a young person like yourself. Someone full of life and hope."

"Well, I don't often feel like I'm full of life and hope. Are you sure you don't mind putting me up for tonight?"

"It's no trouble at all," Roger said.

***

Roger's wife prepared tea and cookies for them, and they spent the rest of the evening talking, laughing, and sharing stories about their lives.

It was the kind of easy conversation that friendly strangers sometimes have, when there is no past history to intrude, and no future expectations to skew one's honesty.

Roger's wife told Rochelle that the guest room was ready for her and that she'd laid out towels and a washcloth if Rochelle wanted to shower. "It was a pleasure to meet you darling, and I hope you get home safely to your mother," Roger's wife said before going to bed.

Rochelle hugged her and told her how much she appreciated both their kindness.

Roger locked up the house, and then he showed Rochelle the way to the guest room. "The bathroom is just off to the left," he said. She noticed a few Vikings football posters on the walls.

"This used to be my son Garret's room. We were both Vikings fans," Roger said.

"I'm so sorry, Roger. I can't imagine how hard it must be to lose a son. And I'm honored that you invited me into your home. I think your son is very proud of you, wherever he is now," Rochelle said.

And then she hugged Roger, and it felt like a little light had chased the shadows of despair from the corners of his heart.

"Good night, my dear, and sleep well," he said.

***

Roger awoke early the next morning and brewed a pot of coffee.

He brought a cup in for his wife and asked her if later in the day she'd like to go shopping with him for a Christmas tree. They hadn't put up a tree last year, after losing Garret. They didn't see the point.

"Oh honey, it would be nice to get a tree. We can pull out the old ornaments. Remember that silly Sponge Bob ornament that Garret always loved?" his wife said.

"I remember, sweetheart. It was the goofiest ornament we had, but he sure loved it," Roger said, and they both chuckled softly.

Roger went into their bedroom closet and pulled out his old cigar box, where he kept his father's watch and the money he'd been saving for that new Leica Summilux lens. His wife listened silently, and when he emerged from the closet she smiled at him.

"Are you sure? You've been saving up for a while," she said.

"I've never been more sure in my life," he said.

Rochelle was already dressed and flipping through a photography book in the living room when Roger joined her. "Good morning, would you like some coffee?" he asked.

"That would be heaven," Rochelle said.

They sipped their coffee and then Roger looked at his watch and said, "We'd better get going." His wife joined them in the living room, gave Rochelle a hug, and told her to write or call anytime.

The morning air was crisp, the rain had stopped, and a fine mist hung in the trees as they made their way to the interstate highway. They spoke of many things. Life, family, and how you never know how lives will intersect.

"I was thinking about that song we heard in the brewery," Roger said.

"The Eagles' song, New York Minute?" Rochelle said.

"Yep. Those haunting lyrics:

'But men get lost sometimes as years unfold
One day he crossed some line and he was too much in
this world
But I guess it doesn't matter anymore'

"And it hit me, after meeting you, what you said about, 'It always matters. What we do always matters.' And that we can't be throwing ourselves in front of trains. And that Pablo Neruda poem I recite, the bit about, 'the heart moving through a tunnel,' and, 'in it darkness, darkness, darkness,' and, 'like a shipwreck we die going into ourselves.' See, the thing is, that was me. I was a shipwreck, dead inside myself." Roger used the sleeve of his Carhartt jacket to wipe the moisture from his eyes.

"You know, Roger, my momma always says we never lose the

people we love. They're just somewhere else, cheering us on. Hoping we find the path forward, to help ourselves and help others," Rochelle said.

"Your momma sounds like an amazing woman," Roger said.

They drove on, and when Roger passed the exit for the Greyhound Station, Rochelle said, "Roger, I think you missed the exit. Don't we want to head downtown to 5th Street?"

"Well, my wife and I decided to give you an early Christmas present, as a way to thank you for reviving our spirits," Roger said.

"I don't understand," Rochelle said.

A few miles further Roger took a different exit, navigating his Peterbilt downtown, until they reached the outer perimeter of the International Airport. Roger pulled into a commuter lot, parked, and turned off the truck's engine.

He reached into his jacket and pulled out an envelope.

"What's this?" Rochelle said.

"There's a little over $2K in that envelope. It's for you. I checked last night online, and there are plenty of flights to New York, including several direct to Jamestown. I'll wait with you here until the shuttle comes by, and then you'll be on your way back home," Roger said.

Rochelle broke down in tears.

"No one has ever done something like this for me before. But I can't take your money, Roger. What about your fancy Leica lens?" she said.

"Oh, Rochelle. This is so much more important to me than a camera lens. I don't want to be a shipwreck dead inside myself anymore, and helping you is how I can help myself. And my wife agrees, so please do us both a favor and take the money. And maybe, after you're back home and on your feet again, you can write us sometimes, and tell us how you're doing."

Rochelle leaned over the seat and hugged Roger.

"And one more thing, before your shuttle gets here. May I take a photo of you?" Roger asked.

"Don't be silly, of course you can, Roger."

The two slipped out of the big rig, and Roger held up his camera as Rochelle flashed him a bright smile. And then the shuttle arrived, and there were more hugs and tears, and soon she disappeared into the shuttle.

Roger waved one last time and returned to his truck.

***

Two days before Christmas, a pickup truck drove into Roger's driveway, and the doorbell rang.

Roger's wife opened the door and then called for Roger. He came from the bedroom and immediately recognized the young hipster fellow who works at Willy's brewery in town.

"I've got a delivery for you," the young man said.

"But you guys don't make deliveries?" Roger said.

"Well, we made an exception. We got a phone call from New York. That lovely young lady you met in the brewery, Rochelle. She was very specific, and she said we had to deliver it before Christmas."

Roger looked at the box on his welcome mat.

"It's a case of nut brown ale. Rochelle knew it was your favorite. Anyway, enjoy, and Merry Christmas," the young man said.

"It's going to be a good Christmas," Roger told his wife.

They sat on their porch chairs outside the front door, eyeing the case of beer. "You did good, Roger. I know you wanted that new camera lens, but this was bigger than that, wasn't it?" his wife said.

"Yeah, you're right. This was bigger," he said with a smile.

Chapter Twenty-Eight

The Gift Wrapper

"Children begin by loving their parents; after a time they judge them; rarely, if ever, do they forgive them."
—Oscar Wilde

Attitude is everything. No matter what life throws at you, you decide how to react. But sometimes, your emotions betray reason and sound judgment. Such was the case for Natalie Parker.

As CEO of a leading advertising and design firm, Natalie was a busy woman. Recently home from a three-day, out-of-state conference with a new client, Natalie was exhausted. It had been a difficult but successful negotiation.

Christmas was only a week away. There had been no time to shop. Leaving her downtown office late that afternoon, Natalie drove her Mercedes along the boulevard toward the city's commerce district. She needed to find some gifts for her family.

Calm before the storm
The skies were beginning to darken as Natalie drove down-

town. She was still thinking about work when her mobile phone rang. On the speaker was her sister, Michelle.

"Natalie, welcome home! How did your business trip go?"

"It was a long three days, Michelle, but we got the contract. Come January I'm going to be buried with work." Natalie noticed raindrops on her windshield.

"Well congrats, Natalie. But I'm concerned that you're working too much. You need to slow down. Oh, and I wanted to ask you about Mom." Michelle let the statement linger, knowing that their mother was a delicate subject.

"I told you, Michelle, I don't want to see her. She's never supported my career. She thinks I'm a bad wife and mother. I'm not gonna have her ruin my Christmas!" Natalie pulled over to the side of the road, too angry to keep driving.

"Ah, Natalie. I know you're angry at her, but she's always been old-fashioned. I think she just wants you to spend more time with Tom and Steven." Michelle knew that Natalie loved her husband Tom and son, Steven. But she also knew that the rift between Natalie and their mother was eating away at Natalie.

"Michelle, I gotta go. It's almost Christmas and I'm running out of time! We'll have to talk about Mom later. Talk to you soon." Natalie hung up, closed her eyes, and leaned back in her car seat. It was then that she heard the pelting raindrops on the hood of her car, followed by lightning and the crack of thunder.

An unexpected detour

Natalie made it downtown and headed to Nordstrom. The place was a madhouse, bustling with shoppers. Holiday music played throughout the store. Despite the pandemonium, Natalie found gifts for her husband, son, and sister. She already bought gift cards and wine for her friends and a few work associates.

Pleased with her productivity, Natalie got in her car and started the long drive home. The storm was raging now, and some streets were beginning to flood. Natalie drove past repair crews and police officers dealing with downed power lines and tree limbs.

Natalie's husband Tom phoned. "Hey honey, where are you at?"

"Well, I went shopping but traffic is terrible from the storm. I'm trying to get to the bypass." Natalie noticed a sea of red lights and motorists ahead of her, going nowhere fast.

"The bypass is shut down, Natalie. I heard it on the radio. Some kind of major wreck. You might as well get a coffee somewhere and sit this out for a while. I'll make dinner for Steven, and we'll save you a plate for later." Tom was always thoughtful that way.

"Okay, I'll take Swanson Street and hit Starbucks," Natalie said.

Big things come in small packages

Natalie's heart sank as she pulled into the Starbucks. They were closed, due to a power outage. Natalie had time to kill and nowhere to go. It was then that she noticed Lind's Art Store down the street. The lights were on, so she drove there.

"Good evening, can I help you find anything?" the young woman by the cash register said to Natalie. The art store was busy with shoppers.

"Oh, thanks, but I'm just going to browse. I'm stranded because of the storm. I can't get home," Natalie said.

"Well, we've got free coffee in the back." The saleswoman pointed to the rear of the art store. Natalie thanked her and meandered past shoppers toward the coffee stand.

They say that big things come in small packages, and Natalie was about to discover the truth of that saying. Near the coffee stand stood a gift wrapping-station.

There were reams of elegant wrapping paper, ribbons, boxes,

and bows, and in the middle of it all was a short, thin, elderly man. He was smartly dressed in dark slacks, a matching suit vest, a crisp white shirt, and a red bow tie. His name tag read "Stanley." He looked like an elf.

"There are no strangers here, only friends you haven't met yet," Stanley said as he looked directly at Natalie. Then he added, "William Butler Yeats. I wish it was my line, but a guy my age needs all the help he can get!"

Natalie smiled, immediately disarmed by the charm and warmth of Stanley. Another customer approached Stanley, with some items to be gift-wrapped. Stanley smiled, took them, and got to work.

"I used to be an illustrator for Hallmark," Stanley told the customer, "But I retired a few years back. I got Parkinson's and the tremor in my right hand made it impossible to draw and paint. So, I'm wrapping gifts now. Gift-wrapping is an art form, too."

Natalie watched as Stanley expertly wrapped the customer's purchases. She was struck by the elegance and artistry of his efforts.

"Gifts are expressions of love. Gifts need thought. Purpose. How they're wrapped matters. There's no fast way to make a gift look great under the Christmas tree," Stanley said. "We move too fast these days. We miss things. But when we slow down, life resonates more." Stanley winked at Natalie, which made her laugh.

This charming old gentleman somehow radiated a comforting calm and generosity of spirit. So much wisdom and kindness in such a small old man.

Smoothing out the rough edges of life
"I like to use 100% cotton rag paper for wrapping. It feels like

cloth. The key to good wrapping is proper measuring and never exposing rough edges. Always fold and smooth them out. And you gotta use double-sided tape, so it's invisible on the outside. Also, you want to crisply crease all the edges and use colorful ribbons. I sometimes like to tie flowers or tree leaves to the ribbon, so the gift has a touch of outdoor life to it." Stanley handed the beautifully wrapped gifts to the customer, whose delighted smile said everything.

"You're such a chipper fellow, Stanley. Do you ever get angry?" Natalie asked.

"Oh sure, when I was diagnosed with Parkinson's. And when my wife Ethel died. But I came to understand that life is too short to hold onto anger. We miss out on what's important. Life is a lot like gift wrapping. We need to smooth out the rough edges." Stanley smiled.

"I want to believe that, Stanley. But sometimes life is just a mess," Natalie said.

"Life is a shipwreck but we must not forget to sing in the lifeboats," Stanley said.

"That's beautiful, Stanley. Poetic."

"Voltaire. I wish it were mine..." Stanley offered, but then Natalie added, "But a guy your age needs all the help he can get." And the two of them laughed.

A phone call before Christmas

Natalie picked out a lovely leather day planner and had Stanley gift wrap it. "Is this going to be for someone special?" Stanley asked.

"It's for me, Stanley. Thanks to you, I'm going to reevaluate a few things. Starting with my schedule this coming year. I want to set aside more time for my family."

"What a lovely idea," Stanley said, adding, "Merry Christmas, my dear."

Just as Natalie thanked Stanley, her phone rang. It was Tom, letting her know that the bypass was open now. "Tom, do you think we could plan a trip in January? Maybe you, me, and Steven could get away somewhere tropical?"

"Uh, yeah. That would be amazing, honey," Tom said. "What brought all this on?"

"The gift wrapper. Such a darling man. I guess there are angels on earth if we slow down long enough to experience them," Natalie said.

"The gift wrapper?" Tom asked.

"Yep, the gift wrapper. I'll explain later. Oh, and Tom, I have one more thing to do before I come home. I'll be there in a bit."

The rain had cleared, and Natalie strolled outside and got in her car. She leaned back, took a deep breath, exhaled, and gazed at the perfectly wrapped journal she bought. She thought about missed opportunities and the future. And then she picked up her cell phone and called.

It rang a few times and then, when the voice on the line answered, Natalie said, "Hi Mama, it's Natalie. I was wondering what you're doing for Christmas?"

Also by John P. Weiss

What Life Should Be About: Elegant Essays on the Things That Matter

An Artful Life: Inspirational Stories and Essays for the Artist in Everyone

About the author

John P. Weiss is a writer, artist, and former police chief with twenty-six years of law enforcement experience. He lives with his family in Nevada. Visit John's website at JohnPWeiss.com.